Silver - 2024 Jules Verne Award for Historical Fantasy and Sci-Fi - The Historical Fiction Company

5 Stars and the 2022 and 2024 'Highly Recommended' Awards of Excellence! - The Historical Fiction Company

2023 and 2024 Historical Fiction 'Distinguished Favourite' Awards - NYC Big Book Award

2023 Finalist - Chaucer Award for Early Historical Fiction - Chanticleer International Book Awards

"...Haviaras handles it all with smooth skill. The world of third-century Rome...is colourfully vivid here, and Haviaras manages to invest even his secondary and tertiary characters with believable, three-dimensional humanity." - The Historic Novel Society

"With vivid descriptions and real dialogue... The author's skill in fusing vivid storytelling with historical detail is astounding, resulting in an engaging and educational story." - The Historical Fiction Company

reader, novice to advanced can enjoy and become fully immersed…"

"One in a series of tales which would rank them alongside Bernard Cornwell, Simon Scarrow, Robert Ludlum, James Boschert and others of their ilk. The story and character development…are superb and edge of your seat! The historical environment and settings have been well researched to make the storylines so very believable! I can hardly wait for what I hope will be many sequels! If you enjoy Roman historical fiction, you do not want to miss this series!"

"… a very entertaining read; Haviaras has both a fluid writing style, and a good eye for historical detail, and explores in far more detail the faith of the average Roman than do most authors."

"I can't remember the last time that a book stirred so many emotions! I laughed, cried and cheered my way through this book and can't wait to meet again this wonderful family of characters. Roll on to the next book!"

Sign-up for the Eagles and Dragons Publishing Newsletter and get a FREE BOOK today.

Subscribers get first access to new releases, special offers, and much more.

Go to:
www.eaglesanddragonspublishing.com

For my good friend, Andrew Fenwick

Για τον καλό μου φίλο.

THE ASP OF SAQQARA

A Novel of Alexander the Great

KILLING A GOD
BOOK I

ADAM ALEXANDER HAVIARAS

"Through every generation of the human race there has been a constant war, a war with fear. Those who have the courage to conquer it are made free and those who are conquered by it are made to suffer until they have the courage to defeat it, or death takes them."

— Alexander the Great

L ast night was violent, the winds more vocal than I can remember. When I came outside just before dawn, I expected to find my home destroyed, but in open contrast to what I believed, all is quiet and there is an air of serenity in the pink hue cast over the desert this morning.

Today is a day like any other, I suppose; I have risen, and checked on the passing caravan that is arriving at the shrine at the oasis. Greater numbers of pilgrims and merchants have worn the path into the desert since the Persian invaders were defeated so many years ago.

For me, however, today is not a day like any other, for I am not going to the shrine. Today is the day that I begin to set it all down, as I saw it. Everything.

Last week I purchased fourteen rolls of the finest Nile papyrus, twenty phials of ink, three bronze styluses, and a cedar writing desk. I may not appear so, but I am a wealthy man, more than most, and did not feel any regret for my purchases, for they will be put to good, if not difficult use.

I am not one for an ostentatious life, though I have lived as such. I prefer to use my riches in other ways such as maintaining the shrine, or helping the people of my village who have become my family. In the present case, my goal is to begin my record of the years I spent in the East, years of wonder, of blood, of love and horror.

All that I have seen, felt, and done, haunts me, and it is my hope that this work will distract the Furies from their pursuit. Most of all, I hope to please him and his shade.

I am speaking, of course, of the only man I have ever truly respected, loved, and hated. I speak out of honour and fear of Alexander.

Even now, when I utter his name, it echoes across the years.

Alexander…

How can one name conjure a million images? The task I have set myself is titanic, and my mind is a maelstrom of emotion as I sit in the sand beneath my favourite palm. The morning light of Amun anoints and warms my face now, a sign for a beginning.

I suppose I should start at the time when the Gods chose me to enter the scene, the day when two Athenian noblemen appeared at my door and offered me several talents to do one thing: kill Alexander.

Part One

THE SLAYER OF PERSIANS

CHAPTER ONE

DEATH AND A BEGINNING

Before I go any further, I should relate a bit about myself. Not that I am of any true and meaningful consequence, for we mortals are all dust in the end. No, I wish to lend some credibility to what I am going to say, to show that I am not some puffed-up philosopher who has not lived beyond the confines of the arcaded gardens of his pupils' homes.

Nor am I one of the thousands of sycophants who heaped praise upon the man about whom I shall speak, a man whom, I believe, no one ever really knew for certain. How can you know such a man?

But let me begin in earnest now…

I am Hanbal, son of Akil and Chione. My father was a horse tamer and breeder, something the men in my family had been for generations. My ancestor, Badru of Memphis, had his pastures beyond the capital's necropolis, on the western side of our Mother Nile.

Badru was foremost in equine husbandry in his day, and supplied mounts for Pharaoh Ramesses II's campaigns, including Kadesh and the Syrian Wars. Badru's son carried on the tradition and supplied Pharaoh Ramesses III. It was at that time that the Hellenes became known to our family.

After the war at Troy, of which we had heard rumour, King Menelaus and his beautiful queen, Helen of Sparta, were washed upon our shores on their journey back to Greece. Pharaoh is said to have welcomed them, and he enjoyed their tale so much, felt such sorrow at the affairs of their lives, that he sent them back laden with gifts, including a stock of our family horses so that the Greeks could rebuild their cavalry.

This is all by way of saying that my father was the inheritor of the longstanding success established by Badru over a thousand years ago.

My mother, Chione, was a priestess-dancer in the temple of Hathor, a most sacred duty that she loved above all things, save my father and I. Where my father was short and overly muscular, my mother was tall and lithesome, and appeared even more so in her long, red priestess' robes which contrasted with the long strands of her black hair.

It was the combination of my parents that gave me an unusual physique that set me apart. I have always been tall, like my mother, and strong and heavily muscled like my horse-wrangling father. I kept my black hair long, and because of my speed and agility, my father would have me run down particular mounts when needed, my own dark mane flowing behind as my adolescent legs carried me on the wind.

The home where I grew up was relatively modest, though it might have been more due to the success of my father's business. While other, wealthier families had granite and limestone palaces along the Nile, we were happy with our mud brick home. It was not gaudy, but it was certainly not poor. It was our own, our home, with four bedrooms flanking the entrance hall, a living area, a shrine, and a kitchen. We had storage for food on the lower level, and were most fortunate to have our own well, the water of which was clear and sweet.

The rooftop was broad and flat and allowed us an unimpeded view of the stars and the white river in the heavens at night. During the day, we could see the horse pastures where the green verge of Mother Nile began to the east, and then the rocky landscape of the great necropolis to the west. The dust blew constantly in our direction from Saqqara, coating our walls, the palms, and even our horse herds. I can still see the dust gathering on the reed mats that covered our windows on the western wall of our home.

It was a wonderful world to grow up in, and that was in no small way due to the love my parents heaped upon me.

I loved my parents. They were my world, and I was theirs, and it was their deaths that first tore my world asunder.

As I recall that day shortly after my twenty-first birthday, I do not now feel anything, for I have hardened myself against that memory, and long-since sated my thirst for revenge.

The Persian dogs, under Artaxerxes III, had recently reconquered the Nile valley. His agents were relentless in their yoking of the Egyptian people, and daily we would receive word of yet another desecrated temple.

My mother's own temple dedicated to Hathor had been looted only recently, and so she now performed her sacred dances in the light of day, in a field adjacent to the horse pastures. That particular day, my father had said I could absent myself from duties to spend time with my beloved Eshe, whom I had been wishing to marry. Father had told me not to go to the river because of the Persian patrols, but I was young and, well, the lush riverside along the Nile was the only place where Eshe and I could explore each other in complete privacy.

Oh, how we enjoyed ourselves in those days along the sacred waters. She was my other half, and I hers, and so neither of us felt any guilt or compunction.

When the sun began to dip toward the West, and the papyrus reeds began to shiver in the evening breeze, Eshe and I began to walk back to my home to give my parents the news that we had decided to marry. I was young and naïve enough to think that my joy was enough to outshine the perils of our Persian world.

It was the neighing of the horses that alerted me. Something was not right. Their voices were urgent and scared. Then the smoke came into view, and I ran with Eshe. When I heard the scream of my father's voice, I pushed Eshe into a row of tall grass.

"Stay here! Don't come out until I come back!"

"No, Hanbal! Don't!" she cried.

I wrenched my arm free and ran on toward the pastures where the yelling was growing louder and more harried. Though I ran with all my force, I felt like I would never get there. It was as though someone was holding me back with a rope about my waist. I pushed on and arrived to see my father riding across the pasture wielding a short sword at a group of Persians.

My soul froze when a torn, red object fluttered up into the air – my mother's robe.

The Persians, six of them, were holding my mother down and even through my father's battle cries, our horses' neighing, and the jeers of the aggressors, I could still hear my mother's shrieking as they violated her.

It happened too quickly, in the time it took me to reach the edge of the pasture. My father rode into the Persians, his sword slashing down on the head of one of them. Then, came the thud of a bow, and my father flew from his mount. He was quickly surrounded, beaten, and brought to where my mother was being held. They made my father watch for a few moments before running him through with their long blades.

That's when I came into view, running at them wild-eyed and full of fury. I threw a stone I had picked up and hit one in the face, sending the man down in an explosion of blood.

They immediately stabbed my mother through the heart, and turned to me. An arrow flew past and nicked my naked shoulder.

I grabbed the mane of a white mare that was running past, and when I was close enough, I hurled myself at them. Like I said, I am a large person and that must be why the first two Persians I landed on did not rise. I snapped the neck of another. The remaining two squared up to me, and in that moment I felt more animal than man, so strong was the shock of fury in my limbs, and in my veins.

When they came at me, I reacted without thought or fear, spinning, grabbing, and stabbing.

It was my mother's choked cough that brought me to myself again, to the beginnings of inner pain. Blood bubbled from her mouth, and her glassy eyes pleaded with me.

I knelt at her side among the Persian dead, and covered her nakedness with her torn priestess' robes.

"Han…bal…" she sputtered my name, and my vision

blurred with tears as she reached up with a bloody hand to stroke my long hair and cheek. "You…must…r…run."

"I will give you the rites, I'll not leave you," I cried.

"No…time. I am…desecrated. Love…"

In that instant I felt someone next to me, and looked up to see my mother smiling at me in her gleaming robes, her hand out to help me up.

But her body lay still then, in the clotted sand.

"Ah! Ah! AH!" I yelled to the falling sun.

Now that I think on it - those visceral, painful moments - I now know that that was the moment in which my heart was filled with unfathomable hate. All my ideals, hopes, and dreams were shattered. They disappeared like a handful of sand in a sudden gust of cruel wind.

After despairing beside my parents' massacred bodies, I rushed to our home to gather what gold and silver we kept in two large jars, some weapons, and some food. I do not know how I was able to think in such a state, but I can only assume it was my mother's Ka guiding me, just as she had bidden me to rise when she died.

Most of our horses had bolted, a fortune lost, but I gathered the ten mounts that remained, including a large black stallion named Ra, and loaded up my provisions, my heart racing all the while.

I rode a distance beyond the line of the Nile plain and on into the desert to a secret canyon where I was sure the horses would not be found. When you spend your life in a place, and are curious by nature, you come to know every part of it.

Once the horses were secure, I strapped on one of my father's swords, slung a bow over my shoulder, and took Ra along with another mount to go back for Eshe, praying to Isis and Hathor the entire way that she was unharmed.

When I arrived near the tall grass where I had left her, it was close to the middle of night, and I had only the light of Yah to guide me.

"Eshe," I whispered into the darkness of the tall, swishing grass. "Eshe!"

I heard a rush, and then she slammed into me. When I turned, she screamed and I thought I had cut her with the blade of the sword at my waist, but then realized she was scared of me. I had not washed the blood off of my face and body, my parents' blood. I clamped my hand over her mouth and looked into her eyes.

"Eshe, my love. It's me! Hanbal!"

She crumpled in my arms, shaking, and I carried her to Ra and set her on his back.

As if recounting a nightmare, I told her what had happened and she wept silently in the moonlit night until we arrived at the bodies of my parents, which I wrapped hurriedly with linen and put on the back of the other horse.

It did not take long to reach the edge of the Necropolis.

When we arrived at the Anubeion, the embalmer, a man who knew my parents, was reluctant to undertake the ritual for my mother because of what the Persians did to her.

Fighting back my tears, growing despair, and my anger, I reminded him she had been a favourite of Hathor. I also offered him the second mount I had brought them on. Everyone knew the value of my family's horses, and so he eventually agreed to the proper ritual for both my parents that they may be entombed together.

Eshe bid farewell to the people she had hoped would be her parents, and then I stepped up to touch each of them. I put my hands on my father's chest and on my mother's cheek. I then turned and walked out of the City of the Dead.

AT TWENTY-ONE YEARS OF AGE, I HAD BEEN UNSURE HOW TO handle the tragic change in my life. When a man is young, he thinks he has the wisdom of the Gods, but when faced with such a feeling of hopelessness, the young man's temple to himself crumbles to dust, and must be built up again with layer upon layer of experience. I had lived an idyllic existence to that point, living with my parents, running free on our lands, learning from some of the finest tutors in Memphis, Egyptians and Greeks.

Yes, even then, there were Hellenes in my life.

But all my learning was for naught. I had not been able to save my parents from the Persians. From that dark day, my priority was to keep Eshe safe.

Her family decided to move farther south in the hopes of avoiding the Persians. They wanted us to go with them, but I could not bring myself to leave, and Eshe did not want to leave me.

You see, I wanted to be near the Persian invaders – I wanted vengeance.

When it became apparent that nobody ever came to, or happened upon, the small canyon where we had been hiding, we made that our permanent home. Every night, for several days, I had travelled back to my family's home to salvage what I could – clothes, linens, pots, pans, mattresses, tools, horse harness – everything I could think of, everything that would make life more bearable for Eshe.

We had far less in the way of moveable wealth for my family's fortune had lain in the horses we bred, and my father's skills as a handler. Well, those days were done, and so, with the Persian attack on our home, so ended the business my family had upheld for generations.

As I said, most of the mounts had bolted and were not seen again. I kept three horses for ourselves – Ra, Zahra, and Jamila, and either sold the rest in my possession for a large amount of wealth, or bartered for food, supplies, and materials so that I could build our new home.

Eshe braved our new life with a smile, and despite my removed state of mind, she loved me more than I deserved. A month after the attack, she informed me that she was pregnant, and suddenly, beyond the joy I felt, was a deep fear of bringing up my child in a Persian-dominated world, a world in which our ancient gods were spat upon, and in which the sanctity of women was never acknowledged.

Images of my mother's end dammed up the rivers of reason in my mind, and I was possessed by fear for Eshe and my child-to-be, by rage and by my never-ending need for vengeance.

That is when I decided on my chosen profession.

CHAPTER TWO

GENESIS OF AN ASSASSIN

Every few days, we would hear of another Persian atrocity, and my blood would boil at the thought of others experiencing similar pain to my own tortured experience.

One day, a young girl wandered into our secret home, bloody and alone. She could not have been more than twelve. Through red, weary eyes, she told us that her family - some small farmers, an hour's ride distant - had been slain by Persian troops, and their corn crops were being cut down to take back to Memphis to feed the garrison soldiers.

The girl had run and escaped, and when she had finished her tale, I stood and went over to the wall where my sword, bow, and daggers hung.

Eshe rushed to my side. "What are you doing?"

"I can't take this anymore. I have to do something!"

"What? What will you do, Hanbal? Get killed?" Eshe leaned close, gripping my arm, her swollen belly nudging me. She put my trembling hand on it. She knew my mind and heart, how I had been nursing my hate, how I had been thinking of the Persians I had killed on the day my parents died.

What she did not know was that I had enjoyed the memory of killing those first few, and wanted to do it again. But that was not enough for me. Nobody was acting on behalf of our people!

I rushed out before she could stop me, and rode away on Ra in the direction of the girl's farm.

THAT DAY I LEFT ESHE BEHIND, WAS THE DAY I WAS FORGED A killer.

I rode up slowly to the small piece of lush farmland the girl had described, and found five Persians remaining, loading up the last of the corn. I left Ra in some tall grass and crept up the side of a rocky outcrop to spy on them.

The bodies of the girl's family members lay smouldering next to their dwelling while the Persians stood around a laden cart.

I had not really thought through how I would attack, but knew that eliminating as many as I could from a distance would better my chances of success. I had practiced with my father's horn bow, so I nocked an arrow and drew back. My heartbeat and breathing slowed. Then, I loosed.

My arrow found its mark in two of the closely packed Persians, through the temple of the first and on into the eye of his neighbour. It was a powerful bow.

These were soldiers, however, and immediately, they spread out, having guessed where the arrow had come from.

I loosed again, and lamed a third whose screams of pain made it hard for me to hear the movements of the others. I put my bow down and drew my sword, making my way barefoot and wearing only a linen kilt, around the rocks. My blade plunged into the abdomen of the fourth as he came around a bend, but just as I withdrew the blade, my head jerked back violently when the final Persian grabbed my hair and twisted so hard that I fell onto a rocky shelf several feet below.

I felt a rib crack on impact, and before I had time to gain my feet, I was parrying sword thrusts.

The Persian was fast, and kicked at me between sweeps of his blade. My speed and agility saved me from being impaled, and when he knocked my sword from my hand, I cast a handful of sand into his eyes and plunged two of my daggers into the sides of his torso.

He squirmed and coughed, but there was just enough life left for him to look into my eyes as I slit his throat, cutting off his prayer to Ahura Mazda.

I finished off the remaining Persians likewise if they were still moving, and watched their dead, grey eyes close with terrifying pleasure. As I said, that day I came to enjoy the momentary relief that came of killing one's enemies, and Persia was Egypt's enemy.

By the time I returned home, I could barely breathe without it hurting for the pain in my broken rib where a bruise had already settled over my skin. I let Ra find his way back to his stable and then I collapsed next to a small fire beside the stream that bubbled up from beneath a rock wall within our dwelling.

Eshe's eyes were red from worry and weeping, but I could tell she had held back for the sake of the girl who now slept curled up in our home. When Eshe walked up to me, her stare was cold, but she broke upon seeing my state, the chunk of my hair that had been torn away, and my blackened side.

This time I had washed away the blood.

She filled a small clay pot with cold water from the stream, sat cross-legged next to me so that her belly rested in her lap, and dipped a sponge in the water before holding it gently to my skin.

I flinched and eyed the beer pot that sat in the shade of one of the rocky outcrops.

"Hanbal, please tell me you will never rush off like that again. I…" Her hands began to shake and she covered her face which disappeared behind the screen of her hair.

I put my arm about her, despite the pain.

"Worry not, Eshe. I'm here. I've had broken ribs before-"

"From horses! Not from Persian warriors." Her eyes blazed now, and the tears receded. "Are they dead? The Persians?"

"Yes. All of them."

"For the Love of Isis, Hathor, and Osiris, please do not do this again."

"I can't promise that, Eshe."

"Why not? Don't you care about me, or our child?"

She took both my hands and put them on her belly, and I felt the now-familiar kicking.

"Of course I care about you. Both of you. That is why I went. Not to avenge the deaths of that girl's parents alone," I motioned to where the girl was curled up. "Nor for my parents alone. I did it for all of us, for everyone under the Persian boot."

"You mock the Gods with your dishonesty, for if you look within your heart," her hand burned on my breast where she laid it flat, "you will see that you do not truly believe what you are saying. Anger alone has taken hold of you, my beloved. Do not fall so far, I beg you."

Eshe rose uneasily, and brought me an earthenware jar of beer sweetened with date. "For the pain," she said before going to check on the girl.

Despite the growing chill outside as Ra's all-seeing eye dipped away in the West, I remained next to the fire, alone, still wearing only my kilt. The bloody daggers and swords lay on the ground across from me. I sat there stubbornly, drinking, and resenting what Eshe had said. I knew, of course, that she was correct in her insight. She always had a keen mind and strong intellect. She could make me look within myself, at the places I did not want to go. For those inner realms of darkness can be as terrifying as any spear point, or cataphract charge. I know that now.

But I was young still, stubborn, and inexperienced, and Hathor forgive me, I held out against my beloved's wishes and warnings. As a result, I was cutting a life-course away from hers and that of our unborn child.

I stared up at the stars and the milky mirror of the Nile that flowed across the heavens, praying to Hathor, Isis, and Osiris for direction.

No answer came. I had only the sound of distant jackals, and my recently ingrained images of death. Perhaps Anubis smiled at my thoughts of death and dying?

In my half-sleep, I saw myriad images of tall trees, swaying saplings, horns, and endless miles of road and dusty plains. There were what seemed to be clouds of locusts before the sun, and rivers of blood. Persian faces came into my vision, but quickly fell away until I came to a sun brighter than any other, so blinding that I fell to my knees and wept.

I woke to Eshe nudging me urgently. The sour smell of beer was on me where I lay in the sand next to my smouldering fire.

"Hanbal!" she whispered. "Wake up!"

"What? Are you all right?" But I quickly spied the root of her urgency. At the entrance to our secret place stood two haggard-looking men, and two weeping women. I reached painfully for my sword and stood up, in front of Eshe.

"Who are you?" I demanded, though no one answered. Then, all at once, the four of them fell to their knees.

"Thank you for avenging our brother and sister," one of the men said.

"What do you mean?" I asked.

"We followed you here yesterday. Forgive us, but we wanted to thank the man who brought low the Persians who murdered our family."

My throat caught and I found myself speechless.

"Auntie!"

Suddenly, the girl who had shown up at our home came running out and threw herself into the arms of one of the women. A river of tears ensued and when the rush abated, the lot of them heaped more thanks upon me.

"May the Gods bless you, always," the lead man continued. "We had thought her body lost when we went to retrieve the others."

Behind them was the cart that the Persians had loaded with amphorae of corn and grain.

The other man went to it and proceeded to unload twelve or so containers. "Please accept these from our family. It is the least we can do to express our gratitude."

"Thank you, but-"

"Please," the leader continued. "Your example of bravery and compassion," he put his hand on his niece's head, "has given us a measure of hope in the midst of our grief."

They turned and left, leaving me and Eshe in wide-eyed shock as we watched them go, a backward glance from the young girl.

THAT WAS HOW IT STARTED, HOW I BECAME WHAT I convinced myself I was: a killer of wrong-doers.

Unlike my ancestors, I no longer made my family's fortune in breeding the sacred horses, but rather in feeding the chambers of the Underworld. For after that day, other people came to me seeking help, seeking relief from the agents of Artaxerxes, seeking vengeance for the wrongs committed by the occupiers of Egypt.

People paid me what they could in the form of food or beer, weapons, and silks. Anything they had. The richer merchants whose caravans had fallen prey to the Persians also came to me for aid and paid much more, sometimes in gold.

How did they find me? How did the Persians *not* find me? I believe that my fellow Egyptians were so grateful and loyal that they never even thought to betray me to the Persians. So great was the hurt and disrespect from the occupiers, that I was rendered completely safe from betrayal.

Over the years, since that first, sloppy attack of mine, I became much more adept and stealthy in my work, employing poisons and Ethiopian darts, as well as brute force. I perfected my marksmanship with my bow and throwing daggers.

In essence, I became a ghost to the Persians, and when they would seek to make an example of an Egyptian in an effort to draw me out, I would always be warned ahead of time, and arrange a trap for the trappers.

I became known as 'The Asp', and such creatures were tattooed upon my arms.

This violent aspect of myself took its toll, however. It was as if with each kill I felt small pieces of my being hacked away, to be ferried away into darkness by the Boatman of the Greeks, the dreaded Charon.

When Eshe gave birth to our little Jamila, with help from a priestess and midwife from Memphis, how was I to know what I would become?

With shaking hands and a quivering heart, I held my daughter close beside my Eshe. I stayed there for hours, overwhelmed and awed by the life I held, the life I was determined to keep safe.

I realized only much later, now, even as I write this beneath my whispering palm among the dunes, that Eshe, Jamila, and Femi, our second girl born three years after our first, had been the force of love that had held back the tide of my madness.

The sadness, however, in Eshe's once-bright eyes betrayed the worry the changes in me had caused her. Despite the great joy I felt when playing with my daughters, my mind was often elsewhere and I spent the majority of my time making preparations, repairing weapons, or drinking, the latter of which was something I did quite heavily after every kill.

I suppose my Ka never really got used to my actions for it tortured me with violent nightmares.

One day, when Eshe looked at me, after eight years of

darkness, she took the decision I had inwardly feared she would take, and I did not have the will to stop her.

I was standing before her, my black mane shorn long ago, my body overly-muscled and scarred, as she looked into my eyes and held my face in her soft hands.

"I must go to my parents, Hanbal." Her gaze held me in all seriousness. "They have only seen Jamila once in eight years and they have never even met Femi. I want them to be able to play along the Nile and walk between the great monuments built by our ancestors. I don't wish for them to have to live in a cave, in hiding all of their lives. In Upper Egypt, it is possible for them to live without as much worry about Persians."

"Please don't go, my love" I said, though weakly. "We can move somewhere else."

"No, Hanbal. It is not safe. Rumours of this young Greek king are rampant, but one thing is certain: war is coming to Egypt. And I do not want our girls in the middle of it." She placed her hand on my heart as she always did, as if it reached me more. "You are determined to take a journey which we can not possibly follow you on."

For the first time, her gaze broke and she looked down.

"When you have finished what you set out to do, when you are still once more, come to us and be our husband and father again. We will always love you, as long as the stars, sun, and moon light the heavens."

I held her close then, regretting my choices of the last several years, but still too weak-willed - or perhaps too stubborn - to turn from my chosen path.

Three days later, on a morning streaked with pink light, my Eshe, Jamila, and Femi joined a small caravan that was headed south. I gave them Zahra and Nathifa to carry them and some supplies. I would send the rest of their belongings later.

I knelt down to hug my girls in turn.

Jamila was sullen and stiff to my touch, and Femi wept convulsively. I picked them up, set them on Zahra's back, and covered each with their favourite cobalt blankets to ward off the morning chill. The two of them looked down at me with a mixture of confusion and fear, of me and of the situation that was turning their world over.

And I was the cause of that turmoil.

"Hathor and Isis watch over you, my girls. I *do* love you, so much."

Jamila, who looked like I had with her long black hair and long limbs, seemed unconvinced.

Femi, tears in her eyes, shook her head. "I love you, Baba. Please don't send us away…"

"Your father will join us later," Eshe put in, comforting our youngest with a soft touch before turning to me. "I love you, my soul. Remember that and us, and may Osiris, Hathor, and Isis guide you to us again…" Her voice broke, and I held her close.

My eyes and my heart burned, and my soul shook in the moment. I kissed Eshe, the salt of our mingled tears on our lips, fear in my heart. She stepped back to look at me, as if to burn my image into her memory, as if to give me a chance to change my mind, to stop them from leaving.

I did not, however, stop them. I stood there at the top of a dune near our dwelling, watching the caravan leave for their long journey south into Upper Egypt to a place apart from me and my chosen path, away from my chaos.

For an hour, I stood numb in the same spot in a kilt and tunic Eshe had woven for me. It was in that state of utter sadness that the Greeks found me.

Two men wearing chitons and Greek swords and daggers beneath desert robes emerged from the dust and called out to me.

It was in that moment that I took my first step down what would turn out to be a very long and trying road.

CHAPTER THREE

MEN OF ATHENS

The two Hellenes introduced themselves as Creon, son of Demitrios of Athens, and Demophon, son of Eurymachus, also of Athens.

I looked them over quickly, decided that they were not yet a threat, though I could draw the daggers at my sides if the need arose.

They were both solidly-built men, about my age, and warriors, from the scars on their arms. Creon was blond and Demophon dark, and both had curling hair and neatly trimmed beards.

The one named Creon stepped forward. He spotted the tattoos on my forearms.

"Forgive the intrusion, but are you the man they call 'The Asp'?"

I didn't speak right away. What I wanted was to watch the last of the caravan wind its way over the distant dunes, but I could not let my attention waver. I was no stranger to the Greeks and their ways, for I had had Greek tutors, some of whose students were also Greek. The Hellenes had been coming to Egypt for many years as traders, and as mercenaries. The Athenian general, Phanes of Halicarnassus, had been hired by Pharaoh Amasis to train Egyptian troops for the war with Persia.

By the look of them - the strong, even build of their muscles - I decided that Creon and Demophon must be Athenian hoplites, citizens.

"We've come a long way to seek your help," Demophon added. "Are you 'The Asp'? The slayer of Persians?"

"I am," I replied, suspicion and curiosity contending within me. "What is it you want?" I risked a glance back at the caravan, but it was gone from my sight.

"To speak, friend. That is all." Creon smiled as I pointed the way to the entrance of my home. Creon went ahead while Demophon stared out to the dunes.

"Was that your family you were seeing off?" Demophon asked.

I did not answer.

"I have not see my own wife and children for a couple of years now." He sighed and went after Creon.

"You must leave your swords and daggers outside if you wish to speak with me," I ordered.

The two men looked questioningly at each other and then back at me.

"You have no need to worry," I reassured. "The people here know who I am and honour me and my guests. Your weapons will be safe."

When they had leaned their swords and daggers against the rock face, I walked past them into my now empty home.

When they were seated around the fire in the middle of

the enclosure, I went to get three cups of beer and bowls of olives and dried figs which I set between us.

They did not eat or drink yet, but rather allowed the tensity of the silence to dwindle a bit first. These men weighed their words carefully, I could tell.

"You have no slaves," Demophon observed, looking around my home.

I shook my head and cracked my knuckles loudly. "No. My wife and I prefer to do everything ourselves. Slaves are inherently unhappy and easily bought for information. I require a degree of secrecy in what I do."

"Understood." Creon nodded sagely.

"Forgive me," Demophon put in, "but I could not help notice the beautiful woman and children you were bidding farewell to… You have sent them away?"

This comment immediately roused my suspicions. I knew I had to be cautious. "This region is not as safe and I would like, and we have family in Upper Egypt."

"Very wise," he added.

"What is?" I demanded.

"That you have sent your family away from Lower Egypt."

I stood up then, anger building in my limbs, but I held myself back. "Gentlemen. Do not think for a moment that you are dealing with just another oaf with a knife. I can see through you both. In a short time, you have discovered where I live, obtained knowledge about my family, gained entry to my home, and now sit at my fire to gain more information." I reached down to the soft sand at my feet and drew out a short sword which I levelled at them.

They froze.

"We came here for your help!" Demophon protested. "We left our weapons outside!"

"Then speak plainly or I will have your throats slit before you can draw the knives from beneath your belts."

"Please forgive us," Creon said, his hands up in a gesture of peace. "We meant not to insult you, and harm is not on our minds." He removed his belt knife, as did Demophon, and they tossed them in the sand at my feet. "We truly did come seeking your help, for your reputation has preceeded you in…certain circles."

"What circles are those?" I asked suspiciously, my sword still up.

Demophon stood, his air confident despite the point of my blade. "Let's just say that we are not *regular* troops. Let's say that Creon and I are warriors behind the scenes, in the greater war behind the war."

"You're spies then."

"Let's just say that we are intelligence gatherers and men of action on behalf of the greater good."

I shook my head in frustration. "You speak cryptically, Athenian, and I don't trust such. Pretend you are Spartans and just spit it out!"

"Enough of this!" Demophon turned away, his patience cracked by my intended jibe.

"Ha!" Creon laughed and smiled as though we were life-long friends. "You do have a way of getting to the heart of a matter…Hanbal, son of Akil."

That stopped me.

"How did you find that out?" I demanded.

"We have our ways and you, Asp, would do well to listen and know that we are not just any sword and spear-wielding grunts, as are our Laconian counterparts. Now, can we three sit and talk, plainly if you like, although I myself am partial to intelligent, philosophical discussion…"

"We don't have time for philosophy!" Demophon interrupted.

"Then plainly it is," Creon finished, his annoyance with his colleague well-masked.

I sat down, as did Demophon, sticking my sword into the sand beside me. I raised my cup to them.

"What do you want?" I asked evenly before drinking.

They both took their first sips of beer and Creon leaned forward, his green eyes never leaving mine for a moment.

"Have you ever heard of King Alexander of Macedon?"

It was my turn to laugh. "Of course I have! Who has not heard of the young king?"

"What do you know about him?" Creon sat back.

"Alexander, son of Philip and Olympias. His father strengthened the Macedonian army and planned an invasion of Persia. When his father was murdered, Alexander became king." I had picked up a lot from traders who came to Saqqara. "Two years ago, Alexander crossed the Hellespont and immediately defeated a combined force of Persians and Greek mercenaries at Granicus, moving to Miletus, Halicarnassus, Issus, and Tyre. He's crushing the Persians every step of the way, the Gods praise him."

"Gods praise him?" Demophon spat in the sand.

I looked questioningly at the pair of them. "I thought Athens was now Macedon's ally and the Hellenes united against the Persian dogs?"

Creon put a hand on his colleague to ease him back down. He then looked at me. "Hanbal, let me tell you something more about Alexander of Macedon."

"What more is there to know? He is defeating and killing the Persians, as I am."

"Yes, he is," Demophon said, more calmly. "But to what end?"

"Indeed," Creon continued. "Alexander is a many-faceted man, a man of extremes. What you do not seem to know is that Alexander of Macedon is every bit as dangerous as the Persians, even more so, for he will enslave the rest of the world to Macedonian rule."

"Come now, gentlemen. I am not so out of touch as you think. Alexander's war is waged on Persia and those loyal to Persia. For hundreds of years, Greeks have had dealings with Egypt. I hear news on a regular basis. There has been an Egyptian advisor in Pella for some years now, apprising the Macedonian king of the situation in Egypt, of the rebellion of Khabash in Lower Egypt, which ousted the Persian governor from Memphis."

"You knew Khabash?" Demophon asked.

"Of course I did!" I exclaimed. "He too asked for my help in harassing the Persians, hacking away at them."

"Yes, well," Creon came in, "Khabash is dead and the Persians are still here." He took a fig from the bowl, turning it over in his thickly-veined hand. "And let us not forget that in Greece's fight against the Persian invasion of our lands, Macedon co-operated with Xerxes and the Persians."

"Yes," I said. "And if I'm not mistaken, both Athens and Sparta sought aid from Persia during your own internal wars."

Both men glared at me, but I pressed on with another thrust.

"I suspect that the dead heroes of Thermopylae, Marathon, Salamis, and Plataea would spit at the thought that their brothers had gone open-handed to the Great King after such crushing defeats as they had delivered to Persia." I fingered the handle of my sword casually.

"Our forefathers were great, but also mistaken in many things," Creon conceded. "Politics is a much more complicated beast than open battle, a chimera of men's own creation."

"We're talking in circles here!" Demophon stood and turned to me from across the fire.

I held the sword ready.

"You think Alexander is simply out for the good of the world, ridding us of Persians in vengeance for all the Greeks, or even for the betterment of humanity? Let me tell you what he has done to some of the cities that stood against him. During the siege of Tyre, eight thousand Tyrians were killed, and thirty thousand survivors, including women, and children were sold into slavery. And in Gazzat, most of the male population died fighting while the women and children were all sold into slavery to fill the royal coffers of Macedon even more!"

I glanced down at the sand momentarily and Demophon went on as if reading my thoughts.

"Women and children, Hanbal! Perhaps you will think on that the next time you think of your darling family with whom you have so recently parted?"

In a moment, I leapt across the fire, my hand connecting with his smug face.

Before Demophon could roll away, my sword was at his neck.

"If you ever speak of my wife or children again, I will slit you from your neck to your navel!"

The rage started to take hold of me, and before I could do anything, Creon spoke up.

"I had spoken of our need for your help, Hanbal! We came to ask you for help."

I threw the other man aside and returned to the fire.

Creon watched his companion closely before continuing.

"Then speak your words now," I said.

Demophon stood beside Creon, like an enraged bull, with murder in his eyes.

"Yes," Creon said calmly. "I will speak our words, and to show our good will, I will include information to sign our death warrants."

"Creon, no!" Demophon protested.

"It is the only way he will believe us, my friend. Hanbal is honest and trustworthy. I can tell. If he choses to betray us, then the Gods have abandoned us." He turned back to me. "Hanbal, you are correct to decipher that we are spies. We have been a part of Alexander's campaign since he took Halicarnassus, and are now a part of his advance intelligence gatherers. Now," he leaned closer, "when I say that we are spies, it is not for the king of Macedon, but for Athens."

I sat back, almost wishing I had not asked.

He continued. "You see, Hanbal, there are many free Greeks of Athens, of Sparta, of fallen Thebes that was destroyed by Philip, and others who know that a world run by Alexander is not a world in which we, and our sons, and our daughters, can safely live. It is a world of tyranny in which free citizens will be slaves to a very few. For myself, I am an Athenian, and I love my polis and my people as much as I suspect you love this bright land of Egypt and your fellow Egyptians. Let me finish before you speak!" He held up his hand. "Alexander will arrive in Egypt in one week's time. The Persian governor of Egypt, Sabaces, was killed at the battle of Issus, and Mazaces has taken his place."

"Yes, I know." I had rejoiced at the news.

"Mazaces will not oppose Alexander when he arrives in the land of Egypt to take control. Who knows what will happen, or how long he will stay with King Darius and his forces still in control of Babylon..."

Creon took a long draught of his beer as though he was suddenly weighed down with a heavy burden. His confident shoulders slouched and he licked his parched lips.

"Now, before I tell you what it is we will need your help with, I must tell you something more about Alexander. The young king is not like other men. He is a force of nature. He is a warrior, a poet, a leader, and a strategist. He is highly intelligent, a scientist, an explorer, and he is physically perfect. He believes he is descended from Achilles on his mother's side, and Herakles on his father's. He takes the Iliad to heart and believes in the deeds recounted therein, just as many Greeks do. But Alexander sees himself as Achilles - young, skilled, brash…and immortal."

"No man is immortal," I added.

"I am inclined to agree, for to believe otherwise is hubris. But some say he is the son of Zeus."

Creon let that sink in and drank some more. His composure was back, but I had a question.

"You say Alexander believes you are here doing reconnaissance for him? However, you are spies. So, I would like to know who, in Athens, *really* sent you?"

"This is information that would get us killed." He paused and nodded. "Very well… We are working for Demosthenes of Athens," he said unflinchingly. "Do you know of him?"

"I have heard the name, but all I know of him is that he is one of Macedon's most outspoken opponents. An orator, not a general."

"True, and true. Demosthenes is also a very great man, and a patriot of Athens. He is the mind that, with other Athenians, can repair this broken world."

"Athens, or Sparta…" I mused, "or Macedon? What's the difference?"

They looked at me quizzically.

"They are all alike to me. They are all states of the Hellenes, all with shifting loyalties. Macedon just happens to be the one who is wiping out the Persians at the moment, and I find little fault in that."

"How can you say or believe that?" Demophon finally spoke for the first time since we had grappled. "Haven't you heard anything that Creon has said?"

"I have, yes. But what I still have *not* heard is what you want of me." I stared hard at them and they knew they had to tell me now or I would have no more of their presence in my home.

"Demosthenes met an Egyptian official in Athens not long ago and spoke with him about this land. He told Demosthenes about many things, including you, 'The Asp', and how you were paring down the Persian population of Egypt, a perpetual thorn in the Persian governor's side. Demosthenes was intrigued by you, the rumours about you, and asked us to make contact with you."

"To what end? What does Demosthenes offer for my help?"

The two men looked at each other and nodded agreement. Creon spoke.

"We are to offer you ninety-nine Attic talents of silver to kill Alexander, King of Macedon."

MY WORLD WENT QUIET. SUCH A SUM... I REMEMBER thinking that that would replace my family's lost horse fortunes several times over. My family would be forever safe and secure. I thought even of rebuilding the temple of Hathor where my mother had danced the sacred rites, but bigger and more beautiful than before. So many thoughts around such a sum of coin. Over eight-hundred years' worth of wages for a mercenary soldier!

The two men continued eating and drinking as I thought this over. They were watching me keenly, though they tried not to appear to be doing so. The wind picked up and swirled sand about my feet where I had stood. The sun was descending. I looked up at the sky. Somewhere out there to the south, my family was moving farther and farther away from me.

Or was I pushing them away?

Perhaps both were true at the time.

This was not a light decision, for if I accepted, I might not survive. What little I knew of Alexander told me that this would not be like slaying a Persian governor or satrap. And did I really want to slay such a man as that? Alexander was poised to destroy the Persian Empire, Egypt's oppressor, entirely. Was that not what I wanted?

My semi-Greek education was causing me endless inner debate, and I was becoming frustrated. I needed time to think. I turned to Creon and Demophon.

"Why would I want to kill the man who is on the verge of destroying the Persians? Why do you? Indeed, we all despise the Persians and Medes."

"We have told you why," Demophon spoke in a calm manner, oddly enough. "A Macedonian hegemony would not be an improvement."

"I think I can ease your mind on that point, Hanbal," Creon said, rubbing his chin in thought. "There are some conditions to this sum Demosthenes has offered. Ninety-nine talents is not something offered for a job such as you have done to this point. You want the Persians defeated, as do we. So, we want you to infiltrate Alexander's inner circle. Demophon and I will introduce you as one of the living forces behind Egyptian resistance to the Persians. We will say that you wish to join his campaign to go east."

"Why would I go east?" I was even more suspicious now.

"Ah, my point is that we don't want you to kill Alexander until he *has* defeated Persia. After that, you are to drive your assassin's dagger deep and painfully."

"And what of the other Macedonian nobles?" I asked. "Surely they will take control. From what I hear, they are all capable men."

Demophon waived this off. "They will fight over the scraps Alexander leaves behind. Without him, they're done, leaderless and-"

"And the reason of Athens will prevail," Creon finished confidently.

"How would I even get close to the king when all of his advisors and courtiers are crowding around him, which I assume they always are?"

"You are right. It is a near impossible task. Though Alexander is a very thoughtful man, for a Macedonian, and often wanders alone in thought. You will have to bide your time."

This did not inspire confidence. So many conflicting thoughts, and my head had begun to pound. *Don't rush this!* I told myself. I turned to them. "I need time, men of Athens, to think about your offer."

"What is there to think about?" Demophon demanded, clearly unable to maintain his feigned calm any longer.

"Much." I said no more, but my thoughts immediately flew to my family, Eshe and the girls, and my homeland which I would have to leave for so long. My own life would be under threat at all times.

Creon nodded carefully. "Very well. You have one week to decide. But," and here he let fall his mask of democracy, "we have revealed much to you…too much. Be warned that if you speak of any of this to anyone, you will regret it all of your days."

I felt a chill at that.

They stood then, and turned to go out. "You have seven days."

And with that, they were gone.

Chapter Four

A CUT OF THE HEART

When the night's veil was nearly fully drawn and the starry sea was bright above, I climbed to the flat, rocky outcrop above our home where I usually went to think.

Below, all seemed so empty and quiet, unbearable. I could not hear Eshe humming softly anymore, nor Jamela and Femi's laughter. Such a decision was before me that my head pounded even under the soft sighing of the night breeze around rock and palm. Next to me was the beer jug that I had carried up with me.

"Isis, Hathor, and Osiris…" I prayed. "Help me to decide on the right course of action. I feel lost. Guide me…"

Huddled under my black cloak, I drank from the jug, savouring Eshe's honeyed beer. I drank and drank, more and more until the jug was empty and I was in a graver stupor than I had been after any killing, which was my unfortunate habit in those days. I watched the stars swirl above me in the heavens, the great dragon, the twins dancing, and I waited for the Gods to speak to me.

It is my theory that the Gods are always willing to help you out or give you a sign of sorts when the matter is of lesser importance, such as which horse to purchase, or whether a journey to Memphis is to be undertaken or not. For the decision with which I needed help, the Gods, to my drunken state of mind, were silent. For the Bacchae of Greece, their god speaks more to them when they are at the heights of inebriation. Not so for me.

Isis and Osiris, I believe, were disappointed at my weakness, my cowardice. Hathor, Beloved and Loving, only infused my heart and soul with a longing to be with my family. This was one of those decisions which the Gods intended for me to make on my own, the decision that all the lesser ones in which I had their aid were supposed to have prepared me for.

I passed out only to be tormented by a night of terrible imaginings, of dreams of thousands and thousands of men and spears, all of it punctuated by the screams of my family.

I awoke with the dawn, shaking, and vomited against the rock face. I then picked myself up and climbed back down to the ground, my mood dark and fearful. Something was not right.

Those next six days before Creon and Demophon were to return were tortuous in and of themselves. I had hoped for some new commissions to keep me occupied, but there was no need expressed by any Egyptian from Saqqara, or Memphis, or elsewhere. Word had come that Alexander had departed Gazzat and arrived in Pelousion as a liberator. He received a warm reception.

I thought of Demophon's description of what had

happened to the people of Tyre and Gazzat in the wake of Alexander's victories.

The Persians occupying Egypt were now fleeing in droves like migrating swallows before the falcon. What need had anyone for my services now?

So I spent the days riding and training, and the nights drinking to escape my burning thoughts and nightmares. By the morning of the seventh day, I was quite certain of my decision, having let Hathor override all thoughts of vengeance, money, or glory. I had made a mistake, I knew, and now I wanted to be back with my family. Even three thousand talents was not enough to dissuade me from that. And so, I prepared myself for the Greeks' visit.

They would not take kindly to my refusal of their offer and Demosthenes' silver. In fact, I knew they would likely kill me for all the precious information they had spilled before me like so many grains of wheat. When they arrived at my home toward midday, I was armed and ready for a fight.

"Greetings, Hanbal," Creon spoke first. He took notice of my weapons immediately.

Demophon stood beside him with a satchel over his shoulder. Both were armed with short swords and daggers and made no attempt to hide their muscled cuirasses now that all knew the Hellenes had arrived in Egypt.

"I do believe he has made a decision," Demophon sneered. "So, Egyptian Asp? Are you so arrogant that you think you can simply refuse Demosthenes and Athens' ninety-nine talents?"

"Wait, Demophon," Creon put out his arm. "Perhaps Hanbal is simply ready to ride out with us." He turned those cold eyes on me. "Hanbal? It has been seven days. Alexander is now in Egypt with his army. You have had time to think. So? What is your answer? Will you help us rid the world of its greatest tyrant?"

I stared at them, so sure beneath their cloak of democracy. *They* were the allies of arrogance, not me. I drew my sword and answered.

"I will not help you. I do not care for you, or your private battles with Macedon. I will remain in Egypt and let you go abroad to fight or betray as you see fit. Now, leave my home."

Both men simply stood there, smiling at me, and I felt a terrible foreboding in my gut. Neither of them drew their weapons. Creon walked a few paces to the side and came back to where he had stood, his arms behind his back as though delivering a verdict in the Areopagus of Athens.

"Sadly, we suspected that you would say that, Hanbal. A Nile frog like yourself can hardly be expected to understand the broader implications of actions in the world outside of your pond. Athens is the only civilized polis with such understanding, and that is why it is Athens who will rule at the end of the day. Athens *is* the alpha and omega of this world."

I moved toward them, sick of their talk and haughty demeanour. Just as I raised my blade, Demophon held out the satchel he had been holding. "Not so fast, Hanbal!"

I stopped short at the sight of something protruding from the bag - a splash of cobalt.

Demophon opened the flap and threw two cobalt blankets onto the sand at my feet. "I believe you recognize these?"

My heart stopped and it took all my will not to leap at them and cut them down. "Where did you get those?" I demanded, my throat burning with the bile that had risen in my gullet.

"Don't be coy, Hanbal." Creon stepped right up to me now, unafraid. "Your precious daughters were wrapped in them as they travelled with your wife the day we met you."

"You should be more secretive with your family, Asp," Demophon chuckled. "They are quite beautiful."

"If you've harmed them, I shall kill you long and painfully!" I roared.

"Peace now!" Creon stepped in front of Demophon. "Your wife and daughters are well for the moment, and can remain as such depending on your actions from this point on. For now, they are our hostages against your good behaviour and completion of the request asked of you."

"You mean *forced* upon me!" I gritted my teeth.

"Call it what you will. The fact is that you only have two choices open to you now. To complete your task by helping us, or, to have your wife and daughters live out their days as slaves in Athens while you yourself are killed."

My head began to spin and I fought for control of myself as rage and helplessness poisoned my being. *Eshe, Jamela, Femi... Gods help them!* "How do I know you haven't already harmed them or that you will even keep your end of the bargain? I doubt very much you will pay what you said you would."

"Oh, there will not even be one talent for you, as you do not value the money enough," Creon continued. "Your family and their lives will be your payment. And if you think to deceive us, or that word of your betrayal will not reach Athens, you are mistaken. I have a thousand men in my network, known only in full to myself, Demophon, and Demosthenes. Swift riders and archers can send word quickly. My orders can be easily carried out. Your choice is simple: kill Alexander, or kill your family."

I knew that the Gods were punishing me for my hubris,

but also for my blindness in sending Eshe, and the girls away. It was a punishment for all the times I had ignored Eshe's embrace or the girls' pleas for my time in favour of killing another Persian oppressor. I had deceived myself for so long that I was right in my actions, that I was doing it all for Egypt and my ancestors, that I had begun to believe it. I had ignored the heart of my life, and now I was in danger of paying the ultimate price and having that heart cut out of me for all time.

Creon stepped up to me again and put his wretched hand on my shoulder. "Come, Hanbal. I swear by Athens and all my ancestors that I will uphold my end of the bargain if you will uphold yours. Do you also swear?"

I could hear the blood pounding in my ears, as if it would drive me mad, but I breathed through the blood haze before me, fought down the urge to kill them right then and there. I stepped back and picked up the two blankets that had so recently warmed my daughters' skin. *Eshe, forgive me my love…*

"I swear that I shall do what is needed to bring my family back to me. I swear that I will kill King Alexander of Macedon…*after* the world runs red with Persian blood."

THE SON OF ZEUS

CHAPTER FIVE

THE CITY OF PTAH

When I think of Alexander, I am wracked with emotions, not because of the man, nor what he stood for, but rather for the times. It was a new age of heroes in which men surpassed the deeds of those who fought at Troy, or of those who sought out the Golden Fleece.

Alexander and many other Hellenes lived by these tales, measured themselves by them, mimicked them. Only Alexander was more than a hero, he was a force of nature, wondrous and terrible.

The emotions that attack me when I hear his name are hatred and loss, fear, anxiety, and deep sadness. Not the hope and elation felt by those men around him. My experience was, perhaps, more complicated. On top of it all, however, was an ethereal blanket of sheer wonder and anticipation of what would come next. When I think of Alexander, I also hear things - sighing winds, the thunder of horses' hooves, and the drums of war. I hear pain and praise beyond reckoning. I hear music and screeching eagles.

Now, beneath my languid palm tree so many years later, I wonder if that is how the Gods themselves feel as they watch mortals, taken daily through the showers and shine of this world. How can the immortals bear it?

I HAVE BEEN WISTFUL THESE LAST FEW LINES, AND THIS BELIES my true state of mind at the time. When I set out from my home with Ra, my weapons, and what few belongings I could carry, including my girls' blankets, I was anything but calm and filled with remembrance. I was more like a lion, hunting and hunted, in an unfamiliar place, though I was not one mile from home. I wanted to kill the king and be done with it, but then Eshe, Jamela, and Femi would be killed. I was to wait until Persia was defeated outright.

I wanted to kill the two Hellenes who rode in front of me, the hateful bastards who had turned my life upside down, but if I did that, my beloved Eshe and our daughters would be killed. It seemed death was around every corner, an outcome chained to every decision.

There were more and more Hellenes in Egypt then since the Persian governor, Mazaces, had handed over Egypt to Alexander when he arrived in Pelusium at the head of his conquering army. Apparently, Alexander was welcomed by throngs of Egyptians waving palm fronds and tossing flower petals in his path. He was their saviour, their liberator.

I felt helpless as I rode with Creon and Demophon toward Memphis, helpless because I could feel my family close, though I was being watched at every moment. One wrong move would alert their captors immediately. Creon had been sure to point out that if anything happened to himself of Demophon, one of the many other Greeks watching us would send the message immediately for my family to be executed. In all the nightmares of my life, that one possible outcome was the most terrifying.

Hathor, beloved and loving, kept my hand at bay, and so as I rode and listened to the smug dialogue of the two Athenians, my whole being was pulled as taut as a Syrian bow. It was a bow I could not loose myself.

My only comfort as we rode was the familiar feel of Ra beneath me, the strong flanks and steady breath. The last of my family's horses, he and I were in it together. I leaned down to pat his neck, and when I sat up again, I spotted my old home in the distance. I shot off toward it without a word to either of the Greeks. I could hear their shouts and the galloping of their horses' hooves in their pursuit, but I didn't care. When I reined in before the dwelling, yet another wave of nostalgia washed over me. I had not been back there over the years since my parents' murder. The land was reclaiming what was once our home. The roof had caved in long since, and the long fences of the horse paddocks were dried and cracked, tumbled in the dust.

"What in Hades do you think you're doing, Egyptian?" Demophon raged as he stopped roughly beside me in a cloud of dust.

Creon arrived more calmly to join us. "I think," he said, "that this may be our friend's childhood home." He turned from Demophon to me. "Am I correct?"

I made no answer to either of them, merely walked Ra in a slow circle, taking it all in. After a few moments, I spurred back to the main road to Memphis.

. . .

IN THE YEARS OF PERSIAN OCCUPATION, THE GREAT CAPITAL of Lower Egypt, Memphis, city of Ptah the Creator, always a focus of the building activities of Pharaoh Ramesses II, was largely asleep. Not that it was in disuse, but rather Egyptians did not throng the markets, streets, and courtyards as they once had. The smoke of the offerings to the Gods was thin and perfunctory, enough only to keep the local population satisfied. Our people, cities, and even our gods had slept for years, but as we rode into Memphis that day it became apparent that the hibernation was at an end.

People were laughing and dancing, and children were playing. Not a Persian was in sight as vendors plied their wares with great exuberance. Everyone took to the streets to sweep away dust and debris, regaining their pride with every action of choice. The priests of the various temples processed, and thick plumes of smoke spun skyward from the altars in all quarters.

I had not been to Memphis in many years for fear of being recognized by Persian troops. I wanted to feel elation at the sights, the life before and around me, but how could I? The axe that hung above the heads of my wife and daughters leached away all possibility of joy. Then there was the smaller matter of reconciling the scene before me with what I was being forced to do.

The men of Alexander's army mingled with my people along the avenue of the Sphinxes and around the colossi of Ramesses the Great. People were not afraid to approach the Greeks, and it was as if the age-old friendship between our peoples had begun again where it had been broken by the men of Babylon and Persepolis.

I looked to where we were headed, in the direction of the large palace complex that sat on the promontory to the north, overlooking the city. I knew then that Alexander must be there with Mazaces, the former Persian governor, under his boot.

Amid the cheering, singing crowds, I followed Creon and Demophon to the top of the promontory. I suddenly felt very small. The world had taken on a different lustre, beautiful and foreboding, which I still can not rightly explain. The golden sandstone walls along the ramp leading to the pylon gate on the east side of the rock shimmered as we rode, wavering at the edge of my sight.

I felt for the daggers criss-crossed on my chest. *Hathor, watch over us…* I prayed as we were halted by a large group of Macedonian soldiers with silver breastplates and shields, holding spears that were at least eight feet tall.

"Hold!" one of the guards said as he blocked our path. "No horses or weapons beyond this point."

Creon looked down on the Macedonian haughtily from his saddle. "Tell the king that Creon and Demophon of Athens have brought the one they call 'The Asp' to join our ranks."

The guard looked me up and down and though I was taller and brawnier than all of them, there was not an ounce of doubt in him, or in any of his companions, that they could take me in a fight. After all the swift, appraising looks of men I had fought and killed, I had become adept at discerning their assessments of me, and using that to my advantage. However, these were true, battle-hardened men of war, each and every one of them. They were not Persian slaves. I knew I had to be careful. I knew I had to win some of them over. I nodded a greeting to the guard and he turned back to Creon.

"The king is in a war council right now and is not receiving anyone except his Companions and generals. Leave your mounts here and come back later."

"You dare turn us away?" Demophon nudged his horse forward, but the guard was unfazed and even ventured a smile.

"Careful, Athenian. You're a long way from the marble of Athens. Now, get off your buggering horse before my mates here plunge you head first up its ass!"

The Macedonians behind him laughed heartily and Creon quickly dismounted to speak to the guard. "We will comply with the king's wishes, of course. Come, Demophon," he urged calmly. "Let us leave the guards to their duties. We will return later."

I noticed that Creon took a long look at the guard, as if to burn his face onto his memory. We dismounted and walked our horses to an area shaded by palms, just to the side of the great ramp. There, several street urchins were lined up, hired by the guards to hold people's horses and camels. Ra shied from the camels, as all horses do, but not as much as the Athenians' mounts who were less used to the dromedaries.

One of the urchins, a boy of no more than eight or nine years, approached me, grinning wildly. "Are you really The Asp? I heard the Hellenes call you that."

I smiled and undid one of my leather arm guards to reveal the serpents around my forearm.

"I will take good care of your horse and possessions. No one will get close to steal anything."

I reached up to pat Ra reassuringly and to unhook my satchel containing the cobalt blankets, slinging it carefully about my shoulders. "Thanks, little one," I said to the boy as I made my way down the ramp ahead of Creon and Demophon. I could feel the Athenians' simmering anger at my back, anger at how the Macedonians had ridiculed them and at my presumption at leaving first. I had taken a risk leaving, but there was one place I knew I had to go, a place of smoke and song and dance.

"Watch yourself, Asp!" Demophon spat. "Remember what you stand to lose!"

I stopped and waited for them. Just then, I noticed several other men hovering at the periphery, watching us. The rest of the crowd took little notice of us, and flowed around us like the river around a clump of rocks.

"Do you think I'm going to run?" I asked Creon, ignoring Demophon. "You should be smarter than to think I would care so little for those whom you have as hostages." I knew I showed weakness by saying that, but I could not chance my family's safety.

"Where are you going, Hanbal?" Creon asked.

"Not even you would risk the Gods' displeasure if you wish for me to succeed in the task you have demanded."

I turned away from him and kept walking.

CHAPTER SIX

THE TEMPLES

It had been many years since my last visit to a shrine of Hathor, Lady of Love. The temple of Hathor at the southern edge of Memphis, the smaller shrine, had always been a source of comfort and consolation in my mind. On my last visit many years before, I had been with my father who was in the city to negotiate the sale of one of our broodmares. He had left me at the temple where he knew the priestesses because of my mother. He knew I would be safe there while he conducted his business.

With Creon and Demophon trailing me, I passed the grand temple complexes of Ptah and Apis, rich in ornamentation, their high walls resplendent with hieroglyphs and images of bow-wielding Ramesses the Great.

I felt a shudder through my heart as I approached the small temple, and stopped in the street before the entrance. Sweet smoke wafted skyward from the enclosure and the tinkling of sistra and song reached out to me.

"I will not be long," I said over my shoulder to the two Athenians. "Sit, drink, and wait." I pointed to a small grouping of tables outside a tavern at the edge of the square, and stepped through the sandstone arches into the temple.

SERENITY WASHED OVER ME AS I PASSED BETWEEN THE pylons and into the outer court and the world of the sanctuary. Everything was immaculate as I remembered, and the familiar smells of incense and flower petals blanketed me in comfort. I felt I should not have been armed, but did not dare to leave my weapons with the two Greeks outside.

A cool breeze swirled about me as I walked hesitantly like a stallion on an unstable Nile barge, through the soft sand. The laughter of children reached my ears and I turned around quickly, hopeful.

But it seemed to be a waking dream. I was alone.

I moved to a shrine at the periphery and knelt there, beneath the cedar roof painted with golden stars.

I was at a loss as I sought any words or thoughts that I could offer up. All I had were my emotions which raged inside of me, and covered all aspects of earthly existence - despair, love, hate, and hope. Anger vied with my dying joy, and violence crept in to be washed over by self-pity.

As if on cue, a sistrum from the inner court roused me. I raised myself up to be met by a white-clad priestess. She spoke not, but gazed into me knowingly, reached out and touched the snakes upon my forearms.

Uncomfortable, I realized I had not purchased an offering for Hathor, something to be taken by the priestess and offered to the goddess. Then, it struck me hard. I reached into the satchel I had been carrying and removed the cobalt blankets that belonged to my daughters. At that moment, they were dearer to me than anything, and my hands shook as I handed them over.

"These belong to my two daughters, and were woven by my wife." My throat caught and stung. "They are in danger, taken from me. Please ask the goddess to keep the three of them safe." I began to turn, but the priestess spoke then, holding the offerings with great reverence and a love befitting the goddess.

"Come," she said. "Hear the music and see the dance in honour of Hathor, Lady of Love."

I followed her to the second pylon gate that led to the roofless inner court. The space was bathed in sunlight and surrounded by columns topped with capitals that were earthly representations of the goddess. She smiled down with care and comfort. The walls were painted with depictions of various pharaohs and their eternal deeds.

What had I done but kill and push my family away? And like a dagger to my gut, I knew I had to kill again to bring them back to me. I did not know it then, but I would have to wade through rivers of blood for longer than I would have imagined.

From where I leaned against a column, I watched the sacred dancer twirl in the cleansing light of the sun to the sounds of a sistrum and reed flute, cymbal and voice. When I was young, the rituals had always soothed me to sleep and wistfulness. Now, I felt like I did not belong, that the only pure things about me were the cobalt blankets cradled in the priestess' arms as she smiled and carried them through to the hypostyle halls beyond where I could not follow.

The dancer was reaching the end of her ritual now, her movements speedy and smooth as her red robes spun and swirled like the clouds of sacred incense about her body. When she stopped suddenly, she was facing me.

In a second, she morphed into what I believed was my mother. There she stood, clear as day, the rest of the court a blur. My mother…alive again.

I was struck dumb for moments, staring at her as she had been the last time I had seen her dance for Hathor. Her robes were as red as they had ever been, her hair long and straight and black as jet.

Hanbal, she whispered, but her mouth did not move. She reached out a lithe, olive-coloured hand to touch my face, but before she reached me, the voice changed and the younger dancer stood once more before me, a questioning look on her face.

"Are you unwell?" she asked, slightly afraid, or maybe compassionate, for the two seemed similar in that moment.

"I…I…forgive me." I could see the priestess returning, watching me, as were the musicians on the other side of the court. I looked at the girl again, seeing my young mother, and fought the tears that burned the inside of my lids. "I'm sorry…" I turned and ran out, leaving behind the shocked priestess and dancer, the musicians, the goddess' sanctuary, my girls' blankets, and my mother's Ka.

I STOOD DAZEDLY IN THE MIDDLE OF THE SQUARE BEFORE THE temple, hot tears burning down my cheeks. With my back to the two Athenians, I tried to regain my senses, breathing deeply, but the buzz around me, the increasingly frenetic energy of the outside world, made me nervous. Something was happening. People were running north up the street, and for an oddly selfish moment, I thought they were fleeing me, for I must have looked quite a sight, wild-eyed and weeping, armed to the teeth. I did not care, lost as I was in the misery that had taken hold of me.

Creon's cold voice brought me to. "We've spent enough time here. Let's move. Back to the palace."

However, we could not manage a route back to the palace. We were swept along by the flow of citizens and soldiers all headed to the same place - the Temple of Apis.

Flanked by Creon and Demophon, we were pushed to the temple's monumental gate, people shouting "He's here!" and "He pays respect to our Gods!"

"Who is here?" Demophon demanded of a nearby soldier.

"Alexander, of course!" the man returned over the din of excitement. "The king is making offerings to the Apis Bull inside."

Another cheer went up from the crowd and the press became tighter.

The soldier laughed. "They love him for it!" he yelled to us as he moved through a crack in the crowd to get a closer look.

In its frenzy, the mass of people was becoming dangerous, and I crossed my arms over the daggers at my chest. I could see the nervous frustration on Creon and Demophon's faces and realized how easy it would be for me to kill them in this confusion. My fingers tapped at the hilts of my throwing knives, but I knew I had to control myself. If these two were lost, so too would be my lifeline to Eshe, Femi, and Jamila.

My dark thoughts dissipated when one, then two, then countless other arms about me pointed to the cloudless sky and there, rising on the thermals of that heated day, was an eagle. It circled directly above us, that symbol of Zeus, with all eyes upon it as it drifted downward to land next to the image of the Apis Bull atop the great pylons of the temple. There was a stunned hush at this sight and then, as if a part of some immortal drama, Alexander, King of Macedon, and leader of the Greeks, strode out of the temple flanked by the priests of Apis, his own seer, and his companions.

The people of Memphis, along with the men of his army, erupted at this auspicious sight, of the eagle and bull directly above Alexander and the high priest of Apis.

I felt the hairs on the back of my neck prickle coldly and strained to get a better glimpse of Alexander through the crowd that showered him with flower petals. I had not been prepared for this, as one encamped in a long-dry riverbed is suddenly swept away by a flash flood after summer rains. Though I could not yet see him clearly, I felt that the world about Alexander was entirely different, and part of me wanted to melt away into the crowd. There was, however, nowhere to go in that sweaty press of adulation. I spotted the eagle taking flight from its perch and then, without warning, the crowd parted effortlessly to form an avenue.

Between the rows of smiling, cheering Egyptians and Greeks, walked Alexander.

At first, I was taken aback at his short stature, but realized that despite that, we were in the presence of a Titan. Every rumour I had ever heard surfaced in my mind, and most seemed impossibly true. He spoke to the people, floating between Greek and Egyptian without pause, and he addressed those he recognized by name, without a secretary to whisper their identities into his ear. His golden gaze took all life in and lit the faces of all around him.

Then, those eagle eyes fell upon me where, to my dismay, I found myself standing alone in his path in the middle of the avenue. I quickly backed away, head bowed - I knew not why - but he smiled and strode toward me.

Long, slightly curling auburn hair framed a vibrant, youthful face. He wore an ornate Greek thorax of white, red, and gold, cavalry boots, and a crimson cloak. His heavily muscled arms were bare and scarred, and a quick assessment led me to believe that any man, no matter his size, would meet his match against this king of twenty-four years.

But it was those eyes, unlike any mortal's, that bore into me and made me shudder, that I remember most.

He was fearless and likely had no need of the body-guards at his back, but they were there and they were heavily armed. I wondered if I moved my arms if they would cut me down then, so I kept them crossed over my chest.

Alexander's eyes darted to the snakes tattooed on my exposed forearm. "I have heard of you," he said, not quietly. "You are the Asp of Saqqara."

"Yes, sire," I said, not daring a long look.

"You need not bow… Please." Alexander reached out for my arm and held it aloft as he spoke high and loud. "This man is a hero, and one of Memphis!"

The crowd now focussed on me, abuzz with curiosity.

"For years he has harassed the Persians who held sway over Egypt. He has let them know that Egypt would not give up its defiance! *This* man - The Asp - is such a man as I need in my army!"

The crowd roared and people cheered me where I stood next to the King of Macedon.

Alexander lowered my arm and a cloud passed over his face as he noticed Creon and Demophon behind me. The smile, however, returned, though it was different than before.

"My Athenian friends. Thank you for finding this man

for us. My man, Nestor, told me you had come to the palace earlier." He turned back to me and placed a friendly hand on my shoulder. "Come and dine with all of us at the palace tonight, and we will talk of killing Persians and of your family's horses."

"Sire," I bowed my head and stepped back as he moved on to trade banter with a pocket of Macedonian veterans a little farther ahead.

And that was it. As brief a meeting as any, but as momentous and terrifying as anything else, for that was the instant I was thrown headlong into the Greek war machine.

"And so it begins," Creon said coldly.

I knew then that he was more dangerous than Demophon or the countless other Athenian spies lurking in the shadows of my new world.

I turned away from them and began to make my way back to Ra to see him properly stabled.

"Where do you think you're going, you piece of shit?" Demophon's hand grabbed at the shoulder of my tunic.

My own hand reacted and before I knew it, I had his wrist bent painfully, my face in his. "I am *not* your slave or your inferior, you arrogant bastard!" I twisted his wrist harder. "You came to me for help, remember?"

Demophon's face was red with rage then, but a smile creased his lips and I felt the prick of a blade at my back.

"And do you remember what is at stake for you, Hanbal?" Creon whispered in my ear. "Release him."

I did, and stepped back, not taking my eyes off him.

"Now, you have an opportunity to begin your work and get into the inner circle. The Gods themselves could not have arranged a better meeting with Alexander." Creon lowered his dagger.

I relaxed a little, but was still uncomfortable at meeting

the man I was forced to get close to and kill. "As I said before," I told Creon, "I know what is at stake."

Before I could say more, a large group of citizens had begun cheering and I was pulled away amid laughter and praise.

"Let's hear it for The Asp!" they yelled.

"Praise Isis and Osiris!"

"Our own hero!" they continued. Demophon and Creon stood there in the centre of the square staring at me with mingled confidence and hate as they receded from my vision and I was hauled away by the grateful people of Memphis.

THE PEOPLE ACCOMPANIED ME BACK TO WHERE THE BOY STILL held Ra on the ramp to the palace. The boy was surrounded by folks plying him with questions and as I approached with my forced entourage, more cheers went up. The boy waved to me and held up Ra's reins.

"Thank you," I said, ruffling his hair and flipping him a tiny copper piece.

As the crowd about us dissipated, waving to me as they went, I turned to Ra who was in obvious distress, stomping his hooves. I whispered so that only he could hear me and the timber of my voice immediately soothed him. I think we both felt better then. I closed my eyes momentarily, my forehead resting against his muscular neck. I did not want to open them. That's how overwhelmed I was in that moment. I became keenly aware of the lack of my girls' blankets, and was shattered by loneliness.

"Erm…" came a voice.

I turned to see the Macedonian guard, Nestor, who stood before me. The rest of the guards watched from a distance. I nodded to him.

"I've been informed that the king has invited you and your Athenian friends to the banquet this evening."

"It appears that is the case," I responded. "But they are not my friends, the two Athenians." I stood taller as I said it, holding to what pride yet remained in me.

"That's good," Nestor said, more friendly now. "I don't like the feel of those two. How did you happen to join up with them?"

I knew I had to be careful here, that this was the first of many questions I was to be wary of. "Circumstance, I suppose. I believe they were sent to find me, to engage me as a killer of Persians."

He was silent, observant for a moment, and then he nodded. "Aye, so I've been told. Anyway, when you come tonight, leave your weapons just outside the palace doors. They'll be safe. Where are you billeted?"

I had not thought about where to spend the night until then. Demophon and Creon had not spoken of accommodation. "I do not know. I don't think the arrangements have been made."

"Typical of the Athenians." He spat off to the side and continued. "Most of our forces are encamped to the north of the city and barges continue to arrive daily from Pelusium and Heliopolis for the games the king will hold. Here." He handed me a scrap of papyrus from a scrip filled with similar pieces. "This will get you free lodging and stabling for your horse in any inn in the northern enclosure of the city."

"I know a good place!' the little boy jumped in.

"What's your name, boy?" Nestor asked, hands on his hips.

"I am Anum, and I've lived here all my life. My father is a fisherman."

"What inn is it?" I asked.

"The Falcon."

"Hmm. I've heard of it," Nestor confirmed. "Good, clean, and secure."

"All right, Anum. Lead me there and I'll give you another copper piece."

"Done!" Anum clapped his dusty hands and set off down the ramp with me following.

"See you tonight, Egyptian!" Nestor said before halting an approaching cart full of provisions for the banquet.

I WAS TREATED WELL AT THE FALCON, AND SHIED UNDER THE lavish praise the landlord offered me for my bloody work. Word had spread quickly and I was given a fine room. I doubted that this attention was doing me any favours, but knew that there was little I could do about it.

At first, I worried that the Athenians would take offence at my getting my own lodgings, but I quickly dismissed the thought as I could feel eyes on me everywhere as I followed the boy to the inn which, as it turned out, was filled with Greek officers anyway. Creon and Demophon knew exactly where I was at all times, and my family was probably the safer for it.

For the remainder of the afternoon I sat alone in my room with a plate of food offered me by the proprietor. I ate quietly as my mind raced with thoughts of Eshe, Jamela, and Femi, and the king's banquet that night.

CHAPTER SEVEN

DINING WITH LIONS

As dusk began to settle over Memphis in hues of pale orange and purple, the first of the night's stars winked above the Nile, Giver of Life. Celebrations had not waned during the day, and even then the sound of laughter and song increased. It seemed that the whole of Egypt was caught up in a circle of celebration and elation while I stood apart, outside the bounds of happiness.

I roamed outside this jollity, quite apart from it, and my heart cracked at the thought of my family being in the same predicament, in a place I did not know. Dazedly, I had washed and dressed in a belted, knee-length, black tunic and my high brown riding sandals. I had brought only two large satchels with me on Ra when I left home, in addition to my weapons.

The man, Nestor, had said I would have to leave my weapons outside, but I did not plan on going anywhere unarmed, however safe the streets may have been at that time. I always expect something. I wore my short sword and daggers. Beneath my leather forearm guards, I kept two small daggers in their hidden sheaths. These I would not relinquish. How could I trust anyone?

I am not, nor have I ever been, a very social person. Indeed I would always shy away from crowds and discourse. Not that I was not intelligent, for I was, as I have said, educated in my youth by Greeks and Egyptians. Though I had never actually been to a proper banquet or symposium, I thought I had an inkling as to what I could expect. My Greek teachers had always stressed manners and proper dialogue, watering of wine, and debate. It had been many years since I had read or discussed Plato or Xenophon, whose horse manual my father had always praised.

I arrived at the palace entrance to find a long line of guests awaiting entry to the king's banquet. To my annoyance, Creon came to stand beside me.

"So, you're still here. Very wise." He did not look at me, opting instead to observe the crowd and note those who were present.

"I told you, I am not going anywhere." I looked about. "Where is Demophon?" I did not like *not* knowing where he was.

"He was not invited. He has other work to do anyway."

In the torchlight, I noticed that Creon had shaved and dressed in a clean white and blue chiton with gold borders. He seemed quite wealthy to me, but then I had never required much more than my family. The irony enraged me.

The line began to move and we shuffled up the ramp. We passed a few groups of revellers whom the guards had turned away because their names were not on the list. Alexander's scribe had been compiling one as he followed the king about. The palace was surrounded by heavily armed troops who stood stock-still, the firelight reflecting off their bronze and silver armour.

I could understand the precaution of tight security, of course. The fact of the matter was that Darius, Persian slave master that he was, was still at large and still commanded an enormous army. I had heard the soldiers saying the Persian force was growing more and more.

For the time being, the Hellenes were happy to be in Egypt. From what I gathered, however, the bulk of the Greek forces were stationed at Pelusium while Alexander, and Egypt, celebrated.

For myself, I doubted whether I would ever feel celebratory again, and so I focussed on listening to conversation and gathering what information I could about my new world of war and politics. I would learn much of Alexander from his soldiers.

I prayed to Hathor to give me patience, though I do not know if she heard me, for the very act I had to wait to carry out was contrary to all that the goddess' loving nature dictated.

When Creon and I approached the pylon gate to the palace, Nestor and three other guards stepped forward.

Creon held his arms out to the side. "I am unarmed," he said confidently. Indeed, he did not even have a leather pouch.

"Check him anyway," Nestor grunted at one of the guards who stepped forward to frisk the Athenian.

The disdain each man felt for the other was palpable. To Nestor's credit, he was unperturbed by the arrogant aristocrat and even managed a smile as he waved him on.

It was my turn next and I unhooked my sword and daggers and handed them to Nestor.

He stared a moment at my forearm guards but did not

say anything of them. "I'll take care of these for you," he said, holding up the weapons I had given him.

"My thanks," I replied. "Where am I going?"

He laughed. "Just follow the noise!"

I started through the gates.

"I hope you can hold your drink, Egyptian!" he shouted after me.

THE CORRIDORS OF THE ANCIENT PALACE COMPLEX WERE covered in hieroglyphs, the images providing a level of comfort to me, but also inspiring the necessary awe as one made his way to the great court where the banqueters were gathered. Torches and royal guards lined the entire route beneath the high cedar roof until we spilled out into the open air of the court.

It became immediately obvious that when it came to the banquet of the Hellenes, Dionysos was the true ruler and patron.

Beneath the massive stalks of potted palms at the four corners of the court, ivy-crowned slaves flitted among the guests with kraters of watered wine, ensuring that no kylix remained empty in any one person's hand. At the far end of the court was a dais with one ornate couch draped in purple silks, flanked by four other couches, all of which were empty. On the ground, however, were several rows of couches radiating out from the dais.

There appeared to be about forty or so couches in all, and these were almost filled. We were told that the inner circle was reserved for Alexander's Companions, the middle for the generals and officers, and the outer circle for allies and local men of importance.

Creon and I were assigned to a couch on the outer

circle, yet only three couches from the end of the as yet empty dais. I sat down reluctantly next to Creon, and a young Egyptian boy who had obviously been recruited for the evening thrust a ceramic kylix into my hand and filled it with wine.

"Don't you have any date beer?" I asked, but the boy only shot me a frenzied look, shook his head, and disappeared amid the other servers.

Creon laughed and spilled some of his wine on the floor before drinking. "Beer? In civilized company, even among the Macedonians, the only proper drink is wine, Hanbal. Beer is for barbarians."

How could I sit next to this person whom I hated? "Surely, Creon, you do not disdain wheat, from which beer is made, and which is sacred to the goddess Demetra who watches over the harvest? Long may we avoid the starvation that would arise from her wrath."

He said nothing and turned to talk to a Carian official whom he recognized on his other side.

Though I knew I had to stay alert to everything, I was happy for the bottomless drink in my hand, as were most others present. The volume of speech was very high, so much so that when the young flute girls and aulos-playing boys were about, I could only hear them if they were directly in front of me.

Greeks drink to excess, especially the Macedonians among them. In my studies, I had learned of the proper etiquette at a symposium through Plato and other works, but those ideals of behaviour seemed from a distant age. Men groped at the musicians' buttocks as they passed and a few platters of food were dropped by unpleasantly startled slaves.

Despite the increasing drunkenness, it all came to a

sudden and reverential silence when the surrounding guards slammed their spear butts on the flagstones and Alexander emerged, golden cup in hand, from the royal apartments onto the dais.

His royal Companions in the inner circle stood and raised their cups to their king.

"Hail Alexander!" they cried in fiery unison.

"Hail Dionysos!" Alexander replied, spilling some wine. "And hail Alexander's army!" he yelled.

The court erupted and it seemed that the stars above shuddered. The king reclined and all followed suit. On the dais with the king were several people. Next to Alexander, on the same couch, was a woman of great beauty with whom the king spoke in hushed tones at times. This was, I later found out, Barsine, the king's mistress and widow of Alexander's late enemy, Memnon of Rhodes, who had fought relentlessly for Darius. Barsine was haughty and beautiful, and her Persian half shone through more than her Greek, despite the emerald coloured peplos she wore.

To the right of Alexander's couch was one of the king's childhood friends, and someone I would come to know very well. This was Ptolemy, a solidly built man, slightly shorter than myself with laughing blue eyes and sandy hair above a hooked nose. He reclined with the only other female guest at the gathering, the well-known hetaira, Thais. The latter captivated all who looked upon her, so much so that if one contemplated an earthly face for Aphrodite, Thais' face, blonde hair, and voluptuous body would be what came to mind. She was intelligent and could engage easily in conversation. She could also be quite dangerous. The sound of her laughter trickled through the greater noise as if the Gods meant for it to be heard.

Next to Ptolemy and Thais sat the king's grizzled

veteran general, Parmenion, and Alexander's official historian, Callisthenes, cousin to the king's famed teacher, Aristotle.

To Alexander's left was young man all his equal in appearance and demeanour, except that he was more pensive looking. He was just as handsome as the king, but taller and darker. This was Hephaestion, Alexander's best friend, supposed sometime lover and, more importantly, his most trusted advisor. Hephaestion was always on the look-out, watching his friend's back, scanning the surroundings even as he spoke with the former Persian governor of Egypt, Mazaces, who sat with him.

I confess that I was truly disgusted to see a Persian official, and a defeated one at that, sitting in such a place of honour at the king's banquet. I imagined feeding his fat carcass to the Nile crocodiles, rather than sitting where he was, head on his shoulders. On this, at the very least, Creon and I agreed.

Of all the people seated either side of the king, however, it was the seer, Aristander, who disturbed me the most. He sat nearest us, with Harpalus, the royal treasurer. He was white-bearded when I saw him up close that first time, but he seemed ageless. His eyes were as pale a blue as possible with overly large pupils that suggested he indeed saw beyond the veil to the realm of the Gods at all times. He said nothing to Harpalus or anyone else, but once in a while he and Alexander would exchange a look that communicated the proper time for an action. He linked Alexander to the Gods directly, or so it seemed to me that night. After such a look from Aristander, Alexander stood and the assembled mass stopped eating and drinking.

Dressed in a rich robe of purple, crimson, and gold, Alexander looked up to the heavens for a moment, silent, even whimsical, as though searching the stars for a sign. His golden eyes fell down to sweep over us all and, it seemed, to connect with each person. I looked down as his gaze rested upon me. I found it hard to look back. Then, he spoke.

"My fellow Greeks," he began. "We are a long way from home."

There were murmurs of approval.

"And our adventure has only just begun." He stepped around the front of his couch to the edge of the dais, still, completely sober, though he had been drinking non-stop. "With the liberation of this ancient land, a land with which Greece has had good relations for ages, the entire eastern half of the Middle Sea is now secure. Our back is safe now for when we press on to meet Darius, the coward who fled the field as Issus!"

Here, the Companions roared.

"We will see that the Persia of old, who invaded our lands and burned our temples, will cease utterly to exist." He allowed the cheers to die down before continuing. "Though we are only at the beginning of our Odyssey, we have seen more than most could ever dream of. We have, by the will of the Gods, achieved much. The heroes have been marching along with us, from Granicus to the holy gates of Troy itself, to Halicarnassus and to prophetic Gordium. We have moved forward, freeing the cities of Asia. At Issus we succeeded in routing an army three times larger than our own. And at Tyre, despite the impossibility of it all, your courage, your blood, and sweat, and determination bridged an impossible sea to victory over our enemies. Gazzat too, learned that Alexander's army is not to be opposed!"

"Hail Alexander, descendant of Achilles!" someone yelled at the back, referring to his act at Gazzat in which he dragged the rebel leader's body behind his chariot around the walls of the city, the same as Achilles had done to Hektor at Troy.

Alexander waved the praise away, but there was a definite light in his eyes when it was spoken. He continued.

"Now, in this ancient land of Egypt, we have found beauty, culture, riches, and new friends." At that, the king's eyes lighted on me, or so I thought, though other Egyptians were present. It was then that Mazaces' hateful gaze locked onto me, and I felt a choking sensation of sorts by the force of his hate.

"And here in this land we shall rest, celebrate, and rejuvenate for the final battle that must come and which must be won. Over the next three days, we shall hold games here in Memphis, in honour of the Gods of Greece and of Egypt!"

Everyone cheered, and men began to boast about their prowess in various events and how they would win the laurels at the games. Boasting was something, I was to discover, that was also a part of banqueting.

Mazaces' gaze returned to me and he spoke heatedly with Hephaestion, pointing at me.

Creon spotted this too. "I think, Hanbal, that the Persian has a problem with you."

He was not mocking me. Creon, who was also adept at reading men, could see the hatred emanating from the former governor.

Hephaestion leaned toward his king and spoke with some gravity.

Alexander's face darkened and he looked at the Persian who seemed to be explaining something.

All the while, Aristander stared at me. Then, the seer nodded to me.

My blood froze. I wished I had not drunk so much.

The king then stood and all fell silent once more.

Mazaces also stood.

"Honoured guests…friends…" Alexander began. "Mazaces has invoked the ancient right of complaint and vengeance against one of you." The king nodded to me. "Hanbal, son of Akil, the Asp of Saqqara…please stand."

Everyone looked about, trying to see whom the king addressed.

I felt ill.

"Hanbal," Alexander said, looking directly at me. "Come forward."

I rose from my couch and grew hot under the gaze of so many. What was the Persian playing at? *I will not be cowed by the dog!* I swore to myself. Chest out, head back, I strode toward the dais and bowed to the king, ignoring Mazaces. "Sire."

Alexander nodded and spoke to the vast room. "Many of you have heard of Hanbal and the resistance he had put up in this area. He is a hero to many." He glanced sidelong to his left. "Mazaces believes otherwise."

The Persian could hold his tongue no longer. "The Asp is a thief, and a coward in the dark!"

There was a collective gasp as the Persian cut off the king.

Hephaestion rose quickly and I saw the Persian wince under the grip that the young warrior had on his arm.

The king spoke to me again. "Hanbal… I will not violate the laws of xenia, sacred to Zeus, by allowing this Persian to have his way. The custom he invokes requires a contest to the death as payment for the grudge he bears you. I will command you to do no such thing."

I nodded, unsure of where this was going though, admittedly, I was willing to squeeze the life out of Mazaces.

"Sire," I said, "I will give satisfaction and fight this Mazaces here and now if required."

There was an approving murmur behind me from the Companions.

"My king!" boomed a voice to my left. "Let me crush the Persian oaf! I'm hungry for more of their blood!"

"Easy, Craterus! You will have other opportunities!" Alexander smiled at the giant of a man who sat back down. "Hanbal, tell us how many Persians you have killed over the years."

"Sire, I was righting the wrongs done to my people and to my family. This Persian offends me by calling me a thief."

"How many?" the king asked again.

My mind raced. I took a breath. "At a guess, sire…three hundred." There was a disbelieving gasp. "I lost count, so many were the Persian dead beneath my blade." Here, I stared directly at Mazaces. "Come here, Mazaces, and let me whisper death in your ear!"

Every Greek soldier in the room clamoured approval. It was thrilling. I was sobering up quickly.

But the Persian laughed haughtily at my words. "Oh, you will not be fighting me, Egyptian thief. I would not dirty my hands so."

He was booed by many at that point.

"You will fight my former head of cleansing operations in Saqqara, Sohrab."

From a side door, flanked by guards, stepped a muscular, scar-faced Persian with a bald head. His limbs looked hard as bronze, and his muscles jumped as he moved. He wore only loose-fitting breeches and was bare-chested.

"What say you, Hanbal?" the king asked.

Calm, Hanbal, I told myself. *Just another Persian…* "Sire, may we push the couches back?"

The Companions cheered and each moved his couch back from the inner circle to make more room. The giant, Craterus, moved me off to the side, slamming his great paws on my shoulders.

"He's not so scary, that one. Fast, but I doubt he's killed three hundred Greeks."

"You are correct," Mazaces piped up. "Sohrab has not killed three hundred Greeks, but he has slain far more Egyptian dogs! He has raped his way up and down this land-"

Before the Persian could finish, Alexander was in his face, his hand on the man's throat gesturing to the two ladies present.

Mazaces sat down, shamed, and then nodded to his champion.

The stern-faced Macedonians about me spoke words of encouragement. Some even placed bets.

But I did not care. I removed my tunic and tried to settle myself into a killing state of mind. If I lost, the consequences were unthinkable. *Eshe…* I thought of my love for strength. I was defending her and our girls now.

"Don't worry, Egyptian," Sohrab said to me, smiling. "Soon you will join your mother and father. Did you know I was the one who ordered your farm burned, your horses taken, and your mother raped? Of course, I never heard from my men again, but I'm sure they enjoyed it."

His tactic worked, and he drew me in.

I felt his knee in my ribs as I charged forward, rage and hatred in my veins like Promethean fire. He grabbed hold of my hair and wrapped his forearm over my eyes and nose, blinding me while on my knees. I tried punching, but could not find a vulnerable target.

Finally, true to my name, I struck hard and fast with my

pointed fingers up into his open arm pits. His grip loosened slightly and in that moment I hoisted him so quickly that he flew over my head to land against the edge of the dais.

I was on my feet now, fully sober, my rage under control, my body on fire.

The Persian got up and darted toward me, screaming.

I repaid him with a broken rib with my own knee, stepped out of the way of his return attack, and then stepped inside his swing to elbow him on his temple. He staggered, but swung up and landed a punch in my jaw that sent me backward. When his next punch arrived, I caught his arm with both of mine and hyperextended his elbow until I heard the joint break.

He screamed and came back with a high kick that brushed my hair. His good arm then followed up quickly, but I caught that too and inflicted the same injury. Then, I swept his legs and he landed face first on the flagstones breaking his nose.

I immediately straddled him, wrapped my arms around his neck and pulled back with my knee on his spine. His legs flailed and he sputtered, but it was no use. True, I had snuck up on groups of Persians, but always after the initial surprise, more often than not, it came down to deadly grappling.

Mazaces stared at me as did all on the dais whom I was facing, including Alexander, whose eyes I was not now afraid to meet.

Then, all else melted away and it was only me and the victim I held, the man who had murdered so many, including my parents. I hated him then.

"By Sekhmet, The Destroyer, Goddess of Vengeance, Daughter of Ra, may you have everlasting pain in the Underworld for all that you have done!"

Then, I pulled with all my strength and snapped his spine and muscled neck.

There was a momentary silence, and then a roar of men from all around me. I was hauled to my feet and back to my couch, and given wine and praise.

Truthfully, I do not remember much else except the screams of Mazaces as he was dragged cursing from the court.

CHAPTER EIGHT

ALONG THE BANKS OF THE NILE

I t was a sort of gateway to the sky that I opened my eyes to, and I thought momentarily of death. Soon, however, woken by the increasing volume of Memphis life, I realized that I was gazing out of the window of my room back at The Falcon. The blue of the sky blended softly with the sandstone window frame out of which I had been looking.

The pain in my side surfaced like a crocodile's snout out of calm water, and I instantly remembered the fight, the evening - Alexander's Companions all about me, draughts of less-watered wine - and little else.

I felt no elation at the vengeance I had exacted on the man who had ordered my parents' murder. It was minute repayment for so much loss.

Now, I found myself back in my room, my ribs bandaged with fresh linen, and myself dressed in a clean tunic. Figs and honeyed goat's milk sat waiting on a small table, but my lurching stomach cried only for a cup of fresh water which I poured from a small clay pitcher.

With some effort, I then bent over to lace up my sandals and stood, allowing a few moments for my head to adjust. My body was in good form, however, and apart from the broken rib, I was feeling well enough, though I did wonder how I managed to get back to my room at the inn, and who had cleaned and bandaged me up. Even all of my weapons were present, retrieved from the palace guard post and laid out on a small couch in my room.

I strapped on my daggers, slung my sword belt over my shoulder, and opened the door.

Two guards stood at attention outside. They startled me and I jumped back into the room, my hand to my daggers. But, a friendly voice called me from down the corridor. The guards outside my door had been saluting the fair-haired man who now strode smiling toward me.

He wore what looked like parade armour, a red thorax with gold ornamentation in the form of gryphons and Nike, the Greek goddess of victory. He carried only a cavalry sword which hung down his left side.

"Good! You're awake!" he said as he stopped before me. "No need for your daggers, Hanbal." He nodded to the guards. He saw the confused look on my face. "Please, forgive me. I am Ptolemy, son of Lagus. I am a general in the king's Companion cavalry."

I remembered him then from the banquet, seated on the dais between the women Barsine and Thais. "Am I under arrest?" I asked.

"By the Gods, no!" He laughed and clapped me on the shoulder. "After that magnificent performance? No. The king ordered you brought back here, cared for, and put under his protection just in case there were any Persians lurking about. Mazaces was enraged at your victory!"

I was silent, remembering the rage I'd felt.

"You were quite ill afterward," Ptolemy said. "Does that happen often?"

He was not prying. In fact, I felt a genuine curiosity in his nature. Ptolemy struck me as a good man immediately.

"I was sick?"

"Yes. You rushed from your couch and puked your guts in the hallway. Then, you passed out."

"It happens every time I kill someone," I admitted. "I meant no offence to the king."

"Ach! None taken! We Macedonians like to drink to excess, and with that comes puking. You fit right in!" He laughed again, like a school boy. But this was no naive youth. A couple of years perhaps younger than I, Ptolemy with his broken hook-nose and scarred arms, was a hardened general and warrior. "Come," he said. "The king would like to speak with you."

I followed him out into the sunlit street where a unit of twenty guards escorted us to the stables where Ra had been readied for me. I began to grow angry at the liberties taken with my possessions, including my horse, but I realized that I had little choice, and so I played along.

Ptolemy was obviously very close to the king, and a good person to know.

"Where are we going?" I asked once we were both mounted. I stroked Ra's neck to soothe him and let him know I was well.

"The king is down at the river's edge right now. He finds it difficult to stay in one place when there is so much that is new to see." Ptolemy kneed his mount into a slow trot, and I followed.

We took the road the short distance to the Nile, groups of Egyptians and off-duty troops passing us and waving along the way. I actually remember it being a beautiful day.

Ptolemy was careful not to speak too much, although he was very amiable. He asked me about my training and how I came to be what I was.

I did not mention my family then.

We both stopped talking as the Nile came into view. Its waters sparkled in the sun as though the surface had been set with diamonds. Tall palms swayed lazily in the gentle breath of wind that rustled the papyrus beds.

The number of armed soldiers increased as we approached the river. A vast, white, open-walled tent stood on the near bank, before which bobbed a pharaonic barge decorated with lotus blossoms. A melodic voice reached out to us from the tent, and as we rode through a thick perimeter of guards, I saw that within the tent were a dozen or so people around a poet who recited some verse.

On a couch draped with linen was the king. As he listened, couriers and pages came and went with messages and instructions like myriad ants to a massive mound. Despite the business of the attendants, the air remained calm, soothed by the lapping Nile, and the call of water fowl around the poet's words.

Ptolemy and I reined in along the other horses, and some guards stepped forward to take our mounts.

"Be calm, my friend. We are safe here," I whispered to Ra, patting his neck. When we dismounted, I noticed a massive black stallion, unbelievably large - bigger than Ra! - set apart from all the other mounts. Four guards kept watch around him while he ate his oats.

"Ah! Of course you know your horses, Hanbal," Ptolemy said.

"He's magnificent," I responded, my voice almost a gasp.

"He should be. That is Bucephalus, the king's horse… and his friend. When King Philip was offered the stallion, he was wild. No one could tame him or even approach him. King Philip wanted to send him away, but that is when Alexander came forward. Though we were all quite young at the time, Alexander said that he would tame the stallion." Ptolemy smiled at the memory. "King Philip laughed, but told him that the horse was his should he succeed."

"What happened?" I could not help but ask.

"With the entire court watching, Alexander stepped into the paddock. The stallion reared dangerously, but he was not afraid. Alexander moved around until the beast calmed. You see, he noticed that Bucephalus was afraid of his own shadow, so now with the sun at the proper angle, and hence the shadow out of sight, Alexander approached and spoke softly to him, stroking his mane."

I looked at the massive animal and wondered at the courage of a child who would approach such a beast where most men had been afraid. "What did the king say to the stallion?" I was curious, having developed such a relationship with Ra myself.

But Ptolemy shrugged. "I do not know. Nobody knows. That is between King Alexander, Bucephalus, and the Gods. Come, let us go before we miss the rest of Choerilus' recitation."

I followed Ptolemy down the short path to the king's tent. Listening to the reading with the king were several of the Companions, including Hephaestion and Craterus, as well as Barsine and Thais who sat on either side of Alexander.

Ptolemy and I stood at the edge of the tent to listen to the court poet.

"Then when Briseis, lovely as golden Aphrodite, saw Patroklos lying there, torn by the sharp bronze, she threw herself over him and shrieked loud, and her hands tore at her breasts and soft neck and beautiful face. And the woman beautiful as the goddesses cried out in lament for him: 'Patroklos, more than any the pleasure of my poor heart, you were alive when I went away from the hut and left you, and now I come back, leader of your people, and find you dead. So it is always in my life, pain following pain. My father and honoured mother gave me to a husband, and I saw him torn by the sharp bronze in front of our city, and my three brothers, borne by the same mother, my beloved brothers all met the day of destruction. But when swift Achilles killed my husband and sacked the city of godlike Mynes, you would not let me even weep, but you said you would make me godlike Achilles' wedded wife, and take me back in your ships to Phthia, and celebrate my marriage-feast among the Myrmidons. And so I weep endlessly for your death. You were always gentle.'"

The poet weaved a spell, of that I am sure. It was beautiful, poetic, and sad, and the silence among the listeners lingered, especially the king who had held up his hand for the poet to stop.

I noticed the seer, Aristander, standing at the water's edge, still as could be. I wondered if I should warn him of the risk he took with crocodiles and hippopotami lurking beneath the surface, but thought it best to remain silent. He was a seer after all.

"Thank you, Choerilus," the king finally said. "An excellent reading. You move me as ever."

The poet bowed. "You honour me, my lord." He then took his seat.

Alexander cleared his throat. "Perhaps with the guest who is now in our midst, it would have been better to finish with 'His heart had been raging to do battle with the Trojans, but now three times that fury took hold of him, like a lion, whom a shepherd tending his thick-fleeced sheep in the wilds has wounded as he jumps the wall of the fold - a graze does not bring him down, but rouses the strength in him and then the shepherd can resist no more, but the lion penetrates the pens and the sheep run in panic, defenceless. They are left tumbled on each other in heaps, and he in the rush of his fury jumps back out of the wide enclosure. Such was strong Diomedes' fury as he joined with the Trojans.'"

Alexander smiled and looked at me where I stood. Next to him, Barsine stared darkly at me. I could tell the Persian in her hated me.

"Welcome, Asp. Hanbal, son of Akil."

I bowed. "Thank you, my lord." I knew nothing of the proper protocols, so I remained where I was and the king seemed content with that.

"You were fast and deadly last night," Alexander continued. "We were greatly impressed. How are your wounds?"

"Minor, sire. I have had much worse. Thank you for your care. Though, I fear I am no Diomedes."

"Really? Which passage would you prefer?" He smiled, but the question was in earnest.

I remember Creon had mentioned something of his obsession with the Iliad and his ancestor, Achilles.

"There is one passage that is always in my mind, lord." In truth, it was the only one I remembered from my studies. I looked around and saw the expectant faces, including the king's. "So Automaton brought the fast horses under the yoke for him, Xanthos and Balios, horses that flew swift as the blowing of the winds: they were born to the west wind, Zephyrus, by Podarge the Storm-mare, as she grazed in a meadow beside the stream of Ocean. In the side-traces he put the excellent Pedasos, a horse that Achilles had brought back when he took Eetion's city: mortal though he was, he could run with the immortal horses."

I was embarrassed at the shortness of my passage, my barely passable Greek.

But, the king smiled. "Of course you would remember that passage, being a man who understands horses. Come, sit with us." He motioned to a space next to Craterus. The big man slapped me clumsily on the shoulder as I sat, sending a wave of pain through my ribs the way an earthquake shakes a home.

Alexander leaned in excitedly. "Tell me…is it true that your family dealt with Menelaus, King of Sparta, and gave him fine horses when he and Queen Helen came to this land of Egypt?"

"Yes, sire. My family had raised and bred horses from before then until the Persians killed my parents some years ago now. I have only my companion, Ra, who remains of our great horse herds. The Persians took the rest."

"They have taken much from Egypt, and from many other lands." Alexander was thoughtful.

I noticed that no one else spoke, that they hung on his every word.

"After we eat, perhaps you could introduce me to Ra?"

"Of course, sire," I replied. "I have heard of your abilities with horses."

He laughed. "Yes, well, Ptolemy does weave a good tale. I suppose I do have a bit of skill with them. But Bucephalus is different. The Gods sent him to me, and we are together by mutual consent." He clapped his hands and servants brought platters of fruit, flat bread, and meat. "Come, everyone! Let's eat along this beautiful river Nile while we have the luxury of peace at our fingertips."

Conversation struck up again as the king and all present took food and wine. My appetite had returned and I ate and drank with the others. It was good I sat with Craterus as nobody noticed how much I ate next to him. The roasted meats, fresh bread, and goat cheese were just what I needed.

Unlike the Athenians, these Greeks of Macedon were people of excess in all things; food, drink, war, and love. In those early days of exposure to their ways, I was ever uncomfortable, aware of my differences, though I was never made to feel so when the king was present.

You see, Alexander had a great respect fuelled by his curiosity for cultures more ancient than their own Hellenic past. Though his was a culture of heroes, of tales of glory and human achievement, ours, that is Egypt's, was a culture of mystery and monument. I was surprised by the calm, meditative, young king in whose company I now found myself. Quite different from the gifted leader of armies, armies which had been crushing the largest empire in the world at every engagement.

Alexander's men bragged for him, and it was a testament to him that he did not need to elevate himself with bluster. From the tales I heard along the Nile that day, and every day thereafter, Alexander's deeds spoke for themselves, and those around him spoke willingly and enthusiastically of Alexander.

Sitting there that morning along the Nile with Alexander and some of his closest friends and advisors, I was able to observe the fabric of the inner circle. This small group around the king sought to reshape the world. I sat uncomfortably under handsome Hephaestion's scrutinizing gaze and avoided argument with willful Cassander. The young nobles, Seleucas and Perdicas, were amiable enough, though they had apparently bet against me the night before.

Some of the others, the more stoic veterans Parmenion and Cleitus, were absent, apparently on their way to Pelusium to drill the troops.

However, my conversation always returned in the company of Ptolemy who, alone of Alexander's Companions, shared the king's enthusiasm for Egypt. Even Thais, whom I learned was Ptolemy's woman, took an interest in the little things such as the way the Nile embraced the papyrus reeds on the banks, or the different shades of yellow and orange in the land. Thais was utterly charming, not least because she found beauty in the smallest of things, things which I had long taken for granted.

At one point I realized that I had briefly forgotten about Eshe, Jamela, and Femi, and the danger they were in. I froze, overcome with a profound guilt and hate of myself.

Alexander noticed the shadow across my features right away.

"Hanbal. Let us go and meet Ra and Bucephalus." He stood up and immediately, Hephaestion and the king's bodyguard, Coenus, were there. Perhaps they took my mood for something else? At any rate, the king waived them off and walked toward the horses, Ra first of all.

"He is truly magnificent, Hanbal." Alexander smiled and moved to the front of Ra where I stroked his muzzle. Ra shifted, a little restlessly, then calmed. Alexander just looked into his eyes a moment, then reached out to stroke the strong neck. "Has he ever seen battle?"

"No sire. He has been my constant companion in my pursuit of the Persians, but never has he seen outright battle, not of the sort your armies engage in. My fights were always on a smaller scale."

"It is well to meet you Ra," he said. "To think that his ancestors served the King of Sparta after Troy…magnificent… Come! Let us go and see Bucephalus. He will be jealous."

We walked to the lavish paddock where the stallion was tethered. From a distance, Bucephalus had looked huge, but up close, he was now titanic.

Alexander spoke some words to him in Greek, and the stallion turned and came to him instantly, tenderly. Alexander, who was shorter than myself, reached up to grasp the neck and hug him. They grappled playfully a moment, and then Alexander stepped back.

"He is a god among horses," I said, and I meant it.

"Isn't he?" Alexander beamed with pride. "We have been through much together… He is family to me, and I am his brother."

As we spoke, Bucephalus turned to me and I felt dwarfed by him. His coat was as black as ebony and glistened with the heat of the day. He nudged me playfully a moment, and I could hear Ra grunt behind me. He too was jealous.

That was when I let my guard down. For a moment, I was seeing my father on the sandy plain, reaching out to one of our more wild stallions. The sky was a sunset orange behind him and palm branches whisked the dusk air. I was there in my mind, but in reality, I reached out to Bucephalus who had not been playing with me but rather smelling Ra, another stallion, on my person. The moment my hand touched him, his ox-like head wheeled and slammed into me.

The impact was that of a battering ram, and worse still,

it sent me crashing into the king. This maddened Bucephalus and he reared above me.

But Alexander was on his feet with lighting speed and the stallion immediately stood down, docile once more.

On either side of me stood Coenus and Hephaestion, swords drawn and pointed at my head.

"Stand down, all of you!" Alexander shouted and walked toward me as his friend and bodyguard sheathed their blades. His voice rumbled angrily and a change flashed in his eyes. He held his hand out to help me off the ground.

"Forgive me, sire. I should have known better."

"You are alive. It could have been worse." Alexander walked away, the peace of the place broken and my ribs aching even more.

I had no doubt that, had my hand even neared the handle of my daggers and sword, even by accident, Hephaestion and Coenus would have killed me before the dust of my fall had settled.

It had been a moment of extremes, from tranquil remembrance to instant aggression. I wondered then at how alike Bucephalus and Alexander were.

When I arrived back in Memphis, I was sickened with guilt and anger, made worse by a run-in with Creon and Demophon who took every opportunity to remind me of the danger my family was in, and what I had to do to see them again.

How long would that be? I dreaded the thought and worried that I had ruined my chances of getting close to Alexander or any of the others ever again.

THREE DAYS OF GAMES ENSUED IN WHICH MEMPHIS ECHOED with the cheers of the mingled populace and troops of

Alexander's great army. During that time, I did not attend the athletic competitions, nor the literary contests. I preferred to remain in my room at The Falcon, drinking myself in and out of sleep. I wondered how I would, among hundreds of thousands of men, get near enough to my target. I despaired of ever saving my family and began to consider capturing and torturing both Creon and Demophon the next time I met them together.

But what of all the other Athenian spies in the shadows?

Some hope arrived on the final day of the games when a royal guard knocked on my door with a letter from Ptolemy. The king wanted to tour the land of Egypt down to the sea and west. And he wanted me to go with him.

I had one more chance.

So it was that on the day after the games, when victors of strength and artistic valour had been crowned with laurels, I made my way down to the Nile once more to join the king's entourage. Thankfully, the aching in my head had finally subsided, but with my emergence out of the fog, my inner pain and worries returned full force.

Once more, I was on my personal mission.

While saddling Ra at the inn, Creon and Demophon emerged from the shadows. I thought I was good at appearing and disappearing at will, but those two had a knack.

"So, you've been invited to attend the king," Demophon stated flatly.

"Yes. We are going down the Nile to Canopus, and from there I know not where."

"It matters not," Creon said. "What matters is that you do not forget your mission."

Oh, Hathor, how I tried to stay my hand then.

"How do I know you have not already harmed them?"

"You don't," he answered coldly. "What you can know is that they are alive and still in Egypt."

My eyes closed, as though I were reaching out to grasp their image…my wife, my girls.

"Why don't you just let me do the thing now?" I shouted involuntarily.

"I would keep my voice down if I were you, Hanbal." Creon came close to my face. "The Persian Empire is on the brink of destruction. It suits us better, civilization that is, if that is done first."

I nodded, willing myself to see it their way, though that was proving to be an impossibility. I was surrounded by necessary evils.

Demophon said, "You will return here before long. The majority of his followers have been ordered to remain in Memphis, or posted to garrison duty at Pelusium."

"Fine." I turned on both of them. "You just keep my family safe, you hear me? For if they are harmed, I will haunt you and yours all of your days."

"Save your curses and threats, Egyptian. As educated men, we don't believe in them." Demophon smirked.

"No harm will come to your family if you do as you are supposed to. It is that simple."

Creon was a dangerous man. I feared few men, but he was one that had a deathly hold upon me.

The two Athenians then walked out into the morning light, and disappeared as they had come.

I inhaled the scent of the stable, let it wash over me and calm me as was always its effect.

"Come, my brother…" I pat Ra. "Let's go from this place together and see what the Gods have in store for us."

The light outside swallowed us as we emerged and were on our way.

CHAPTER NINE

A VISION FOR THE FUTURE

It was not one ship that carried Alexander and his entourage down river, but rather a miniature fleet in the wake of the king's flagship. Special, sturdy Nile barges had been commandeered to carry all the horses, and there were many, including my own Ra who was unused to river travel and took some time for me to steady.

Only Bucephalus rode in the king's ship, calm as could be, bothered by nothing. Many of the closest Companions' horses were on the barge with me and Ra. We were joined by Ptolemy, Callisthenes, and several Agrianes, Alexander's light-armed troops.

The Agrianes were all lean and built like cheetahs or leopards. They carried batches of javelins and a short sword each. One of them tried hitting one of the Nile crocodiles but the point bounced off the reptilian armour with ease. As soon as the man had thrown, a skiff sped from the flagship with orders from the king that no crocodiles were to be harmed so as to avoid offending Sobek.

When Ra had calmed sufficiently, I moved to the bow where Callisthenes sat writing at a desk. Ptolemy and Nearchus stood gazing at the passing shore, marvelling at the size of a particular specimen of crocodile. As I came up, my black cloak flapping behind me, Callisthenes spoke his very first words to me.

"Asp…erm…Hanbal," he said. "What do you know of the mating habits of these crocodiles? How many young do they have?"

I shrugged my shoulders. "I do not know." Ptolemy glanced back and smiled.

"What of the ibises that line the shore? What do you know of their migration patterns?"

"Of ibises, I know only that they are sacred to Thoth. Of crocodiles, I know little of their mating behaviours. I try not to get close to them. I advise you to do the same." He seemed disappointed, and I tried not to laugh. "I have heard that they will either suck the flesh from a man's bones in a second, or take you to the bottom of the river to grind you up and roll in your blood."

He looked back, frustrated at my lack of knowledge, but still jotted down some hurried notes.

Ptolemy laughed and I joined him and Nearchus. "Don't mind Callisthenes, Hanbal. He's always gruff when feeling academic."

"You would be too," put in Nearchus who leaned against the railing, hands behind his head. " Aristotle, our teacher, and his cousin, tasked Callisthenes with measuring the asshole of every beast from Greece to the ends of the Earth."

"It goes somewhat beyond that, Nearchus." Ptolemy

threw a crust of bread at his friend. It bounced off his head and into the river to be gobbled instantly by some fish.

"You were both students of Aristotle?" I asked, curious. I had, of course, heard much of the philosopher and other students of Plato.

"Yes. King Philip brought Aristotle to Pella when we were young, to teach Alexander and many of us Companions. We all learned together." Ptolemy smiled at some memory or other.

"What is Aristotle like?" I asked.

"He has a sharp wit and an insatiable curiosity." Ptolemy thought for a moment. "He can be quite sympathetic to the pressures and expectations upon a young king."

Nearchus sat up. "At the same time, he can be an extremely hard task master, especially if he knows you're not achieving your full potential. I felt his cane upon my back more than a few times, I tell you!"

"Ha! Nearchus, that's because you slept during lessons and spoke only of the sea when we discussed mountains."

"Yes, well… I like the sea." Nearchus took a deep breath and lay back in the sun. He closed his eyes. "Aristotle also has a childish enthusiasm for learning that is contagious. Our king shares this with him and that, I believe, is why Aristotle loves him so. Not because he was Philip's heir, but rather because of Alexander's endless thirst for knowledge."

Both men suddenly stopped speaking and gazed ahead to the flagship.

Alexander stood on the prow, alone with Aristander. They looked out at the land, the water running beneath the hull. One had the impression that Alexander was always going somewhere, that there was purpose behind every action.

I suppose I could not have understated things more.

I watched the shoreline slide past and really saw the beauty of my land for the first time in many weeks. I had been so locked up with my own thoughts and troubles that nothing else mattered. Isis herself could have appeared to me and I would only have seen the jug of beer before me. I began to panic then, for as I watched the fleet sail, listened to the sailors calling, the Nile splash, and felt the sun upon my face, I realized that I was now moving farther and farther away from Eshe, Jamila, and Femi whom I believed were somewhere outside of Memphis, kept close by Creon and Demophon.

I doubted my every thought and decision, and I hated it. How could I be doing the right thing? Should I not trust to Ptolemy in this, tell him? Perhaps Alexander would help? Truthfully, why should he even bother, I wondered. In Gazzat and Tyre, women and children had been sold into slavery by the thousands. What were my own wife and children to this conquerer?

"Hanbal… Hanbal!" Ptolemy was shaking me by the shoulder, holding a jug of watered wine in his other hand. "What's wrong, friend? You look faint!"

"Erm. Nothing. The heat I suppose."

"Here, drink this." He handed me the jug and I drained it in one long draught.

"We'll make a Macedonian of you yet!" Nearchus laughed.

I did not return Ptolemy's stare.

DURING THE LEISURELY TWO-DAY SAIL DOWN THE NILE, MY mood was dark. At night, I sat looking up at the starry river directly above, wrapped in my cloak and leaning against Ra. At times, I felt like a child, comforted only by the slow rhythmic breathing of my pet. Loneliness and worry began once more to seep into my being.

Ptolemy and Nearchus spent more time with the king and his advisors and I saw them little until we disembarked at Canopus, a small settlement in the western Nile delta.

IT WAS GOOD TO BE SITTING ATOP RA AGAIN AS THE ROYAL entourage rode west from Canopus, along the sea which I had never seen.

The brilliant blue expanse was a true wonder to me, its many hues, the way it moved and sparkled under the sun's intensity. Inevitably, as we processed, myself riding between Ptolemy and Nearchus, with the Agrianes behind us, I thought of how nice it would have been for Eshe and the girls to see the sea with me. But I pushed away the weakening sentimentality of the thought, though a part of me wanted to cling to it.

I looked instead about me, at the Companions, elite warriors and philosophers all, at the hardened Agrianes, loyal to their Alexander, trusted by him in battle. Archers flanked the entire column of our march too, but there was little point, I thought, for everywhere we went in Egypt, even the tiniest of fishing villages through which we marched from Canopus, people came out to wave to Alexander with colourful pieces of silk or whatever bright fabric was to hand. Those without colourful homespun banners waved palm fronds instead, taken from the very land he had liberated. Young boys and girls clapped sticks together, and old men nodded approvingly at the young conqueror who had expelled the Persians.

I could tell, however, that despite the sparse population

and general gaiety, Alexander's bodyguards never relaxed. These men were always ready for anything.

After a few hours we dismounted on the banks of Lake Mareotis, just outside a settlement of fishermen and salt farmers. We made camp on a stretch of land between the lake and the sea. Ptolemy told me the time was ours to wander about as we chose, for the king wished to linger in that place.

"I envy you this land, Hanbal," Ptolemy said to me as we walked slowly around the site. It was late afternoon and the sun's eye was closing in the west. "Ever since we arrived here in Egypt, I have been in awe."

I looked at him sidelong. "Is not your land of northern Greece fertile as if placed there for the Gods? Why do you long for other lands when you hail from the very steps of Olympus?" I detected a note of bitterness in my voice which I quickly curbed. Part of me did wonder at, resent even, the fact that people who had their own paradises often seemed to prefer others', and would go to war for such. I was, of course, being somewhat unfair in my thinking, for the Persians had been expelled by the Hellenes and their king. Egyptians had, admittedly, not been able to hold their own sacred land for many years and no doubt, Isis, Hathor, and others had wept for our weakness. But the Gods have a will and a plan in all things, and as I have since found, golden days can spring from fire and death.

I did not know that then.

Ptolemy continued, "Do not mistake me, friend. I love my home, its mountains and forests brimming with game, its valleys and crystal streams. It is a part of me, and I of it. But as with many things, it is changing, and not for the better. Politics at home is unsettling and, besides, a new age of heroes has begun, one that will not be contained within the confines of Greece and the sea of Aegeus.

"What if you never see Greece and Macedonia again? Will you not be saddened by that?"

"No." His answer was decisive, quick. "I have seen my homeland in sun and rain, washed with water and blood. I would see the rest of the world along with my comrades in Alexander's army, the men I grew up with."

"There is much to see," I admitted. "I myself on this sole journey have seen more of Egypt than ever before." I looked again at the sea, the island facing us to the north. "Today alone, I have seen the sea for the first time in my life."

Ptolemy's eyes widened at the thought and he put a friendly hand on my shoulder. "May it be the first of many more wonders to behold." He turned to walk on alone. "I can't wait to describe this place to Thais."

When he had gone, I stood there for a time, watching the lowering sun turn the sea to purple, listening to the waves of that natural harbour lap at the farthest edge of Egypt. I could understand Ptolemy then, his love of the simple beauty of my land. It truly was a wonder to behold the desert with the artery of the green-flanked Nile running through it, life-giving and loving. And the sea… I loved it at once and longed for a day when I might show it to my family.

As I slept beneath the stars that night, I strained to hear the voice of that watery realm above the voices of jubilant soldiers encamped about Alexander's tent. I prayed to Hathor for the first time in many days, and slept peacefully with the faces of my family. I awoke with a feeling that everything might, just might, be well again.

· · ·

PLANS WERE IN THE MAKING THAT MORNING AND, FROM THE bustle around me, grand ones at that. After a breakfast of goat's milk, cheese, fruit, and fresh bread, the men about me rose without further converse.

"What's happening?" I asked Nearchus and Coenus, a cavalry hipparch with an affable personality.

"The king has decided to make a mark," Coenus said as he moved to where the men were gathered round a makeshift altar.

Nearchus leaned in to whisper once we had joined the mass of men at the sea's edge. "Perdiccas told me that the king had a dream. The Gods showed him a magnificent city by the sea, a city in *this* place that would bear his name and long be a beacon of civilization." He paused, looking between the taller heads of those in front. "Ah, shh. Alexander now performs the sacrifice."

I looked easily over the heads of the men in front of me to the centre of everyone's attention. There, in the middle, stood Alexander, an adolescent ram braced under his arm, its curled horns spiralling out from its black head. He placed it upon the altar and stroked it calmly, his mouth moved in whispers as the wind whipped his hair about his head. I waited for the ram to buck and bolt, but it lay there, ignorant of the golden dagger the king held in his other hand.

Alexander spoke for all to hear. "Great Gods of Olympus… Last night you showed me a vision of beauty, of light, and of civilization! In this place by the sea, in this land of Egypt, I will build a city to surpass all others, a city with temples in your honour, a city of learning, a beacon to the world. I will build it here, by your leave, between the lake and the sea, that all may benefit. I offer you this ram, a creature of skill, strength, and daring. Show me the way, Gods of my ancestors…"

When he finished, Alexander pulled back, ever-so-gently, on the beast's neck, and to my shock, it complied without so much as a twitch. The golden dagger sliced through the neck quickly and smoothly, and Alexander laid it down, almost lovingly, upon the altar.

"Was the animal drugged?" I whispered to Nearchus.

"No. Never," he answered. "The king never drugs his sacrifices as he believes in the truth of the Gods' messages, that they are not things to be tampered with."

Nearchus stopped as the tall, white-hooded form of Aristander began to inspect the ram's organs to discern the Gods' message. Crimson blood ran in fluid streams down all sides of the rocky altar as the seer cut with precision and deftness of hand as though sculpting a work of art. It took some time, but in the end, Aristander's haunting voice called out and it seemed that even the sea stilled to hear his words.

"The Gods approve! Here, in this place shall be built the city of…Alexandria!"

The men erupted in a chorus of victorious shouts.

Even I found myself cheering along with them.

Under the mid-morning sun, while the fat-wrapped bones of the offering were roasted over the fire for the gods of the Greeks, Alexander immediately set about marking the layout of his metropolis.

As with many things which his vigour and youthful enthusiasm could not bear to wait for, Alexander commanded that work on the city begin right away. With his companions and soldiers in tow, the king set to laying out the city and various buildings by leading his surveyors around the entirety of the site. And because they had lacked the proper equipment for laying accurate avenues and level walls, Alexander grabbed a sack of meal from one of the Agrianes and, plunging his hand into the sack, began to realize his vision with the contents of his soldiers' rations. Sack after sack of meal gave shape and location to defensive walls which enclosed a market square, barracks, a palace, and temples to Zeus, Poseidon, Artemis, and even Isis on the island of Pharos. A titanic lighthouse was mentioned, as well as a library, and a theatre.

We followed him, as though a part of a religious procession, and I wondered how much of what we were seeing was born from the king's dream, and how much from his intellect. For he moved with such haste and purpose that it was as though it was all pre-conceived, laying out a world as of sand falling in a glass.

There were to be several harbours, a stadium, a hippodrome, civic buildings, and a court. Alexander even indicated the site of the necropolis to the southwest, and the route of a proposed canal that would lead from the royal harbour all the way to Canopus and the sacred Nile.

Only once did the king stop, while discussing linking the land to Pharos island by way of a hepta-stadium. He turned back and we all looked to see large groups of frenzied birds devouring sections of the city where it had been laid out in meal.

Aristander, without hesitation, informed the king that this was a good omen, that the birds represented the mass immigration that would make Alexandria the centre of the world. "People will come and go for ages," Aristander said, "and they will know that this was the city built by Alexander. The Gods favour this place, my king. Keep going."

Alexander nodded and continued until dusk, only going to bathe when he was certain that the surveyors had mapped it all out on sheets of Nile papyrus.

. . .

THE KING HAD NOT YET ADDRESSED ME SINCE THE INCIDENT with Bucephalus and I yet worried about being excluded. However, I had been invited on the expedition and that night was seated nearer the king, among some of the Companions and Callisthenes whom I had not seen since the Nile journey.

I made cursory speech with him, something I was truly unaccustomed to. "Your task is a truly daunting one, I think." I had been drinking easily but then, so were most of the men.

All were giddy, except the court historian. For me, I drank because, as beautiful as the night and the sea were, the future site of this 'Alexandria' made me melancholy.

"Which task?" Callisthenes asked after a few seconds. "I've been charged with many... To catalogue and take samples of the entire natural world east of the Aegean? To record the religious practices of all peoples we encounter? Those are truly daunting yes, but...I relish the work, for myself, and for my cousin, Aristotle. Even as children, we gathered insects to sketch, observe, and dissect." Callisthenes looked sad then, or burdened by an Atlantean weight.

"You also record the travels of King Alexander, do you not?"

He nodded. "Ah, the Titan among my tasks. At first I though it to be the easiest, but how I was wrong."

"How so?" This intrigued me.

Callisthenes looked troubled for a moment and did not answer.

"Forgive me," I said. "I feel somewhat adrift and unknowing in the midst of this host."

"Not at all," he said, more relaxed as he moved closer.

I do not know why he trusted me then, but he did. He stroked his short beard as he spoke.

"You see, so much has happened since we left Greece behind. It hasn't been merely about the crush of battles, though that could fill several scrolls alone. Nor has it simply been a tale of the infancy of an empire. It is, the more I record events, about the building of a legend, about a name that in no false way provides the deeds to match. We have only just begun, and yet I struggle to find the words to describe what I have seen. New words are required."

"What have you seen?" I asked as I drained my cup.

"Beyond the death and mutilation that accompany victory with sword and sarissa, I have seen seas of hard men break and weep like babes, and a lone Greek fight as a lion when facing a hundred of the enemy. I have heard godless men drop to their knees in prayers long-forgotten, and the skyward walls of ancient cities crumble with ease. I have seen the sea pull itself back and part for my king. I have seen…thousands slain, and women and children wail as they were put into slavery without hope of rescue from their own 'great king'."

Callisthenes was visibly shaken then, and I put a hand on his shoulder and offered him more wine. He drank and breathed.

"I have seen much," he continued, "and before this body is ash and dust, I shall see much more." He smiled again, an act which lightened his usually frowning face. "I have also seen Egypt, of which I am very glad. For it is a beauty all its own, especially without the accompaniment of bloodshed." He stopped, unwilling to speak anymore.

I noticed newcomers to the gathering, sitting with the king.

"Who are they?" I asked Ptolemy who had sat down next to me. "They look Greek."

"They are Greek, of a sort. They're ambassadors from Cyrene, newly arrived to pay homage to Alexander." He drank and filled my own cup again from a small amphora. "They will travel with us tomorrow when we set out for Paraetonium."

"We're heading west?"

"I appears so," Ptolemy responded, wiping the wine from his mouth.

"Why?" I asked, fearful of going farther from Eshe and the girls whom I suspected were still in Memphis.

"I don't know!" Ptolemy laughed, slapped my back, and drank some more.

Chapter Ten

THE SAND SEA

The next day, just after the dawn, I was sitting on Ra once more as the procession headed west, the sun at our backs. We hugged the coast, grateful for the crispness of the sea breeze. All eyes were on the king's banners at the head of the column where he spoke at length with the envoys from Cyrene.

The men around me did not seem bothered, having seen countless kings and ambassadors approach their Alexander with pledges of loyalty to him and to his cause. It seemed that wherever Alexander went people wished for his favour. But as the sun is never without the moon, there were always those who wished him harm too.

What did that make me?

After staring at the flapping banners ahead for some time, I fell to thinking about the dream I had the previous night. It was disturbing, and at first I put it down to my drunken state.

In my dream, I stood at the sea's edge marvelling at its beauty and stillness. I blinked with the rising of the sun in my eyes, and there she was, beloved and loving Hathor, standing on the water.

She smiled at me and my heart soared. I made to step into the shallows and wade out to her, but the cool blue of the sea burned my feet as though it were made of fire, and I fell back into the sand which clung to my face and stung my eyes. I looked up again and there too, standing on the water, held lovingly beneath Hathor's lithesome arms, were Eshe, Jamela, and Femi. They all looked at me, smiling at first, and then pleadingly as the sea went from calm to rough.

Eshe opened her mouth as if to scream, but no sound emanated.

I felt a solid impact upon the back of my head that sent me face first into the sand. An iron fist pushed my face downward so I could not rise or breathe, and I began to hear echoes of the Underworld beneath, like the baying of jackals in a cavern. I clung to the thought of my family, of Hathor, and with all my strength, threw off my attacker.

He was faceless and muscle-bound, and blood leached from his mouth as though it were a sodden sponge. Behind him were Persians, hundreds…thousands…laughing and spitting at me. And there too were Creon and Demophon, dark and severe, neither laughing nor baying for my blood.

I stood at the edge of the sea and sand, the place where they met. I stretched my limbs and stood between my family and those who would flay us.

The faceless monster attacked and I moved about him revelling in my speed of limb and the connection of my fists with his rocky torso. Now I could hear Eshe's screaming, and the girls' too. With every punch I inflicted on my aggressor, the more powerful he became, and I was blinded by the blood spurting from his mouth.

I was weakening.

He made to move past me and enter the sea, but I grabbed hold and in my fury set about ripping his arms and legs off. I turned to the enemy host and ripped the head free of its spinal column and threw it at them as a Greek throws a discus. They laughed as the head came back at me, my feet stuck in the clotted sand. There was more screaming as the sea began to boil about my family. I yelled, but the sun went dark and a wave washed over me. I was caught in a maelstrom of sea foam and blood.

I yelled so loudly when Ptolemy finally tossed a bucket of water over me that the guards had come running. He said I was not waking when he nudged me and that he had used the water because my cries were so loud.

I did not ask him what I had said, if the names of Creon or Demophon had escaped my lips. I had drunk a lot the previous night, but that thought did not quell the horror of my dream or extinguish my worries about what it meant.

My mother had told me that the Gods spoke to us in our dreams. My father thought that they were a kind of training ground for our daytime existence beneath the all-seeing eye of the great god, Ra.

I did not know what to make of my own dream. I did not know what meaning to glean from it other than that my family was in danger and that I had to defend them. But how many atrocities could I perform to keep them safe?

"You look as though you think of dreams, Hanbal," Ptolemy said suddenly as we rode side by side.

The question took me by surprise and I fidgeted with the reins. I shook my head and looked at him. "The dreams of a drunken fool with a world of regrets. That is all," I said.

"We are too young yet, my friend, for a world of regrets. It is this land, I think… I have had such dreams since setting foot here in Egypt! The Gods, I believe, are closer here."

"You are blessed to have had such dreams. For me, at times, I have wished for quiet oblivion in a vat of sweet beer."

"What troubles you? We are friends now, you and I. You can tell me."

I knew that I could not, of course. But I wanted to tell him of my situation, to expose the Athenians. "I merely long for blood and vengeance upon my enemies. I owe the Persians much. I…" A pain racked my head then, like a dagger's point pressed into my skull.

Ptolemy did not notice. "You will have occasion enough to slaughter Persians, my friend. Worry not. For now, set your mind to travel."

"What do you mean?"

"The king too had a dream two nights past. He told a few of us that the Gods have spoken to him and that he must attend the Oracle of Zeus at Siwa. Aristander has confirmed this."

I shuddered at the thought of the seer. "Siwa? The Oracle of Ammon?"

"The same." Ptolemy looked up at the sky and then back at me. "Alexander has an overwhelming need to go there, as his ancestors Perseus and Herakles did."

"But it is a journey of many days through the desert. Few attempt such a thing!"

"All the more reason for Alexander to attempt it, and us with him. Have you been?"

"No. I know little of the oracle there." I felt an instant foreboding as we rode on.

· · ·

AT THE COASTAL TOWN OF PARAETONIUM, THE KING PARTED ways with the embassy of Cyrene, having formally accepted their gifts and oaths of allegiance. Being Greeks, it was expected that the Cyrenians would offer their support for the continuing campaign, and this they did, not only in the form of military and political allegiance, but also by providing knowledgeable guides, beasts, and supplies for the three hundred mile journey from the coast to the oasis at Siwa.

Ptolemy explained to me that Greeks had long had ties with Siwa and that the oracle there was revered by many Hellenes past and present, the Theban poet, Pindar, and the Spartan general, Lysander, among them. There was even a temple to Zeus-Ammon in the Athenian port of Piraeus.

The Companions talked excitedly about the forthcoming expedition as we turned south-west from Paraetonium into the desert.

I, on the other hand, did not share their excitement. The stories I had heard of the oracle were mainly of entire armies perishing in the salt-wastes, burning on the earth's anvil. The oracle was highly revered, but also feared, for with knowledge comes not only joy, but all pain and suffering.

No Egyptian Pharaoh had ever made the journey there, to the reaches beyond their power.

IT WAS ESTIMATED THAT THE JOURNEY WOULD TAKE FOUR days, and so a suitable amount of supplies was transported for us on the backs of the camels the Cyrenians had provided. As the dromedaries spooked the horses, the camels were kept at the rear of the line of march, behind the Agrianes.

The journey began with a feeling of wonder, with Alexander ordering camp to be made under the star-clad canopy of the night sky. We camped as youths, as boyhood brothers.

Around the king's campfire, to which I was invited to sit with the closest of his Companions, I listened to the tales of gods and heroes. Alexander spoke of Perseus and how he had flown upon the stallion, Pegasus, above that very land with the blood of the Gorgon, Medusa, dripping from its severed head. There was no irony or mischief on the king's face when he stated that that was why there were so very many snakes in the sands around us, born of the Gorgon's cursed blood. The king was not afraid of the snakes, and welcomed them near him.

Ptolemy whispered to me that Alexander's mother, Olympias, had many snakes in her home.

Alexander went so far as to pick one of the snakes up and describe it to a tremulous Callisthenes for his notes.

All I could think of as Alexander held it, was that that snake could very nearly have robbed me of my family's freedom.

"Does anyone remember from our teachings what Herodotus said of the establishment of the oracles of Siwa and Dodona?" Alexander suddenly asked, his eyes curious. He waited expectantly for an answer to his question as we sat about that fire at the centre of the camp. The stars had exploded in the heavens to cover the sky with silver and blue. In contrast, Alexander's features reflected the red fire-light, his eyes burning with anticipation, with joy, like the embers before us. "Come now," he continued. "Make Aristotle proud!"

"Erm," Perdiccas spoke up. "I do believe, my king, that

two girls who had been serving in a temple of Zeus in Egyptian Thebes were abducted by Cilicians-"

"Phoenicians," Hephaestion corrected, smiling boyishly as Alexander elbowed him.

"Both sea-going peoples…" Perdiccas continued, undeterred. "Yes, Phoenicians. One girl ended up in Dodona, and the other at Siwa where they were inspired to establish oracles of Zeus. At Dodona, the shrine was beneath a sacred oak tree, and at Siwa, it is supposedly at an oasis. According to our Cyrenian guides, it is on a mound in the centre, by a lake."

"And what of the other story, Perdiccas, oh great scholar?" Nearchus laughed heartily.

Perdiccas waived him off.

"Herodotus dismisses the tale, and rightly so." This was Cassander, dark and serious as he was. He suddenly fixed on me from across the fire, about to say something, but was cut short by Alexander.

"Though I admire Herodotus and find him useful, he is less entertaining, *sometimes*. What of the pair of black doves that set out from Thebes at the same time to alight on trees in both Dodona and Siwa? Do not the Gods speak to us in different ways?"

As Alexander spoke, I forgot my dread task and listened intently under the spell of his attention, as was everyone in that circle of fire. He continued.

"The birds landed and spoke in the language of each place, telling them to establish oracles to Zeus and Ammon, fathers of all…" he trailed off, somehow caught up with the licking flames before us.

"I don't know about the rest of you, but a bird has never spoken Greek to me," Philotas laughed, but alone.

"What say you, Hanbal?" Ptolemy brought me to. "You

were educated by Greeks and Egyptians. What did they say?"

"The same tales…" I began, nervous as the king's eyes focussed on me, as did all the fire-lit faces. "Herodotus was told the stories that I was taught. I remember learning of both the birds and the priestesses."

"That does not advance our conversation," Seleucas interjected.

"Let him speak." Alexander's voice stilled him.

I was in no mood for debate. "Birds or women… Does it matter? Both are beautiful and from them both can be heard worthwhile things including, I believe, the will of the Gods."

They were all silent.

I continued. "Does not Zeus favour the eagle as messenger…and Apollo the crow? How much is certain? I am an assassin of Persians, nothing more than that."

"You underestimate yourself, friend." Alexander smiled, while some of the others looked faintly affronted at his words to me. "You also speak wisely, for the Gods' messages may come to us in any form, and so we must be astute enough, faithful enough, to hear them and be able to separate science from the divine."

The fire continued to crackle and spit and I flinched at the eyes that stared back at me from the flames. I shook off the vision.

As the others rolled up in their cloaks beneath the night sky, I walked a short distance to clear my head of the wine, but also I wanted a few moments alone. I wondered if, in that empty expanse, Eshe might be better able to hear me. I could see the rocky outline of an escarpment that skirted the edge of the oasis where we camped. The air that had been so hot during the daytime when Ra shines was now cold and my breath showed in the air. I pulled my black cloak tightly about myself.

Eyes closed, I willed Eshe's face into my mind and imagined my voice carrying over the desert wastes to her. A comfort in the dark. But, in my mind's eye, her perfect face became twisted where she sat, our daughters huddled and sleeping beneath each of her arms. Tears rolled down her soft cheeks, and silent despair radiated from her. I sobbed briefly, fear-struck at that moment.

I was startled by a hooded figure who stepped silently past me, staring up at the stars.

Alexander stood there a moment before speaking. "No matter how many times I stare at the night sky, ever am I filled with wonder." He paused before turning to me. "Is it the same for you, Hanbal?"

I struggled a moment for words, thinking more of the daggers beneath my cloak that might end the madness even then. "I suppose, my lord. Yes. It is difficult to explain, but when I stare at the sky, when it brings me to thought, remembrance, I feel an urge to pray."

He nodded. "I believe it is the same for all men. I see my ancestors in those stars - Herakles, Perseus… Oh, to reach such heights." He turned away for a moment. "Father…"

Alexander was lost in thought then, in a prayer of his own making, and it was something into which I could not intrude. I began to back away, though he spoke again. "Tomorrow we begin a new chapter of life, Hanbal. Is it not magnificent?"

He did not turn to me as he spoke this last, but I wondered what he had in mind.

· · ·

Upon leaving the camp in the early hours before dawn, we had little idea of what the world ahead entailed. As the sun crested the eastern horizon, a patch of pink and orange, it soon became evident that the Gods were going to challenge us.

Our eyes were met with nothing. Not a single palm, mountain, or bit of scrub broke the distance. All we would see was sand, a vast, limitless expanse of sand. I had heard of the great Sand Sea far to the west of Saqqara, but never had I imagined myself marching into that desolation.

The Cyrenian guides conferred in whispers, trying to judge the way in a land with no visible landmarks.

I tapped the hilts of my throwing daggers across my chest, as a sense of unease washed around me.

Alexander, on the other hand, ignored the guides and spoke to those around him without a care. He seemed happy as he reminded his companions of a story Aristotle had told them about an Argive pilgrim who, on a journey to Siwa, starved his body to the limit and travelled weeks to get there without once drinking water.

"Now *that*," the king said excitedly, "is a feat of endurance to be challenged!"

I do not think I was alone in thinking then that we had only enough water for four days.

Nobody spoke.

After a day of listening to the guides bicker, even the king's patience began to waver. The Cyrenians insisted we should be travelling through a shale landscape. We were not.

"Are you lost?" Hephaestion demanded of the guides.

"No, lord. We are just looking for signs of shale outcroppings."

Alexander turned in his saddle. "Do you see shale anywhere?"

The guides lowered their heads.

"I see only sand, friends. Nothing more." The king's stare was as sharp as a sarissa blade. He was not afraid, no. Alexander was growing angry at the delay, his impatience beginning to overflow.

"Sire," the head guide began, but he swallowed his words and stared westward.

A wind began to pick up suddenly, and the sand began to shift around our nervous horses' hooves.

Ra was restless beneath me as I stared at the massive wall approaching us.

"Sandstorm!" I yelled, hopping down from my saddle.

For a moment, Alexander said nothing, but observed the coming storm. Then, he came to action, in control of his awe. "Everyone down on the ground!"

"Sire!" I yelled. "We must cover the horses' heads with our cloaks so they do not suffocate!"

"Do as Hanbal says!" The king ordered his men who followed my lead and, pushing their mounts to the ground, flung cloaks or blankets over themselves and their horses.

Just as I covered mine and Ra's heads with my cloak, the howling wall slammed into us.

The shrieking of some of the mounts was immediately swallowed up in the storm's roaring voice. I lay across Ra's shoulder and neck, speaking at his cheek to calm him, though I was terrified. Together, we rode out the storm beneath the darkness of my whipping cloak, the sand blasting my bare calves all the while.

I had, of course, weathered sandstorms before, but this was unlike any other I had experienced.

Some god was trying to lay waste to the group, and I

imagined one of the Greek Titans' jaws agape, blowing us to bits from the edge of the desert.

The storm lasted an eternity, or so it seemed. No matter how tightly I shut my eyes beneath my cloak, I could yet feel sand attacking the ridges of my lids. Granules of fine Libyan powder made their way into my ears and mouth so that I tasted the grit at the back of my throat. I wanted to cough, but I knew that would only open a breach for the sand. I could not hear anything other than the storm's voice when the winds were at their highest and then, within a heartbeat, it was silent as a necropolis in the dead of night.

When I was sure my mind was not deceiving me, I threw back the cloak and gasped for air, spitting when there was not a drop of moisture in my mouth.

The king was also up, and Hephaestion and the others, the horses, all shaking their heads and coughing.

Only the camels at the back of the dusty column seemed unaffected by the storm, their mouths continuing to move in that lazy, angular chewing motion so typical of the beasts. Their murmur suggested they were mocking our discomfort.

I always preferred horses to camels.

"Hanbal?"

I felt a hand on my shoulder.

"Are you well?" Alexander asked.

"Ye…yes, sire. I am."

"Good. Thank you for the warning." His golden eyes pierced, despite the yellow dust in his auburn hair and on his face. "It was well-done to warn us so quickly."

"Thank you, sire," was all I could say before he slapped my shoulder and continued all the way down the line, to check on his men.

.   .   .

WHAT LITTLE THERE HAD BEEN IN THE WAY OF RECOGNIZABLE dunes before the storm had been completely obliterated, the desert landscape wholly changed. With the sun directly overhead, the guides were at a loss and admitted their failure.

Alexander did not kill them, but nor would he heed their counsel blindly.

The humiliated Cyrenians made a guess and, after some discussion with Aristander, the king concurred for lack of a better plan. We mounted up and set off into the heat, each step a new, muted outline in the wavy softness of the desert sands. The goal was to ride the rest of the day and long into the night to make some time.

We wandered for four days in that manner. Our water had been used up and we were no closer to our destination.

Sacred Siwa eluded us.

On the fourth night after the storm, Alexander offered the very last of his water to the Gods in a plea for their aid.

"Why doesn't he drink it himself?" I asked Ptolemy in a whisper.

"That is not Alexander's way," he answered, a shadow of a smile upon his cracked lips. He said nothing further. He did not need to.

The next morning, dark clouds gathered in the distance to rush to our aid.

When the storm arrived, it was not of sand but of rain. The men hooted and gazed up at the storm, their parched mouths agape to take in the Gods' gift, their own helmets upside down to catch water to give to their horses. The Hellenes praised Cloud-Gathering Zeus for their full water skins and the feel of the rain on our dusty visages.

I too drank, along with Ra, until I felt human once more for the touch of water upon my skin.

· · ·

After that storm, our water skins full once more, the air seemed clearer and we came to a range of hills that led south through interminable lengths of rocky valley.

The guides believed that Siwa lay not far beyond the end of the range, and so the king pressed on excitedly along towering red cliffs slashed with white markings.

As I looked up at the walls, all I could imagine was a face viciously scarred by some beast's claws.

The final pass led downward on loose rubble upon which the horses struggled for footing. As we rode through a ravine, I could see the men scanning the walls for an ambush, so accustomed were they to watching their surroundings. The echo of our own mounts, weapons, and armour off of the rock faces did not help.

Alexander, however, knew that no army would have cared to ambush him in that remote place.

For myself, I was more distracted by the increasing thrumming in my head which made me flinch now and again.

When we eventually reached the end of that dry valley, the king's roar echoed back the length of the column. Alexander sat atop Bucephalus, perfectly silhouetted by the narrow sides of the ravine and the vast, unending, unbroken expanse of sand beyond.

"Curse it!" Nearchus bellowed beside me.

No one else spoke as the king rode forward, slowly, onto the flour-like consistency of the endless desert.

The heat from the sand plains, for it was high sunlight at the time, slammed into one's face as though standing before the hole of a kiln.

"Make camp until night!" the king said to the air as he dismounted and walked onto the furnace. "We leave at dusk!"

. . .

IT WAS A SHORT REST. I WAS NOT WELL. THE POUNDING continued to afflict my head with increasing annoyance. I did not think it was the heat for I, of all the company, was well accustomed to it. That said, I had heard of men lost in the desert without proper attire, having their brains cook beneath their skulls. But those were tales of high summer, and this was mid-winter.

As the sun dipped mercifully in the west, we headed south once more, shadows moving onto the sun's daytime anvil. I passed the hours trying to distract myself from the pain in my head by wondering with true interest at the brilliance of the heavens in that place.

The moon and star light were unnatural. And the quiet! It was as though the Gods had forbidden sound of any kind. It was so extreme that each man could not help but be locked away with his own thoughts of family, of violence, of love, and hate, and of destiny.

We were moving through another world, and as the ground beneath our horses' hooves changed, it lit up like a vast gleaming carpet of scattered jewels.

Alexander dismounted and reached down for a handful of sand and seashell lit by moonbeams. Men gasped as he walked over to Callisthenes to pour some into the scholar's hands. Even in the darkness, the pure wonder was evident upon their faces.

Frustratingly, with rose-fingered Dawn, as the Hellenes say, we discovered we were lost yet again. The sand plains gave way to a landscape of black rock shot through with jagged peaks and formations that haunted my mind along the way. The black rock seemed to retain the day's heat unnaturally, and the darkness swam before my eyes.

We rode into the morning heat of the next day without stopping.

WHAT HAPPENED NEXT IS HAZY IN MY MIND, AND I DO NOT know to what to attribute it except my desperate longing for my family as my head pounded with pain and prayers to the Gods.

When I slept upon Ra's back, I dreamed of despair. We had been saved by water from the heavens, but we were yet lost, wandering. Beneath the hood of my wind-torn cloak, I felt my mind waver and rush in an effort to see her, my Eshe.

I would come close to madness in many forms over the years, each time a new manifestation. Eshe stood in the distance, on a dune beneath a swaying palm, or on a high crest where the sand met the sky. She waved and I waved back.

The men around me, Ptolemy, Nearchus, Perdiccas, and Coenus, were all oblivious. But, by Beloved and Loving Hathor, I could see, smell, and hear Eshe as though she were but ten feet away from me.

"Eshe!" I called out. "Come!"

The men about me baulked at my words, but I cared not. They did not notice much, so taken up with their own whirling thoughts. I set heels to Ra to achieve the place where I believed Eshe had stood with arms held wide for me, only to find nothing but air. I could hear someone pursuing me, but I rode on, pulling away from them, "Eshe!" I yelled as she turned to leave. "Come back!"

My heart pounded as one with Ra's hoofbeats. I reined in before her, and jumped to the ground a few paces from her.

"Eshe," I whispered. "Thank the-"

In a moment, she vanished as though swallowed by the very light before me.

Little do I remember other than my crying out, my sun-blistered arms reaching desperately before me in the direction she had gone. The tattooed serpents upon my forearms writhed and reached out to where I pointed. Then, all was black.

I awoke to find the king's seer, Aristander, staring down at me, studying me with his terrifying eyes. "Follow the serpents," Aristander said, but not to me.

"Which way did they point?"

The king's voice came into my consciousness, and I opened my eyes then to see Ptolemy who also spoke.

"That way, sire. The serpents upon his arms point toward that range of hills."

"He's mad, lord," said a Cyrenian. "The desert and thirst have corrupted his mind."

"That's ridiculous!" Ptolemy snapped. "Hanbal's fared better than most of us under thirst."

I sat up, dizzy yet able to see the king speaking with Aristander nearby.

"Sire," the seer began. "Lord Ptolemy has it right. Shining Apollo has decided to show us the way. He speaks through the Asp of Saqqara."

"Look!" Callisthenes came running up. "Sire, two crows flying in the same direction!"

"Apollo's birds, sire!" Aristander confirmed.

As I stood, the men all about me gazed in wonder at the two black shadows winging it on the thermals.

"Far-Shooting Apollo has lit the way for us," the king

finally said. "We shall not ignore his aid." Alexander handed me his water skin while he spoke. "We shall ride in the direction the Gods have shown us!"

The men cheered and mounted.

Alexander then turned to the Cyrenians. "You may ride in the rear with the camels!" With that, Alexander, Hephaestion, and the other Companions, including myself, were off on our new course.

For two more days we rode and the Gods of the desert yet made their attempts to hamper Alexander's journey. Snakes plagued our horses' every step, asps and desert cobras.

One of the Agrianes in the rear had collected two snakes in a linen bag to keep, but while the man tried tying the sack more tightly to keep the snakes from writhing too much as he walked, the two reptiles escaped and had at him where he stood - one bite on the neck, and a second on the wrist. He died in a matter of seconds, I'm told, foaming white at the mouth as the venom ran like quicksilver through his body.

The king put a coin in his mouth, had him buried, and moved on.

Thirst crept in on us once more with no relief in sight. It was too hot for even scrub to survive on the sand plain we had come across. Despair began to set in with a vengeance and I overheard Ptolemy and Nearchus saying how Alexander had been praying fervently to Zeus-Ammon all through the journey.

Upon yet another rocky, cliff-top road, on another small range of wind-blown sandstone, the path suddenly opened and fell away from view.

Alexander stopped Bucephalus and raised both hands to the sky.

Hephaestion laughed, and soon all the Companions joined in.

The mirth spread down the column along with word that an oasis of swaying palms lay sprawled in the plain below us. We all kicked our mounts to careen toward the heavenly greens of it all, and the blue splash of water that lay in the midst of the trees.

Gara, as it was called, could have been a filthy mud hole and, for all we cared, it would have been heavenly. But, a mud hole it was not, for there we found clean water, shade, and the warmth and hospitality of the people of Ammon. Most of all, gods be thanked, we had arrived at the final oasis before sacred Siwa. That night, we slept in the groves of Gara to the sound of desert song, beneath a star-riddled sky.

I slept well after a feast of cheese, dates, and goat meat, but my sleep did not go unbroken, for in my relief at coming to Gara, I had forgotten my vision in the desert, and awoke abruptly, whimpering Eshe's name.

"Hanbal…" came his voice from beyond my fire's reach. I turned to see Alexander, cloaked in black, his intense eyes lighted upon me.

"Sire…" I made to rise, but he held up a hand to stop me.

"Please, sit. I wanted to thank you for coming on this journey, for in coming, you have been instrumental in this sacred task of mine."

I knew not of what task he spoke, but did not dare question those golden eyes.

Alexander sighed and I knew then that he had not the

relief the rest of us had had upon entering Gara. In fact, now I know that his anticipation was a burden.

"Sire, I do not recall much of what happened out there." I lowered my head. I could not speak of Eshe. "I am unworthy of the thanks."

"Nonsense," he said, his hand fastening on my wrist.

I shuddered as though his grip burned absolutely.

"Though you may not recall anything, the very fact of you being there was destined. The Gods chose you to show us the way, and I can not ignore the Gods' aid." He shook his head lightly. "Not even Aristander heard them."

"My mother was a priestess of Hathor," I said. "But, she alone of my family was close to the Gods, sire. And she is gone."

"She will never be gone, be it in Elysium or the Fields of Reeds, she is with you, as are the Gods."

"You seem quite certain, sire."

"I am certain of many things…but not of all things…" Alexander was lost in the fire in that moment. Then, he stood. "When we arrive at Siwa, I want you to come with me and my companions when I speak with the god. Will you join us, Hanbal?"

For some reason, I bowed my head. "Yes, sire. Of course."

"You have my thanks again."

When he left the fire, I tried my utmost not to sleep for fear of the visions that would plague my mind. I thought of Isis and Osiris and wondered with horror whether Eshe or I would have to travel the earth in search of the broken bits of the other. It was a sacrilegious thought, to be sure, and one that gave me utmost terror. Such thoughts do just that, I have learned.

Chapter Eleven

THE ORACLE OF SIWA

Rested, watered, and fed by the people of Zeus-Ammon, we set out in broad daylight on the final leg of our journey. It was one more day to Siwa.

The king led the way, always a little apart and to himself. He did not utter a word to his Companions, Aristander, or anyone else. He simply rode in thought, uncaring of the heat, the treacherous gorges, and the gravel plateau across which we travelled.

We came to a ravine that, as we had been told in Gara, lay not ten miles from Siwa. White sand gave way to hardened plains where caravans came to take blocks of salt rock from the brilliant crystalline landscape. The natural wonders did not, however, delay the King of Macedon.

Alexander rode on all the while, silent and thoughtful as a statue of some god, until the sudden greenness of the great oasis of Siwa exploded into our vision. He paused and raised his hands to heaven, to Zeus, Protector of Travellers.

The oasis, which was about five miles long and three miles broad, lay peacefully at the edge of the great salt lake. Our senses took in vast groves of swaying palms and fragrant fruit trees along gurgling streams where blue quail plodded through meadow grasses. Above it all, falcons wheeled, rising and falling in a kind of dance.

But it was on the sacred sanctuary of Zeus-Ammon where all eyes eventually came to rest, not to be torn away. The sandstone hill, eroded as it was by the ages, was as a beautiful altar to the sky itself. Siwa truly was a beacon in the desert.

There was a thick screen of trees surrounding the sanctuary and in the shade that was offered, peoples from far and near mingled, interacted, and traded. There were Ethiopians from the east, Troglodytes from the south, the Simmi from the west, and from the north, the Nasamones, a tribe of the Syrtes.

The native people were of the Hammonii, and they welcomed all faithful visitors of Zeus-Ammon. The Hammonii had erected three walls about the sacred precinct, the first enclosing a palace of sorts, the second housing wives, children, and concubines, and the third the Oracle itself.

The Macedonians marvelled that the women and children were housed closer to the Oracle than the palace and men. They had a very different view of women than the Hellenes did.

Alexander was met at the first wall by representatives of Siwa who led us through the oasis.

The Agrianes and Cyrenians were left to settle around the palace with the horses while Alexander, the Companions, Aristander the seer, and myself made our way directly to the Oracle's shrine.

You see, Alexander could not wait. He believed his immediate attendance upon the Gods was more important than a clean appearance.

As we stepped through the sun-dappled shade of the oasis, amid children's laughter and birdsong, I believe each man among us felt the onset of something momentous.

"My ancestors walked this very path…" Alexander could be heard saying.

Hephaestion, Ptolemy, and Coenus flanked him on three sides as they went, their eyes ignoring the wonders about us to prowl the shadows of the mysterious place for any threat to their king.

In truth, I do not believe there was ever any danger to Alexander in that sacred place. The only real danger was disappointment should the Oracle not tell the king what he, I later learned, so fervently believed, or at least suspected. No one knew what Alexander had in mind, what questions, if any, his heart wished to pose to Zeus-Ammon.

Beyond the second wall, we passed the Water of the Sun as it was known, which was a wonder unto itself. This water had the strange habit of being warm at sunrise, cold and midday, and boiling by midnight. The circular pool winked knowingly as we passed on our way to find the enclosure and the shrine.

A silence unlike any other stretched away before us, like the sea at the shore before one of Poseidon's earthquakes.

I began to sweat, and coldly at that, my heart pounding beneath my ribs.

The sacred mound loomed above us where we stood in its shade waiting for the procession to descend toward us. The faint jingle of sistra held by girls and women reached my ears.

White-clad and smiling, the women of the shrine

surrounded an aged priest of Zeus-Ammon, hunched and grey-bearded. He walked before the earthly representation of Zeus-Ammon, the divine Earth Navel encrusted with emeralds, rubies, sapphires and other precious stones glittering to the heavens. Dots of colour spread about us, across the rock faces, the trees, everything. Lesser priests carried a likeness of the divinity in a golden boat decorated with silver cups.

When the procession neared Alexander, the high priest nodded and the women and girls broke into a high ululation to shatter the silence. I was told later that this song was intended to elicit the God's presence for the coming questions.

The procession turned and, as Alexander moved to walk solemnly beside the high priest, wove its way back up the rock-cut path to the top of the high, sacred sanctuary.

"Stay as close as possible to the king upon the rock."

I turned to see Aristander, his daring eyes intent upon me as the Companions filed past. He disturbed and unnerved me a great deal. "Why?" I asked. "Who am I to follow the king closely when you and his closest friends are about?" I began to move away, but the seer held my arm fast and with surprising strength.

"You *must* follow," he insisted. "The king wishes you to be present... And your serpents..." He glanced at my tattooed forearms.

I relented and hurried forward to keep apace with the group, if only just to get away from Aristander. I caught up with Ptolemy and the others at the top of the path where it opened onto the sanctuary plateau.

Alexander and the high priest came to a stop far ahead.

"Which building is it?" I asked Ptolemy.

"It appears to be the small structure at the end of the avenue, the one sitting on the cliff's edge."

I looked. It was a small, rectangular building that jutted out to overlook the oasis and the salt lake beyond. The oracle shrine was accessible only through the main door, before which stood Alexander.

The singing stopped and the old man began to speak to the king through a translator. I moved to the front, just to the left of the shrine's stairs.

I did not understand the Hammonian language and could not make out all that the interpreter said, except that the High Priest of Zeus-Ammon referred to the king as 'his son' and invited him to enter the shrine alone to pose his questions.

Alexander bowed respectfully, thanked the high priest in Hammonian - he was a fast learner - and turned to go in. Alexander paused then and looked back, not at us, not even at Hephaestion. Us, he ignored. Alexander looked at the world about him, as if seeing it a certain way for the last time, the sun's chariot where it raced downward in the western sky above the vast sand seas.

I saw sadness there and, perhaps, for the only time in his life, real fear.

When Alexander, dirty and travel-worn, disappeared into the darkness behind the high priest, not a man among us spoke. The tension was palpable as the Companions exchanged anxious looks. I knew then that the fate of many, one could say the world, rested on what exchange took place inside that shrine.

I felt unwell and dizzy then, my eyes swimming, and so I walked around the other side of the shrine to be alone. My head pounded again, and I began to feel the dagger point of dread as I leaned against the sandstone wall of the shrine.

My forehead pressed against the wall, I looked down at my forearms, my tanned skin, touched the sword at my side. All of it felt unfamiliar to me. I fell to my knees, and in the muteness of my mind in that moment I heard voices, though no one was beside or behind me. Dreamlike and smokey, the words were as clear and soothing as my daughters' long ago laughter.

"Are any of King Phillip's murderers yet living?" came the question.

"All have been punished…"

A pause. Then, a second question.

"Is it my destiny to rule the entire world?"

"You shall rule over all the Earth… You will remain undefeated until you go to join the Immortal Gods."

I could hear focussed breathing, an effort to remain calm, and somehow I knew that Alexander's final question was at hand. My head began to spin, and all sound was receding. I told myself that I should not be hearing this, but I could not help but listen against that cool stone surface.

"Who…who is my *true* father?"

Alexander's words hung there, potent, resonant.

"Who?" he repeated with the uncertainty of a child.

"I am," the voice said, a voice of power, a voice to shake the world and time itself.

I was thrown back at that moment and landed on the rocks, my head catching a large stone. The last thing I remember was Eshe's face before all went black.

CHAPTER TWELVE

A NEW WORLD

If sadness and desperation can drive a man mad, then hearing the voice of a god proclaim a god has the ability to rip one's soul out. How can one understand such an event?

And how else can I explain the mixed feelings of guilt, grief, solitude and unworthiness that I felt I owned so absolutely in that darkness?

The voice…*that* voice…

I am.

The voice of a father to a son.

My torn head shivered with the image of Eshe's face, a mirage to inspire or torture my lost Ka.

Through the thick foliage of the palms, the Eye of Ra dappled my dusty form with flecks of gold, and I felt cool water trickle past the corners of my mouth and down my throat. Then, from the top of my brow, through the roots of my matted hair.

I made to open my eyes, expecting, partly hoping for a glimpse of the land of Aaru, the Fields of Reeds. I shut my eyes tight against the light, fearful. A hand held my forehead and I chanced a look to see a woman with a headdress of horns hugging the sun. When she smiled, the headdress faded and Eshe's face swam there.

"My love?" I wept the words.

A Hammonian maid with black hair and olive skin smiled and gave me more water.

"Rest now," she said, her voice as soft as the rustle of palm leaves in the hot breeze. "You are safe in Siwa, under the protection of Zeus-Ammon."

"Eshe? Where is Eshe?"

"I know not," the girl answered with pity. "Perhaps she is where the Gods intend her to be for now?"

I closed my eyes tightly and it all rushed back upon me, images muted and sharp. From my family's departure into the desert, to the two Athenians, to the sea, the desert…the words on the rocky mound of the shrine where Alexander had asked his questions…

I sat up suddenly, a wave of nausea washing over me.

The girl steadied me, her hands and voice healing. "We are beside the Pool of the Sun. You are safe." Then her eyes looked away to where a man in white sat on my other side.

Aristander looked tired then, as if his strength had finally been sapped. He was not a young man, after all. "You may leave us now," he said to the girl.

"Here," she said, handing me a clay cup. "Drink this slowly. Do not stand yet." She walked away then, avoiding the seer's gaze. I watched her white form disappear into the oasis, and then fought to hold Aristander's eyes. I had had enough of the discomfort he seemed to bring about in everyone. I remember my mother saying that the presence of priests and priestesses should make one feel calm and at peace, if they are of a good nature.

I did not have that feeling with Aristander, staffed and white-robed as always. He was not evil, for I would have felt that too. It was something about his being that just didn't seem to fit in with my world. Perhaps that was the fate of all seers?

I remember stories of Calchas, seer to King Agamemnon, from my studies. A seer who had to tell a father to sacrifice his own daughter was in an unenviable position. I wondered what deeds Aristander had asked of Alexander to this point on the road of conquest.

"Alexander," the seer blurted out, as if plucking the word from my mind the moment I thought it.

"Yes?" I returned.

"What did you hear?"

"Hear?"

He leaned closer, his stare more intense. "Let us not play games, Asp. You were next to the temple when my king entered and asked his questions. I saw you shudder and fall, even before the priests reached the back door of the shrine."

"There is a back door? Why were priests going that way?" I was not a man of absolute faith in all spiritual workings, but it had never crossed my mind that priests were to be hidden.

"Are you so naive, Egyptian? The Gods do indeed speak to us in signs, through oracles and other means, but sometimes they do not, and in those instances they need someone to help their messages along. They need to help inspire the mortals who tilt their ears toward the heavens."

"But the king did not need to hear from Zeus-Ammon through his priests… I am surprised you question this." I was feeling bolder now, but knew that I should stay safe on the side of caution with one so close to the king.

"I do not question the Gods. I only wish to hear from you what words you heard spoken, before I hear it from the others. The truth is, Hanbal son of Akil, that the Gods obviously favour you and speak through you." He eyed the tattoos upon my forearms. "I need to know the exact words the better to advise King Alexander."

I scoffed. The thought of the Gods favouring me felt laughable in every aspect. But I could not repeat what I had heard. Divine words were just that, and not to be uttered again. "The king, I believe, received the answers that he desired."

In truth, I did not know for certain if that were true, but from what I had gleaned of Alexander, no other answer would have been acceptable.

Resigned, Aristander stood up and, shockingly, bowed his head to me, his hair rustled by a wave of hot wind. He said no more before leaving me there in the sun-spotted shade.

I sat for a while, still, the space about the Water of the Sun calming.

The Hammonian girl returned to check my head and give me more water. I did not want to move from that place but, as usual, time marched on, especially with the Hellenes.

Voices came prowling through the trees, and down the path I spotted Ptolemy, Nearchus, and Coenus.

The Hammonian girl took her leave as they approached.

"I see you are well now, Hanbal!" Nearchus chuckled, watching the girl go.

"She's been giving me water and tending my head."

"I'll bet!" Coenus laughed, but I was not amused.

Ptolemy knelt down beside me. "What happened up there, Hanbal?"

"I don't know," I lied. "One moment I'm standing up, the next all is black. I woke up here. What did I miss?" I struggled to my feet as he spoke.

"After the king emerged from the temple, he and Aristander spoke in whispers."

"As they often do," Coenus pointed out.

Ptolemy continued. "Aristander pointed out to the king that you had fallen. Alexander gave orders that you should be tended to, and then he told the rest of us Companions that we were each to be allowed to ask our own questions of the Oracle." Ptolemy grew silent, wandered over to the edge of the Water of the Sun, and gazed at the surrounding oasis.

"I gather the words to you were momentous," I said.

"Yes," he whispered. "And burdensome."

"You both as well?" I asked the other two.

"Nearchus swears it was one of those bald priests speaking to him, not Zeus-Ammon," Coenus said.

"And you?" Nearchus prodded him.

"I heard nothing. I didn't know what to ask. But I did see something. Myself standing over a body in battle. Maybe it was a great Persian giant I'll kill."

"That's all?" Ptolemy asked.

"That's all," Coenus conceded.

"Hanbal, it is a shame you did not get to ask something of the Oracle," Ptolemy said softly.

I did not answer him, for the thought gave me much pain. Would Zeus-Ammon have told me of Eshe, Femi, and Jamila? Perhaps I might have seen my mission's success? Then again, perhaps I might have seen, or been told, of my greatest fear. Knowing and not knowing were both exciting and tortuous all at once.

Standing beside the Water of the Sun, next to Ptolemy, I felt a need to move on, though I did not wish to. As I watched, the evening waters of that wondrous pool began to boil.

THAT NIGHT, I LAY BESIDE A WARM FIRE GAZING UP IN thought at a star-pocked sky. It was a new sky, the constellations now taking the shape of the heroes worshipped by the Hellenes: Pegasus, Herakles, and Perseus holding aloft the Gorgon's head. If there was divine music, I thought I could hear it for all the heartache it gave me.

Siwa was a world unto itself, the sand, the water, the sky, and the people. I prayed to Zeus-Ammon, but had no sign, no whisper that I was doing the right thing. There was no menace from the god whose very son I was supposed to kill.

My soul was as chaotic as a sandstorm then, and I was afraid that, like the desert after the winds howling through, I would not recognize the landscape of my being afterward. So much uncertainty...and yet, of one thing, I was certain.

I knew that if ever there was a single, momentous time for Alexander to come into my life, a time for me to actually meet this young king, it was when he came into this very Egypt. Having matured and settled into his crown, having waded through rivers of Persian blood at the vanguard of his own army, in Egypt, Alexander of Macedon, Alexander the Greek, came into another, completely new dimension of existence.

Alexander had reached Siwa starving and in need of water, in search of answers long-kept in the vault of his own heart.

When we set out for Memphis a few days later, sacred Siwa at our backs, it was not a mortal who led us, but a god at the head of his men. Alexander radiated confidence, purpose, and power, and the men about him basked in its rays.

We left Siwa behind at the end of spring, following the direct caravan route to Memphis. The three hundred mile journey, we were assured, would take no more than eighteen days, but Alexander ordered extra water and food. He never made the same mistake twice.

As our column slithered into the dunes of the east, I kept turning in my saddle to catch glimpses of the oasis. All the men were quiet on the route, especially the king who would remain alone every night we camped, except for Hephaestion's company, or Aristander's council.

"We are living in an utterly new world now, Hanbal," Ptolemy said to me as we rode late into the night.

The moonlight set ribbons upon the tops of the dunes, I noticed, giving them the look of water at night.

"How so?" I asked absentmindedly.

Ptolemy shook his head. "I do not know... I mean, I used to pride myself on my ability to debate, to give a coherent argument, or outline an idea perfectly. Aristotle always said so. But now, in the wake of Siwa, I find myself incapable of describing anything." He adjusted his sword and cloak a moment before continuing. "Imagine all you know, your world and your perceptions of it, being completely changed."

"I can imagine," I said, "and I would not wish it on any man." My thoughts were dark, and I had not meant to snap.

Ptolemy gave me a quizzical look and continued. "I

mean everything changing for the better, all barriers wiped away, and being given a glimpse of what *could* be. I cannot speak of what the Oracle told me, nor what I asked, but I can say that whatever lies ahead, I will return to Egypt."

He looked so wistful then, so full of hope, I had no wish to dash whatever dreams he now cherished with my 'cynicism', as the Hellenes call it. "And the king?" I wondered what Ptolemy knew.

"Alexander is an enigma to me, now more than ever. But I do believe he has come fully into himself." Ptolemy chuckled. "If I were Darius, I would run to the farthest reaches of the Earth. For nothing will save him now."

By the eleventh day of our journey, men became more talkative, the Agrianes more boisterous at the rear of the march.

Alexander yet marvelled at the land about us, grateful for the smallest oasis, awed by the most remote pyramid. It was all beauty to the young king, and it was all his.

That night, when I was invited to sit around the fire with the king and his friends, talk turned to further exploration of Egypt.

"I want to see more," the king said. "I want to sail up the Nile and explore Upper Egypt and Ethiopia."

"But Darius and his army still live, my King," Seleucas said. "Surely we must pursue him and end this?"

"Oh, we will end it, Seleucas. Never you fear. It will end and then, only then, will we bring civilization to the world."

"I'd rather bring them sword blades than civilization," Perdiccas jumped in.

"Then we would have no subjects to help our new realms prosper." Alexander's face grew cold. "I mean to free the world of Persian tyranny. Mark me. And when the fighting is done, we will bring education and order to all. It is going to be a world such as none have before dreamed of."

Some of the faces about the fire looked doubtful to me, others like Ptolemy and Hephaestion looked as though they believed the dream, or at least desperately wanted to.

For myself, I remember thinking that Alexander truly believed what he said, and that given the opportunity, he would indeed make it happen.

I struggled to push the thought of my task far from my mind. Who was I to try and snuff out the sun?

A man who desperately wants to save his family, I told myself.

But that time was not yet upon me, for the Persian king, Darius, yet lived, and by all accounts he commanded as many men as there were stars in the heavens.

A battle was coming, and I could already smell Persian blood.

I just had no idea as to the enormity of the coming fight for the world.

Chapter Thirteen

THE BITTER TASTE OF MEMPHIS

Coming out of the deep desert, I believed my eyes to be playing tricks on me.

The air seemed to be clear, like a skene slipping away in one of the Hellenes' plays. In the distance, I could see it all, the necropolis and the pyramids about Saqqara, my boyhood home. Could the Kas of my mother and father see me coming, dusty and armed in the company of these strangers? Could they see through to my own Ka and read there the distant intent that sat heavy upon my heart? I would not go to the horse farm, not now, for that path was ruined and forbidding.

But oh, when the distant rocky crevices of my own family's home appeared to the south, how I wanted to race there to fall by our cold hearth and sleep, dream of my wife and girls. The place pulled at me and it took all of my will not to weep and run. For what good would it have served? To hold a scrap of a broken toy one of the girls had left, and feel yet more shame? None of it would help them.

"Hathor, help me. Protect them…" My voice was so near to cracked sadness that my throat seized.

"Hanbal? You look unwell." Nearchus came beside me, seemed taken aback by my shot eyes.

"I'm fine," I muttered.

"You know this place?"

"By Hathor and Ammon, I do." And I kicked Ra into a gallop until I could no longer see where my home lay.

As the men whooped at the speed with which I rode, I doubt that they noticed the tears raking my dusty face, or that my eyes were clamped shut as Ra and I charged ahead.

When Memphis and the great green swathe of the Nile lands came into view, we could almost hear it, the chanting, the ululating joy of the population as it hailed its new Pharaoh. For indeed, that is what Alexander became. He was the warrior king, the only Pharaoh to visit sacred Siwa, he was the proclaimed son of Zeus-Ammon, and the liberator of Egypt.

Alexander had sent Hephaestion and Ptolemy on ahead to prepare the city, and the priests and priestesses of the various temples, for his arrival. Word must have spread like fire through dry palm, for before the city were arrayed Alexander's phalanxes, with Hephaestion and Ptolemy, and beyond, the main thoroughfare was lined with smiling people, men, women, and children.

Alexander too smiled. His head high as he sat atop Bucephalus, the King of Macedon, Alexander Pharaoh, was adored. He rode at the head of his Companions, his troops' roar like crashing waves amid swaying sarissas. As he passed, he spoke to individuals, called to soldiers and even local officials he had met only once by name, and pressed on into the city.

The colossi of Ramesses seemed a little less large beside Alexander as he passed, hailing the warrior Pharaoh. Alexander halted at the temple of Apis where he, as he had when he first came into Egypt, mounted the sandstone steps to be greeted by several priests.

Aristander and Hephaestion flanked the king who greeted the priests and turned to the cheering mass of Greeks and Egyptians before him. The sound never abated, there was no need, for at that moment the priest raised a headdress of gilded ram's horns above the king and set it upon his head.

Alexander's eyes closed as he felt its weight and then, when they opened, they shone brighter than ever.

I was not really near to the king, but even from where I stood at the very bottom of the temple steps, I could see a new light burning in his eyes, a life-force which at once awed and terrified me. Would that I remembered enough of those moments to scrawl them in detail upon these papyrus sheets, for that was the true moment in which the people of my homeland came under the protection of a new and powerful father - Pharaoh Alexander.

But my heart still ached from the journey past my home outside of Saqqara. The feel of the tears, and sand, and biting wind upon my face as I rode away was all too acute and chilling, like a Fury's whisper in my ear.

Among the crowd gazing up adoringly at the Pharaoh who had liberated them from the Persians, there were many joyful tears, and a great deal of laughter. Alexander and his Companions processed slowly from the temple to the palace of Apries, greeting the people, many of whom fell upon their knees, reaching out to touch the king.

However, I could no longer remain.

When I saw my chance, Ra and I melted away and I found myself outside the temple of Hathor, Beloved and Loving. I sat staring at the entrance to the goddess' house, but did not approach. Instead, I moved on to the Falcon where I had stayed before. They had been expecting me, and a clean room with food and drink was waiting.

I washed the crust of dirt from my skin, grateful to be clean, and sat to eat, sharpen my daggers, and think.

What madness possessed me to think that there was a way to free my wife and children and still keep Alexander's blood off of my hands? It was insanity. And yet, I was obsessed with the thought of that singular conundrum.

The Athenians, Creon and Demophon, were cold men. That, I knew. I also knew, in the pit of my stomach, that I could not easily sway them.

A recollection of the voice of Zeus-Ammon came to me then, unbidden, through a haze of sun and sand. The words of a father to a son…

Would Hanbal, son of Akil, be such a one as to snuff out the sun? Surely the Gods would be angered by such an act.

As I fell toward exhausted oblivion, I continued searching for ways to keep my family safe while at the same time avoiding the sacrilege of slaying the new-made Pharaoh and avenger of Egypt.

When I awoke, it was to a persistent banging upon the door of my room. I sat up, feeling incredibly hungry, and looked out the rectangular window to see the sun high in the sky. Rarely did I oversleep without having had several draughts of Eshe's date beer.

The pounding started again, impatient now.

I grabbed my short sword and moved to unlatch the lock, the blade levelled out before me.

Demophon nearly walked directly into it, stopped a hand's breadth from the honed point which reflected angled light into his eyes.

I ignored his glare and allowed him and Creon into the room.

"So, Hanbal," Creon began. "You are returned from Siwa."

"Yes. Yesterday."

"I would have expected you to seek us out to report."

"Why?" I asked, my anger already rising. "You gave me no such instructions. I don't even know where to find you."

"You don't need to, Egyptian," Demophon began. "We know all who seek us out."

"I'm sure," I conceded. There was no point in upsetting them, but I had little to say.

"Your name is on the lips of all in Memphis," Creon said as he looked out of the window to the Nile. "They say the Gods spoke to you on this great journey across the sand sea to Siwa. They say Alexander trusts you and that his seer, Aristander, consults you."

"Who is it that says such things?" I wondered if they had another spy in Alexander's entourage.

"I believe things will go much more smoothly for you if you stop trying to hide things from us." Creon turned to sit on the window ledge and face me. "Remember, we have men everywhere, as I have already pointed out. Now, tell us what happened in Siwa."

I did not like being between those two men at that

moment, for their menace felt suffocating. I had to tell them something, I knew. A drop of sweat ran down my spine.

"Tell us!" Demophon shouted.

"What is there to tell?" I began, finally finding my words. "We trekked through the desert in unbearable light and heat. We got lost, and I fell from my horse. I thought I saw something and pointed, and that is the direction the king decided we should go."

"And?" Creon pushed.

"And we arrived in Siwa days later."

"What happened at the Oracle's shrine?" Demophon asked.

"The king went in alone to ask his questions. I do not know what he asked."

"Really?" Creon's eyes bored into me.

"Yes." I held my head up. "Really."

"You were not next to the temple?" Demophon asked.

Obviously someone had talked.

"I was. But I fainted and hit my head on a rock. Next thing I knew, I was being tended by a girl in the oasis." As I spoke, the sound of birds and water crept into my mind, soothed me. "Here, look." I moved to Creon to show him the encrusted blood where I had hit my head.

"Seems you did hit your head, Hanbal…and yet…something tells me you are not being wholly truthful."

"All right. What the men were saying afterward was that Zeus-Ammon confirmed to Alexander that he was indeed his son."

"Hmph! Zeus-Ammon," Demophon scoffed. "A priest whispering through walls, you mean. For a few drachmas."

"No!" I jumped in. "The priest arrived after, looking quite confused." I had made my mistake, and Creon caught it. But before he spoke, as I yet stared at Demophon, I thought I saw a sheet of blood washing down his spiteful face.

"Ah, Hanbal," Creon said, his voice dissipating the vision. "You said you had fainted before the questions were asked."

"I… I did. It is all a blur, but the priest must have come just as I awoke."

"In the oasis?" Creon pressed.

"I…I don't remember. All I know is that, if what the men are saying is true, if Alexander is the son of Zeus-Ammon, is it wise for anyone to kill him?" I had said it. I had planted the hopeful seed of doubt.

But Creon smiled thinly.

"Hanbal, you disappoint me. You are the Asp of Saqqara. Your life is in the killing. And yet, now, your courage wanes? But you are correct. It would not be wise for anyone to slay Alexander."

For a moment, my heart stopped, and hoped.

"It is only for you to do so, Hanbal, as agreed, and only when the Persians have been defeated. I fear that you have forgotten the stakes you play at. The man who kills Alexander will die, that much is certain. If he does not, then others will." He stared at me, so cold, so full of calm hate. "You are the only sacrifice that will save the people you love."

Creon began to move toward the door, Demophon following.

"I do remember," I said to their backs. "I will do it!"

They said nothing as they left.

For the rest of the day, I wandered about Memphis in a daze, worry harrying my every thought, every step. I fretted for my beloved Eshe, Femi, and Jamila. I moved as a wraith through the crowds of people and soldiers who gathered for all the activities and games Alexander had planned to celebrate his return, his confirmation as Pharaoh.

The men of Alexander's army paraded through the streets of Memphis, their gold and silver armour speckling the ancient statues of sphinxes and pharaohs, temples and pylon gates with reflected sunlight. Trumpets blared as their sandalled feet shook the ground, the people of Egypt cheering all the while.

And yet, I was numb with fear, despite the clap of hands upon my back, and friendly salutations of "The Asp!".

As the Hellenes are wont to do, there were also athletic and theatrical competitions followed by bouts of drinking that lasted on through the night. The following day, it all continued with sacrifices being offered to Zeus the King, Apis, and all the other important deities of our land and of the Hellenes. I hovered on the edges, ever watchful for Creon or Demophon to give them reassurance of my determination. But I never saw them, and that worried me.

The town was filled with tales of good omens, of which the seers said could only bode well for Alexander. One particular group of envoys from Miletus came to the king to announce that at the temple of the Branchidae, a spring sacred to Apollo began to flow again after being dry for one-hundred and fifty years since King Xerxes of Persia had sacked it. It was also said that the Erythraean Sibyl confirmed Alexander as the son of Zeus. And so, it seemed that all over the world, gods and men were voicing their support of Alexander the Greek, King of Macedon, and Pharaoh of Egypt.

Yet, as I drank and stewed in my dread feelings, pain

was also Alexander's companion, for several tragedies occurred all at once to rouse the young king.

Once more, I found myself at a state banquet in the palace of Apries, this time among the Companions. I shared a couch with Leonatus, a short, feisty Macedonian noble who had competed in the boxing that day from the look of him. Beneath his dark ringlets, his cheeks puffed out beneath blackened eyes and a newly crooked nose. He smiled however, happily repeating that his opponent, a thick-chested infantryman, now lolled in the infirmary. He found my tattoos most interesting and barbaric, and wanted to know all about the techniques for using my throwing daggers which he had seen me use on the march.

"It's all about the balance," I told him, using an eating knife to mimic the motion.

As he tried it himself, a guard of the Silver Shields came rushing up the aisles to the dais and knelt before the king holding out a scroll.

From the corner of my eye, I caught the Persian, Mazaces, staring at me. He had been put on a lesser couch a few feet from the dais, where he had previously commanded his man to kill me.

I stared back a moment, almost smiling, before returning my gaze to the king.

Hephaestion took the scroll and read it at Alexander's behest. His eyes darkened and he leaned down to whisper in his friend's ear.

Alexander stood up, a rage upon his face which he quickly mastered. But the feel of the room took a dark turn.

I watched intently as Leonatus kept on fiddling with the grip of the dagger.

"Do not stare, Hanbal, my friend," he said as though it were a part of the conversation. "The king must have his moment when bad news arrives. He is forever in the sun and therefore, those who are closest give him shade when possible."

Indeed, as I looked around, all the Companions were looking anywhere but at Alexander, whereas all the foreign envoys and other Greeks continued to gawk.

Among them, I spied Creon.

Not twenty minutes later, an embassy from Athens entered, led by a man named Theron who was met at the doors by Creon.

The companions made no pretence about staring at the Athenian delegation as they approached the king. They were haughty in every way, and I wondered what had happened over the years to the men of that great city-state who had crushed the Persians at Marathon and Salamis.

Yes, even in Egypt we knew the tales of those glorious battles. Why had the men of Athens fallen so far?

Alexander mastered a brilliant smile as he stood and waited for the Athenians to reach him. "Welcome to Memphis, my fellow Greeks." Alexander's voice rang through the palace. "What message from our eternal Athens, my dear friends?"

Theron cleared his throat before speaking. "To…*King* Alexander, Commander of the combined armies of Greece and her allies, from the citizens of Athens and the Boule, greetings and congratulations on your great victories along the road to Egypt."

"I accept your greetings and your congratulations, friends. Your words are kind."

"My lord, Athens is proud to be a part of this most important campaign-"

"I'm sure you are!" Cleitus said from his couch.

Alexander ignored the jab, though he did smile slightly.

"And we are happy to have you, however small your contribution to the war effort."

There were some consenting grumblings among the Companions.

Theron looked perturbed. "My lord, we have brought you two hundred men from Attica to swell your ranks."

"Swell our ranks?" Alexander chuckled and brushed back his hair. "And how many are fully-trained hoplites?" he asked.

"Of hoplite warriors, the greatest soldiers that have ever existed, there are twenty."

"Twenty." Anger once more sparked in Alexander's eyes. He spoke louder now. "Darius supposedly has over a million troops. Perhaps these twenty of Athens will be able to take care of them for us?"

The room burst into laughter.

"And what are the other one hundred and eighty? Goatherds and beekeepers?" Alexander eyed him, and there was fury there, a contempt that exceeded that which the Athenians held for him.

"Peltasts and mercenaries, sire."

Alexander nodded, and his frown was replaced with a smile that had no bearing upon his eyes. "We should not be ungracious to our Greek brothers," Alexander said to his men. "We thank you, Theron, for 'swelling our ranks' with so much Athenian courage."

Theron held his composure, a trained politician and rhetorician. "Sire, Athens is pleased to comply and help to finally chase down the Persian king, Darius."

"Oh, do not fret, dear Theron, for with or without Athens' help, we will cut the viper off at the head and finish Persia once and for all. But we thank you for your…reinforcements. It shall not be forgotten." Alexander gestured to some couches on the right, below the dais, and the Athenians sat themselves down.

Alexander then spoke some words to Hephaestion and the banquet continued.

"Those Athenians," muttered Leonatus. "Too smart for their own good. They think so highly of themselves, even after Philip destroyed them at Chaeronea."

Smart or not, I needed my own Athenians in order to get my family back.

"Sire!"

Another Silver Shield rushed into the banquet hall and fell to his knees before the king.

"What is it, Delphinus?" Alexander addressed the man by name. "What makes you burst in here in such a way?"

"A great tragedy, sire. Forgive me. Out on the river, a boat has capsized and several people have drowned."

Alexander stood up, his eyes sweeping his Companions' faces. "Who is among the dead, Delphinus?"

The trooper stood and his eyes strayed to General Parmenion where he sat on the dais with his son, Philotas. "It is…Hektor. General Parmenion's son."

Parmenion and Philotas were on their feet in a moment, the son with his arm about the veteran father.

Alexander remained seated, and yet all those at the front could see his eyes welling as he spoke. "How did this happen, Delphinus? Where is Hektor's body?"

"Sire, the boat was overfull and the men inside joyous. The boat tipped and…well…Hektor was wearing his armour. Some of the witnesses say Hektor swam in the current for some time before reaching the opposite bank where they say he died of exhaustion. The body is at your pavilion along the river, sire. I've set a guard around it."

Alexander hung his head. "Poor Hektor…a fighter to the last."

"Did my brother say anything before his heart gave out?" asked Philotas who had stepped to the front of the dais, his face a mixture of sadness and fury.

"Yes, my lord," Delphinus looked down, and then to the king. "He said a name… 'Alexander'… That is all."

Parmenion was now on his feet, his grey and white beard mussed where he had been rubbing it through all of this. "Sire," he said. "I must go to see my…my son."

"Yes, of course, General. And I shall go with you, for we all mourn the loss of so great a man at such a young age." The last few words barely audible, Alexander strode from the hall with Parmenion, Philotas, Hephaestion, and others of the Companions.

"This will hit the king hard," a voice said beside me.

I turned to see Ptolemy and the hetaira, Thais.

She observed me, up and down, almost hungrily, much to my discomfort.

But Ptolemy was silent, sad as he watched the king and the others go. "Hektor was a fine young man, a favourite of the king's."

"But not like Hephaestion," Thais inserted.

"No, my dear. But he showed much promise and worshipped Alexander."

A silence hung momentarily while I thought of something else to ask. "What was the other bad news from earlier in the banquet?" I asked.

Ptolemy straightened, serious in every sense. "News from Syria. Apparently, the Samaritans burned Andromachus alive."

"Who was he?" I asked, wary.

Ptolemy's eyes met mine. "Our boyhood friend and the

man that Alexander had given command of the region to." Ptolemy held Thais by the hip with his right arm and gazed to the open sky. He sighed. "I believe our Egyptian holiday has come to an end, my dear." He kissed Thais on the cheek and led her away, patting my shoulder as he went.

I COLLECTED MY SWORD AND DAGGERS AT THE PALACE GATE where I had left them, and made my way down the ramp into the streets of Memphis. I was not yet tired and wished I had drunk more at the banquet, for my thoughts were turning dark and sad again. I passed a brothel that seemed to be enjoying thriving business, but moved on, despite the calls of several pretty women from the doorway. It was hard to see beauty anywhere else.

My steps, as ever, led me to the temple of Hathor's precinct, but I deliberately turned the other way, down an opposite street. It was as if the temple were calling me. I gazed up at a narrow bit of sky between the buildings and began to walk faster. I did not hear the footsteps coming behind me until I entered the next deserted square.

The three men facing me when I came out smiled when they saw me.

"There he is! It's The Asp!" said one of them.

"Doesn't look so tough up close," said the largest of the men as two other sets of feet slid to a halt behind me.

"Mazaces said we should kill him right away."

"Is he mute?" asked one of the men behind me. "Maybe we should enjoy him before killing him," he laughed. "He looks nice and tight."

I felt the familiar race of my heart, that rhythm before a fight, and was then glad I had not drunk too much. *Hathor, help me…* I prayed.

"What's he doing?" the big one just got his question out before my throwing knife planted itself in his gullet.

Shouts erupted all over as I spun and rushed the two behind me, throwing two daggers at the same time. One died, the other stumbled before my sword was out and hacking his life short.

Striding for the narrow alleyway from which I had come, I heard a knife whistle through the air and then felt a slight pain across my arm. I threw my last dagger and took out the fourth, his eye exploding with the hit. Behind him, however, the last had a bow drawn and then-

"AHH!"

Both his arms fell at the elbows, the arrow puncturing the sand a few feet before me.

The Persian knelt, cursed before his attacker lopped off his head.

Leonatus stood, blood-spattered, above the body and then walked over to help me up.

"Thank you," I muttered.

He smiled. "I see the technique now." He slapped me on the back. "You just need more daggers! "I actually laughed then, grateful my wound was just a graze and that Leonatus and a few Silver Shields had shown up. "I saw Mazaces staring at you earlier. When I spotted this lot following you out of the palace, well, me and the lads decided we should check things out."

"I might have got lucky," I joked.

"You did! We showed up!"

I smiled and shook my head.

"Just promise me one thing, Hanbal," Leonatus said.

"What's that?"

"Next time, stop at the brothel."

THE GODS OF WAR

Chapter Fourteen

THE BURDEN OF PAIN

Over the years, I have come to the conclusion that the mighty and powerful are no more immune to tragedy than are the rest of us. Indeed, Alexander had his fair share, and more than most.

Funeral games and sacrifices were held for the young Hektor, General Parmenion's son, the following day, and then it was just as Ptolemy predicted. All joy ran out of Memphis, all sense of celebration evaporated like water in the salt beds by the sea.

The business of Ares returned to the Hellenes as preparations for renewed war on Persia seemed to possess Alexander.

Ptolemy came to tell me that I was to be prepared to leave Egypt on the morrow and I assured him that, despite my slashed arm, I was fit and ready to go.

When Alexander decided to move, it was done swiftly and decidedly.

But how was I to leave it thus, my homeland, the only place I had ever known? A journey to Siwa was one thing, but to go east into Persia? Of course I had lied to Ptolemy. I was not ready to go farther from Eshe and my daughters. On the morrow, I was to leave the land of my mother and father, the temples, palaces, and pyramids. I would be away from the dwelling where my own family was born, away from the life-giving Nile beside which I had first made love to my Eshe. I was to leave the place where my family was likely being held captive. We were going into the jackals' den, Ptolemy had told me, into the heart of Persia.

I set out at once to find Creon and Demophon.

As I walked Memphis' streets searching for the two Athenians, the talk on the lips of all Egyptians was that the new pharaoh was leaving, but was giving Egypt back to the people for safekeeping.

Apparently all Persians in the political organization of Egypt were already replaced by Egyptians. The king would, it was said, return one day to his beloved Egypt, to her people, to explore far to the south as he had wanted, into Ethiopia and beyond to the source of Mother Nile.

This pleased the people greatly.

What the people did not speak of was the fact that men of Alexander's army were to remain behind. The garrison commanders of Memphis and Pelusium who were assigned the task of keeping the peace, and holding Egypt against a possible Persian counteroffensive, were the Macedonian, Peucestas, and a Rhodian by the name of Aeschylus. They would have four thousand infantry to carry out their charge and there were few men who thought they would not be able to do so.

In addition, Alexander was leaving the sea captain, Polemon, and thirty Greek triremes to patrol the mouth and length of the Nile.

Finally, about the new planned metropolis of Alexandria, as it was now referred to, the people were ordered to move their homes within the already growing city walls so as to provide a quick population base. Incentives were provided, I was told, but I could not help thinking that there was a price for freedom.

Still, as I walked through thick crowds of Egyptians and Greeks, Ethiopians and Carthaginians, I could not help but think that for all the powers at play about me, Greek hegemony over our beloved Egypt was far preferable to Persian tyranny.

My mind was at war with my heart, and I cursed myself for it as Creon and Demophon came into view at the tavern in the square before the temple of Hathor. It may have been my racing mind that did it to me, but as I sat down on a third stool with those two Hellenes, I thought I could see the images of Hathor atop the columns of her temple weeping. I rubbed my eyes.

"I've been looking for both of you," I said.

"We knew you would come here, Hanbal." Demophon answered.

It angered me that they could read me so easily. I determined to be firm with them. How naive I still was, despite the men I had met, the violence I had seen, and the death I had caused and dealt.

"Come, Hanbal," Creon said, his face a mask of nothing. "Tomorrow the army moves and we have much to talk about."

The two Athenians rose from their table and moved on ahead.

I followed.

They were not armed that I could see. I was, and I fingered my blades as we went down one street, and then up another until we reached a stretch of the Nile where the papyrus beds grew tall. I imagined a crocodile nabbing them before me, but the two of them moved on, unfazed.

A gentle breeze rustled the reeds, and sailors on a Nile barge sang as they lowered the angular sail of their craft.

They stopped at the water and looked out. Creon turned while Demophon fumbled with something in his chiton.

"I hear you had some trouble last night," Creon said.

"Yes. Nothing I could not handle. A run-in with some Persians."

"Well," he rubbed his chin. "I am glad you survived. I hope, Hanbal, that that experience has strengthened your resolve."

"To see the Persians destroyed by Alexander, yes. I am confident he will destroy them."

"Are you not pleased to be a part of this endeavour anymore?" Both men eyed me. Their questions made little sense.

I had not told them anything yet. However, I decided to cast my lot. "About that. Surely it is best if I kill Alexander when he returns to Egypt. I mean-"

"Hanbal. You are wavering in your resolve, it seems. We were told Ptolemy informed you that you were to join them on the march. Alexander and his seer want you at the front of the army."

"Yes, but-"

"Do you forget what is at stake, Egyptian?" Demophon turned around now, a brown leather pouch dangling from his right hand.

"I have a suggestion you must listen to," I told him.

"Must I?" Creon, for once, lost his composure momentarily, his quick step toward me giving me confidence. I had cracked his armour.

"Let my wife and children go," I said. "You have me. I will go to the ends of the Earth if I must, and I will kill Alexander, but let them go. If I fail, you can kill me and leave me unburied and unmourned." A chill shot through me then, for the words were terrifying, but I had to save my family from any more hurt. "My Ka will wander the Earth, lost. You can take me instead. You will be with me all the while on this campaign."

As soon as I had finished, the columns with Hathor's face came back to my mind, the tears glinting like diamonds in the sunlight.

Then, Creon laughed. "Hanbal, I am sad for you, truly. I fear that we have not made ourselves clear." He turned briefly to Demophon. "Now I don't feel so badly," he said to the other man.

"About what?" I asked.

"Hanbal, you have no other choices, but two. Do what we have asked, and you will save your family. Fail us, and you will never…ever…look upon them again."

A ringing started in my ears, low at first, but slowly getting louder as Creon continued to speak.

"What you propose is too easy. Self-sacrifice is too easy when it comes to loved ones. I thought you knew us better. Demophon, you, and I shall march with all the other thousands of men into Persia to defeat them, and you shall kill as instructed, when we tell you to. You would do well to remember that we are not stupid, that Athens is everywhere, and that it is you who decides if your wife and children live or die. We are the ones who will carry out the sentence based on your action, or inaction. They will be watched, never fear. But by others. Men I trust."

"But certainly-"

"Enough!" Demophon shouted.

"Hush, my friend," Creon held his hand out. "Hanbal, your wife…Eshe, is it? She knows you are leaving, for I have told her, and so she has sent you a memento so that you do not forget your task."

Hathor wept in my heart as Demophon handed me the brown leather pouch.

I looked at both of them, uneasy, wondering what Eshe might have sent.

The Gods have a way of ensuring one never forgets certain things, a way of searing an image into one's mind. A first glimpse of a woman, or of your first newborn child. Even your first kill, be it beast or man.

But a whole world of firsts had not prepared me for what happened next, for when the sticky contents of that pouch emptied into the palm of my trembling hand, a silent scream from my heart pierced the heavens.

The newly-cut finger was that of my Eshe, and the ring the one I had placed upon her finger, the one connected to her heart on the day we were bound together for all time. I recognized the nail, the colour of the skin, the supple knuckle, now bloody and full of rigor, removed from the greater part of her.

"Now you know we are serious," Creon said.

Even as the tears welled in my vision, I was moving, quickly, and hoisting Creon onto Demophon, a great yell bursting out.

Then a thump behind my head brought me to my knees and vice-like arms held me as my vision swam.

"I told you, Hanbal…" I think it was Creon who spoke.

"We are serious. You will march to war with Alexander. You will kill Persians - as many as you like - and then, when *we* say, you will kill the king. If you fail, or if we have even a hint of your dissension, you will never gaze upon your wife and children again."

"See you on the march, Asp," Demophon paused before me and I felt the side of my head crunch before being dropped to the ground, my face in the mud.

I AWOKE TO THE SMELL OF BURNING FLESH AND THE RATTLE of sistra. A beam of sunlight streaked across my eyes from where it pierced the sandy hallway in which I found myself. I vaguely remembered clawing my way back to the streets from the Nile. I know not how I had the strength and figured only that some sympathetic god or goddess must have helped me along. I felt something clenched tight in my fists, held fast to my chest.

The pouch was real and, daring to look, I knew the contents were also painfully real.

Heralds were making their way through the streets, the call-to-arms loud and clear. The time had come, I knew. I got to my feet and went to the square that faced The Falcon.

Stumbling into my room, I found fresh water, bread, and figs waiting. On the small table was a note from Ptolemy to assemble, mounted, outside the northern gates by mid-morning.

Dazedly, I washed with a sponge and the cedar-scented water put out by the tavern keeper's slave. Then, I removed Eshe's finger from the pouch and washed it gently, the skin, the ring, until the only blood was at the end where my beautiful wife had been cut.

I felt sick, but forced myself to look, to know that I had

done that to her, that the only way to prevent worse from happening was to kill a king…a god.

After I dried the finger, my eyes burning all the while, I wrapped it in clean linen and placed it in another black pouch I had in my satchel. This one had a long leather thong with which I hung it about my neck. I then armed myself for war, physically and emotionally. The leather guards covered my forearms once more, the daggers criss-crossed my chest. My sword stuck up between my shoulders. When all my belongings were packed, I left that room behind, the basin of water, the bloody brown pouch, and made my way to the only friend I still had.

RA WAS ALONE IN THE STABLES WHEN I ARRIVED, THE YOUNG boy who had cared for him before there by his side, brushing him down.

"Here, boy," I said, flipping him a Greek obol. "Buy yourself some food."

"Thank you!" He beamed, and the sight of it made me sad for some reason. "Are you off to war with the Greek king, the new pharaoh?"

"Yes," I answered. "Now go, for there may be more money you can make before the city empties."

Without another word, he was gone.

Ra turned to come to me. I had neglected him and yet, he came. I believe he sensed my sadness as he nuzzled the pouch beneath my tunic.

With my head against his thick neck, I closed my eyes and allowed myself a few tears. I prayed to Hathor and to Zeus-Ammon, who had allowed me to hear his words, that somehow I should be allowed to see my family again, no matter what, nor however long it might take.

. . .

THE SHEER MASS OF ALEXANDER'S ARMY STRUCK ME WHEN
Ra and I came out of the northern gates. There was a
rumble of horses' hooves and a grunting of oxen that shook
the earth. Dust clouds rose to the sky as though a sandstorm
were coming, and through the dust the sun glinted off of
bronze, silver, and golden armour. Thousands of wagons
carried new provisions and supplies, siege equipment, and
weapons. I was amazed to see so many thousands of men so
organized and disciplined, Agrianes, peltasts, hoplites,
cavalry and, or course, the thick forests of heavy infantry
with their dreaded sarissas.

Egyptian troops had also joined the ranks, mostly boys
who had never seen a fight or killed a man. But that was the
effect Alexander had on everyone - people would follow him
with abandon, just for the chance to serve.

Then I spotted Alexander at the head of a group of
horsemen, riding along the lines, wearing the ram's horns of
Zeus-Ammon.

Cheers followed as a rolling wave approaches the shore.
His companions were in parade armour, polished, ornate,
and full of vanity. And I was to ride with them, I, Hanbal,
son of Akil, the Asp of Saqqara, all in black, like a shadow
pursuing the sun.

I urged Ra forward to find a spot among the Companions and stopped before the Athenian contingent.

Creon and Demophon stood there with the others,
armed and waiting. They nodded to me, but I made no
acknowledgment.

I stared at them. I cursed them internally, and with every
fibre of my being I wished for Sekhmet and Petbe to give
me vengeance some day.

The sound of cheering came closer and when I turned to see what was happening, I was face-to-face with Alexander. His long hair sprouted from beneath the sacred ram's horns and his golden eyes sparkled with all the excitement that pulsed around him, that orbited him. It was apparent that the previous tragedies' effects were now gone and giving way to a thirst for war.

"What say you, Hanbal, son of Akil? Will you join me in overthrowing Darius and his Persian hordes?" The king spoke loudly for his Companions and so that all others nearby could hear, even the Egyptians outside the pylon gates of Memphis.

I bowed my head, my arm crossed over my chest and the pouch beneath. "Nothing would give me greater pleasure, Alexander, Pharaoh of Egypt!"

The first cheers erupted from the Egyptian civilians atop and below the walls, then the Egyptian troops in the ranks, and spread from there.

The king was pleased, his smile genuine, bright, the kopis he hoisted above his head deadly-sharp. "Then, to war!" he yelled, his eyes on the sky. "And the death of Persia!"

As he and the Companions behind bounded off northward, toward Pelusium, I fell in behind Ptolemy and the others to go and meet up with the bulk of the army with Cleitus and Craterus, as well as reinforcements from Macedonia, Athens, and other Greek city-states.

Barges followed up the Nile, loaded with more provisions and, of course, women, including Thais and Barsine, and other hetairae and boys who went with the men.

. . .

WHEN I THINK BACK TO THOSE FINAL DAYS IN EGYPT, watching the land pass by, one image stuck with me. To my surprise, it was was not watching Memphis fade into the haze and dust behind me. I had forced myself not to look and called out with my soul to Eshe that she might hear me, know that I was not abandoning her and the girls. Nor did I much care for the great pyramids that towered over our land.

What I remember most was my final look at the sand of Egypt, the distant green of the Nile as we marched into Arabia. It was the first time I had left the land that had been all to me and my ancestors. I did not know what lay ahead. I was only keenly aware of what I was leaving behind.

CHAPTER FIFTEEN

THE SCARS OF TYRE

I have had to pause in my writing to collect my thoughts and rally myself for the task ahead. The recollections have not been easy, and revisiting them has been like to opening old, scarred wounds with a jagged, dull and rusty blade.

Never have I felt so lacking in control of my own life as I did on that march north and east out of Egypt. It occurred to me that my path was chosen, that my life was a single lotus leaf upon a broad river. I had absolutely no choice but to be swept away with the current.

This thinking did not help me as I knew I was my family's only hope. How could I, as insignificant as I was or felt I was, hope to save them? And yet, I clung to that hope. I had to, with every bit of strength within. It terrified me to think that if the tiny, thin thread by which I was hanging were cut, or snapped under my weight, that I would lose my family and tumble headlong into darkness.

After a few days of dark thoughts, I decided to focus on violence, on the realization that it was me or them. Such are the workings of a mind that sees nothing beyond its own inadequacies. I had been pulling the bowstring of my self back to its limits, holding it taut for so long that the tension and effort made my soul rage and quake.

And I could not show it. Not yet.

In Pelusium, the army of Alexander regrouped and took on the reinforcements newly arrived from Greece.

Until I saw the entire force arrayed on the sandy plain, I had been ignorant of the great power of the force I now found myself a part of.

Greeks of every city-state and village, except for Sparta, were present alongside Ionians, Thracians, Egyptians, Libyans, Cypriots and others I had not heard of before. And the logistical support for this titan that was Alexander's army, was almost grater than the most populous polis.

I was part of a moving civilization, complete with philosophers and priests, merchants and harlots, and the fiercest warriors the world had yet seen.

The talk on many a man's lips was of vengeance for Persian wrongs of the past two hundred years.

I have come to the conclusion that hatred, and the need for vengeance are longer-lived creatures than the most noble of emotions.

With a force of almost fifty-thousand troops, Alexander set his sights on Syria and Tyre where his next act of vengeance would be played out. After news that the Samaritans had burned the Greek commander of Syria alive, a friend of Alexander's named Andromachus, the young king would not rest until he made them pay.

We crossed into Judaea, the land of the Jews, past the still-bleeding heart that was Gazzat. We rode across dry, rocky land with the sea to our left. There was no emotion among the men as we passed Gazzat where the people who remained quivered with fear, full of remembrance of Alexander's dragging of the body of the Gazzatan leader, Batis, around the city behind a chariot. His ancestor, Achilles, had done the same to Hektor at the siege of Troy. Batis had been no Hektor, however, and yet the message had dissuaded any who were still possessed of a rebel heart.

Tyre was another story altogether. This was where Alexander had conquered the sea by shifting earth and timber to create a massive causeway in the water to take the city. The memories of that siege lingered in the faces around me.

The gaiety that had marked the Companions' days in Egypt had bled away in the face of Ares. They were ready for another fight.

I rode among them, asked no questions, and was asked none. Voices picked up as we approached the island-city where Alexander's military genius had conquered the waves, his stubbornness the city. The army camped on the mainland that evening and thousands of men swam in the sea where months prior they had bled, their comrades drowned. Certainly, a heavy pall had settled on the spirit of that once-great city and, to me, the waves sounded like the screams of massacred Tyrians.

I did not go into the sea like so many others, but went into the city with Alexander and the Companions. The king was eager to mete out justice and demanded the surviving leaders of the populous hand over the murderers of his friend.

"Do not forget what happened here last time the Tyrians disobeyed me," Alexander said to those gathered in the agora. He stood, his gold and red cloak whipping in the sea breeze, dust from remnants of rubble swirling about him.

You could have heard a pebble drop, the silent fear was so palpable.

The perpetrators were handed over to Alexander and promptly burned on the beach, all ten of them.

Memnon, a Macedonian, was then appointed Commander of Syria, to replace Andromachus. Once justice had been done, Alexander made offerings to his ancestor, Herakles, in the temple that was dedicated to that great hero of the Hellenes.

We walked about the city then, as Alexander gave further orders for rebuilding. The city was scarred and burned. I stood before the Agenorium, the fortress where, Ptolemy told me, the Tyrians had made their last stand, facing the Sidon harbour. It was desolate, despite the rush of activity, and I could see Ptolemy and Nearchus, Perdiccas and others shudder at the memories.

The Phoenicians never stood a chance, even behind their high sea-barricaded walls.

"Come," Ptolemy said as he slapped me and Nearchus on the shoulders. "The banquet will begin soon, and I need to drink myself into oblivion."

"Praise Dionysos!" Nearchus echoed. "Maybe we'll even find some Egyptian beer for our dear Asp here!"

I laughed half-heartedly.

I NEEDED TO DRINK MORE THAN I HAD THOUGHT THAT night. It was a raucous evening with the sound of the sea crashing beyond the walls, and the bellowing of the drunken troops within.

Alexander knew the men were on edge and so, as a precaution, he ordered that the Tyrians were to go unmolested, having paid enough. Beatings would be met with lashings, and rapes with execution. The latter, Alexander despised and never tolerated it among his troops. He would not see women and children treated so horribly, nor accept it as a whim of war. That the men obeyed spoke to his mastery of their hearts and minds.

The father and husband in me respected him greatly for this, though, it would make my task no easier.

At the outset of the banquet, embassies arrived from Chios, Rhodes, and Athens. They were admitted before the king, prior to the opening of the wine which then began to flow in earnest.

I drank my beer and listened.

The ambassadors from Chios and Rhodes both complained jointly of outrageous behaviour on the part of the garrison troops that had been left on both of these islands. The theft of livestock did not perturb Alexander, but when the rape of young girls, boys, and the wives of the levies who now marched with the army were mentioned, the king's face took on a grave countenance.

"My brothers of Chios and Rhodes," he said, a hand on each of the ambassadors' shoulders. "You have my apologies for the actions of these base cowards who have attacked your women and children. You also have my word that those who have committed rapine will be executed and entirely new garrisons put in place."

The ambassadors nodded and bowed gratefully, having achieved much more than they had thought possible.

The king turned to one of his secretaries and whispered while the man scribbled furious notes, orders to be carried out. "I do this in return for the loyalty and good faith shown to us by Chios and Rhodes, and for their continued support."

There was a round of applause.

"Hanbal," Ptolemy nudged me and nodded toward the approaching Athenian embassy. "This should be interesting."

I watched as two proud Athenians walked toward the king, heads high, the folds of their himations perfectly set.

"Diophantus and Achilles of Athens," the king said. "Approach."

The two men moved forward among the Companions.

"What would Athens have of me?"

All eyes were on the two men who, to their credit, did not break a sweat.

Hephaestion stood back and to the right of Alexander, ever watchful, ever wary.

I drank down my beer and listened as Diophantus spoke.

"*King* Alexander," he began, barely getting the word out. "Athens and Macedon have not always seen eye-to-eye on many things."

There were chuckles and grumblings on the floor, but Alexander raised a hand for them to stop so the man could continue.

"We have had bloody conflict and lies between our great city-states for far too long, disgraceful dealings with the Persians on both sides."

"Before Thermopylae," Ptolemy whispered to me, "Macedon had yielded to the Persians, allowing them to move south."

I nodded, quite surprised to hear of this, and listened as Diophantus went on.

"The glories of our ancestors at Marathon and Salamis have been sullied by more recent politics."

Here Alexander stepped forward a pace, his ears pricking up like an alert mountain lion.

I understood then that, though defeated, Athens, the idea of Athens, still awed Alexander.

"My king," Diophantus said now without hesitation. "Athens regrets her decision to support Darius with troops at the battle of the Granicus and at other places. We were wrong and, as Athena is our witness, we admit it freely. We ask one thing of you." Here, Diophantus spoke up. "Athens asks for the return of all Athenian prisoners of war taken at the Granicus so that they may return to the field of battle, not against Macedon, but against the forces of Persia, that we may help you in avenging the wrongs done to our Greek peoples!"

The gathering erupted then, making me jump and spill my beer.

"He's good!" Ptolemy said of the Athenian. "He's really good." He clapped me on the shoulder. "This is momentous, Hanbal."

"What will the king say?" I asked, and in answer, Alexander strode forward to Diophantus and Achilles, arms out.

"Granted! With all my heart! Macedon welcomes Athens beside it on the field of battle!"

Even I jumped up at that, caught up in the sheer energy of the moment. I scanned the room and saw smiling faces, heard laughter and relief, for Athens had been a beacon to them all.

Then I saw Creon at the back of the hall, nodding and smiling. I felt the pouch that hung about my neck, and sickness leached into my mood. Such fine, noble, and inspiring words. Was it all a lie, a play? I knew the Athenians were fond of their drama, their theatre, but this…could it all have been a ruse to get Alexander into a false sense of security with Athens? It was a good speech which Diophantus had made, and a part of me hoped that he and Achilles were unaware of the ultimatum that had been forced upon me by Creon and Demophon.

"Amphoretus!" Alexander called to his admiral who stood and saluted.

"Yes, my king!" the grizzled seaman said.

"You will take the fleet back to Greece to support all the Peloponnesian cities who likewise support us."

"What of Sparta?" I saw Creon yell at the back. Others took up the question and Alexander was forced to answer.

"The fleet will flush out Spartan troops from their hiding places on Crete and elsewhere where they plot with the Persians."

At this, the Athenians smiled.

"King Aegis of Sparta," Alexander added, "will regret his revolt, and wish that they too had marched into our enemies' bloody heart with us!"

The Athenians melted into the crowd, nodding and proclaiming justice and victory.

Meanwhile, I sat down on my couch, numb, confused. All sound went out of my ears, and along with all the others, I lost myself in a world of alcoholic stupor.

THE NEXT DAY, I STOOD ON THE MOLE LOOKING AT THE SEA, the sun rising in the east. I had not slept, but wandered the raucous streets of charred Tyre from where we were to press inland into Persia.

Before the army moved on, however, Alexander proclaimed games and competitions to occupy the men, to train them, and to inspire them.

Again games. I was not in the mood for games, for mock fighting, or for sport. Nor had I ever thrown a discus or jumped holding the stones. What odd pastimes the Hellenes had.

I closed my eyes and felt the breeze ruffle my hair. I breathed deeply, tried to feel myself again. All I had was a lurch in my stomach from too much drink and a shaking hand as I wiped my brow. I then heard footsteps approaching.

"Hanbal!" Ptolemy came up beside me, leaving Nearchus and Cassander to continue down the mole toward the beach. "Are you going to compete this time?"

I shook my head. "I had not thought to." I turned to look at him. "Why games?" I asked. "Why now when we are on the brink of battle?"

Ptolemy smiled and nodded. He seemed to understand the question, and why I asked it. For a non-Greek, it was a legitimate query. "Why not games?" he said. "I know many of our customs may appear strange to you, Hanbal. The king calls games not only to train us, but to calm us, to focus our minds before the true test. Every man thinks of and fears death. Thanatos and Phobos are our constant bedfellows, and if we do not think of anything else but blood and death, then we may well go mad. The games have been a part of our lives from the beginning. They tie us to our youth. When we win, we achieve glory before the eyes of the Gods, and that glory we carry with us when we wade through rivers of blood in battle."

Ptolemy walked to the edge of the causeway and stared down at the turquoise water where fish darted back and forth. "I suppose," he continued, "the games are our lives in a microcosm, lived in the space of a few moments. We fight to the limits of our abilities." He turned and looked at me. "That is the 'why' of the games."

I knew I had, despite my limited education, misunderstood this aspect of the Greek mindset. It was such a foreign concept to me. I had only taken it as a frivolous pastime for the braggarts among them, not as a rite performed for the Gods themselves.

Ptolemy had begun to leave when I did not answer, but turned once more before going. "Join us in the games, Hanbal." He smiled. "Show them what the Asp of Saqqara is made of!"

When he had gone with the others, I stood there mulling it over and came to the conclusion that if I were to become one of them, one of the inner circle, I should have to prove myself in their own ways first.

I EVENTUALLY CAUGHT UP WITH PTOLEMY, NEARCHUS, AND Cassander where they lined up to put their names down for events.

"Glad to have you with us!" Nearchus slapped me on the back.

Ptolemy smiled too, but Cassander stared at me from beneath his brooding brow. "So, *Asp*, what events are you trained in?" he asked.

"None but fighting and riding."

"Well, there will be no horse games today, so fighting it will be."

I shrugged. "Then I suppose I should enter the boxing and wrestling."

"Hmm. Two events, eh?" Cassander looked doubtful.

"Is that not enough?" I asked.

"It is. We are each entering one. I am for the pankration."

"What event is that?" I asked.

"Pankration is fighting with no rules, except that you cannot bite or gouge eyes." He observed the surprised look upon my face. "I like to push myself."

I could see that about Cassander. He did not appear to be one who did things half-heartedly. There was a darkness to his personality that made me highly cautious of him. "What about both of you?" I asked Ptolemy and Nearchus.

"It's the discus for me!" Nearchus laughed.

"And the javelin for me," Ptolemy added. "Though I suspect I'll be up against the king."

"The king competes?" This surprised me for a brief moment, but then it made perfect sense. Alexander was no common king.

"Of course," Cassander answered, surprised I would even ask such a thing. "The king most of all! Our leader must remain proven in the games, even as a god." Cassander moved forward and gave his name to the secretary of the games.

Nearchus and Ptolemy followed, and then myself.

When we were finished, we walked beneath the awning onto the broad sand of the beach facing Tyre. The sun was up and I shaded my eyes to take in the view. Men were everywhere stretching and limbering up for the coming competitions which would take place in different areas of the beach which had been divided into fighting rings and fields for the throwing and running events.

I felt my nerves then, especially when it occurred to me that I was really the only non-Greek among the competitors.

"Change your mind, Asp?" Cassander laughed as he made his way to a tent set aside for officers beside the king's grand, white tent which was adorned with golden, Argead stars.

"Come on, Hanbal!" Ptolemy urged. "There is time before our events. Lets get ready and then we can have a look around."

We went into the officers' tent, myself as Ptolemy's guest, and took off all our weapons and armour so that all we wore were short breeches. It certainly felt better with less clothing beneath the sun, but I could not relax. I knew I could not lose because if I did, I would not gain the respect I needed.

Men eyed me warily as we walked, assessed my physique in case we ended up competing. It was explained to me that women were not usually present at the games, but that sometimes exceptions were made. Ptolemy pointed to a great silk awning that fluttered in the hot summer breeze.

Beneath it lounged many ladies who were following the king, including the dark, beautiful Barsine, and Thais, Ptolemy's lover. He blew her a kiss as we passed and she winked back at him before turning to her wine and conversation while boys fanned them in the shade.

The first competition was the discus and Nearchus, as soon as we arrived, set about stretching his arms and shoulders as the first group of men to throw stepped up.

I had, in truth, never seen a discus thrown, had thought it a trifling sport from the little I had heard of it. But after having held one of those bronze discs, and seeing the technique involved in throwing them, and the distances achieved, I changed my way of thinking.

Nearchus came in second, not far behind an impressive throw by a trooper from Elis where the Olympic Games were held. Nearchus swore and said he would beat the Elian at the next games.

The man laughed and raised his cup to his superior officer.

Crowds of men roared at the foot races which were always a highlight. However, it was the javelin that attracted the largest crowd, throngs of warriors turning up to see King Alexander throw against Ptolemy, Cleitus the Black, Philotas, and Menander among others.

I had a feeling that with Homer's words ringing in their heads, each believed he could be Achilles as he hoisted his spear shaft to make the running throw that would win glory. Each would have three throws, and the king would go last, at his request.

There were about twenty competitors in all, but it was Alexander and his Companions who went into the final round. They were at the top of the ranks not only by right of birth, but also by skill, for they had been trained by the very best since boyhood.

I stood at the front railing with Nearchus as Menander made his second throw amid friendly jibes from the army. It was a decent throw, but only matched the king's and Ptolemy's shortest attempts. Cleitus was next, but was surpassed by Ptolemy who hurled his javelin in a high, long arc that crossed the midday sun. The crowd hailed the throw, and I clapped as well, impressed by his skill, though his style seemed more brute than graceful.

Philotas stepped onto the sand then. He was very serious, focused. A few feet away, his father, General Parmenion, was likewise serious. In fact, I don't believe I ever saw either of them otherwise. Philotas stepped back and waited for the breeze to die down. Then, with a great cry, he sprinted to the line and loosed his shaft. It soared like an arrow, arched just enough but winging it perfectly to land several feet beyond Ptolemy's.

Ptolemy betrayed no emotion when Philotas smirked, the crowd shocked by the throw.

All the while, Alexander had been leaning against a back rail with Hephaestion beside him. The king applauded for all of his men, high and low-born, then stepped out to select a javelin from the rack.

Alexander was truly the epitome of physical beauty according to the Hellenes. Every muscle was perfectly proportioned, strong and quick beneath the bronzed skin. Despite a multitude of white scars upon his arms and legs, he was what most men aspired to be in his world. His wild hair danced in the hot breeze beneath the burning sun. He seemed happy and in his element.

The king loosened his shoulders casually, tested the weight and balance of the spear. Then, he was still, his eyes closed. Alexander, amid the hush of thousands of onlookers, raised his arms, holding the spear to the sky.

I heard him speak to the heavens, not for show, but for himself. "For you, father." Then, louder, he said. "For Zeus!"

With that, he stepped back, paused and ran, not clumsy or determinedly, but beautifully as Nile river water, as smooth and quick and powerful as a lion. The spear shaft that had been a part of his body one moment separated from his hand to soar so high and far that I thought it would not come to earth. When it did come down, it was well beyond Philotas' throw.

There was a moment of awed silence, and then the world erupted in cheers.

I saw Philotas curse and kick sand in disgust while the other competitors shook their heads and clapped for the king.

"Alexandros!" men chanted. "The new Achilles!"

Alexander laughed, enjoying the raucous joy of his men,

and then disappeared into the crowd with Hephaestion and other followers.

A herald for the games then rode along the beach announcing the beginning of the combat events, and I knew it was my turn.

"Let's go, Hanbal!" Nearchus slapped my shoulder. "The wrestling is first!"

We moved with the crowd to the area where several wrestling *skamae* had been outlined and the first matches were being announced.

I noticed that many more lower-ranking troops were participating in the next events. Many of them were hardened fighters with broken noses and missing teeth, while others were young men entering the ring for the first time, eager to impress their king who stood with several of the Companions to watch.

I was on my own then, at the wrestling ring assigned to me, waiting for my opponent. Some of the other groups had already begun and bets were being placed, won and lost. I felt foolish standing there alone and unheeded. I considered asking the officiant where my opponent was when the crowd parted to let him through.

Craterus smiled when he stepped onto the *skama* and hoots and taunts came from the Companions about Alexander.

"Go on, Egyptian!" Cleitus shouted. "This one should be easy!"

I laughed along with them, nervous more than anything, as I tried to assess Craterus' bulk. He was easily two heads taller than I, and I was taller than most. His arms were thick and muscled, his thighs like strong tree trunks.

He's big, Hanbal, I thought. *Too big...which means he's slower than most. Avoid a leg lock!*

Craterus laughed and extended his hand to shake mine. "Don't worry, Hanbal. I'll go easy on you."

"Please don't, Craterus. You'll need all your skill!"

He seemed to not know if I was joking with him, or if I was serious.

The referee signalled and we began circling.

Craterus eyed my movements, analyzing everything. I darted and he slapped my hand away like a fly, again and again. Then, I know not how, I was flying through the air to land outside the circle. I could taste grit in my mouth and hear laughter echoing all about me.

How he did it, I can't even fathom, but slow he certainly was not.

"Told you I would go easy on you!" Now Craterus crouched, more intent as I entered the skama again. His long limb shot out to sweep my legs, but I jumped, side-stepped, and moved to grab him from behind, dropping my weight. However, with the sweat drenching us, the olive oil he had rubbed into his skin, and the sheer weight of him, I could not shift him.

The second I released my grip, he swept around behind me, locked my arms behind my back, and drove me face down into the sand.

More cheers, more laughter.

I got up, my body patchy with sand and sweat, my shoulders aching from the hold. I went to the side and splashed water on my face to get the sand out of my eyes. When I came back, Craterus rushed in, sweeping arms and legs all about me, trying to trip me up. I jumped and dove, avoiding each, and then, in a moment, I saw him leap flat out for me.

As he came, I jumped, almost like a Cretan bull leaper, onto his back, grabbed his arms, and pulled hard.

He bellowed as I pinned him in the sand, my knee in his back.

The cry of shock from the ranks was satisfying, and I noticed that even Alexander stood, staring intently. New bets were placed as we circled each other again.

It was a strange feeling to inhabit my immediate thoughts and body. The focus was so intense, it took me by surprise. But the rush of blood through my limbs was like a riptide.

We each made for new holds which we each broke out of.

Craterus was tiring, but only a little.

I struggled to control my breath in the prolonged engagement. But when I saw the big warrior go down on one knee, I lunged, the asps upon my arms darting to flip him onto his back.

But I fell right into this feint and as soon as I was on him, his massive arms caught me, spun me up onto his shoulders, and he flung me over a nearby railing that marked the edge of the wrestling area.

I had lost.

Cheers erupted, and curses flew from the mouths of those who had placed hasty bets on me.

Craterus roared in triumph and pumped the air with his arms.

I struggled to look at anyone, shame running through me, but to my surprise, the assembly clapped and smiled as I rose.

"Good bout, Hanbal," Craterus helped me up. "Sloppy, but good!" He always was Spartan with his words.

"Ptolemy leapt over the fence and came to me. "Magnificent, Hanbal!"

"Magnificent?" I panted. "He tossed me like a child's toy. I lost!"

He laughed, his head back, his hands on his stomach. "Nobody has *ever* won against Craterus! Not even Alexander!"

"What?"

"Craterus has wrestled lions with his bare hands!" he continued laughing, as did others who heard what he told me.

I saw Alexander congratulating Craterus and the two of them smiled in my direction. Craterus shrugged an apology.

Unfortunately, I did not have much time to rest before the boxing began.

Ptolemy, Nearchus and Craterus took me directly to the boxing skamae where I was to fight three times.

You must understand that this was all utterly strange to me, fighting for sport. I had only ever fought to kill Persians, and so I feared killing any Greek in the ring. I decided upon using a minimum of force and effort, depending on the opponent.

The straps and weights the Greeks used on their hands for boxing, which they called 'himantes', felt unnatural and clumsy to me, but I followed the rules of their sport.

My first two opponents, I downed in seconds, much to the shock of some, and the dismay of others who had been hoping for a longer bout.

One thing that fighting for your life will teach you is that the less time and energy you spend fighting, the better. You want any engagement to end quickly, on your terms, and to your advantage.

When it came to the final bout, I found myself across the sand from Philotas.

He looked at me with arrogance, a contempt that I despised, and I felt a deep dislike for him as we stepped in to face each other.

Craterus, Nearchus, and Ptolemy cheered me on while Parmenion, Perdiccas and others urged him to bury me.

I knew in that moment who my possible friends were in my endeavour, and whom I should be constantly wary of. That alone was useful, but I forced myself to focus on the fight, for I suspected it would not be as easy to beat Philotas as it had been the Messenian and Naxian whom I had bested with such ease.

Alexander looked on, Barsine and Thais by his side now, beneath shades held by slaves.

I looked up to the sky and murmured a prayer to Hathor. I said Eshe's name, for its utterance reminded me of who I really was.

"What's that, Egyptian? Worried?" Philotas said. "Don't be. This won't take long."

The referee signalled, and Philotas immediately came at me with a series of feints and punches that set me on the alert. He was lean and quick, and full of anger, and I knew I had to beat him.

When one of his punches connected with my face, I staggered back, my ears ringing as he then hammered my ribs.

I instinctively brought up an elbow and smashed him in the face, but the referee halted the bout and told me that I had to be penalized for that. "This is boxing!" the man said. "Save that for the pankration."

Philotas cursed me above the roar of the crowd.

"Come on, Hanbal!" I heard Craterus shout. "You can take him!"

I shook my head to clear it and stepped up again. I remembered the hand-to-hand fights I had survived over the years. *I am The Asp!* I thought. *I am speed! Coil and strike, dart and dodge!*

Hatred burned in Philotas' eyes. He would kill me if he could, I knew.

When he came, a flurry of punches and swipes, I was ready. In fact, rarely have I felt so alive. As soon as I dodged, my long arm was out, connecting with his face, then twice with his ribs.

He hit me again in the face, but then it was as though I did not feel it. My left hand came out to block his follow-up punch, and my right darted out to slam into his forehead.

For a moment, he looked confused, then he staggered and fell backwards. He did not rise for several counts, and when he did, he stumbled sideways back to the ground.

I was declared the victor.

Even as Philotas' friends tried to wake him with water and the medic saw to his head, I was confronted by cheering men calling my name and a wreath of olive was placed upon my sweat-soaked brow.

In the middle of the crowd, Alexander and the two women also clapped for me as Craterus raised me onto his shoulders. It was not until then that I noticed several of the Hellenes scowling at me. I was the Egyptian who had beaten a Greek then, and no matter how well-deserved my victory, they would always see me as a xenos, a foreign barbarian among them.

I wondered if winning had done more harm than good to my cause.

. . .

As I nursed my swelling face and drank pomegranate nectar with water, we went to take in the final event of the games, the pankration.

The Greeks speak of civilization, but this event, I believe, merits no place in so-called 'games'. It is pure brutality.

Which is probably why Cassander excelled at it.

Cassander was cold and calculating and deadly-fast. The pankration, I realized after the first couple of bouts, was for those who cared not for anyone else. You had to be ruthless or you could end up maimed or worse. Even if biting and gouging were banned, bone breaking and grabbing hold of genitalia were not. Not one person left the skama without some major injury.

Through all the fights sailed Cassander, his face bloody, his body scratched. His cold grey eyes took in an opponent in seconds and he had the measure of the man's skill in that time. He broke arms and legs, and dislocated joints to the audible disgust of some.

I could see the king was angry at losing so many battle-ready men to Cassander's ego, but he could say nothing. This was the pankration.

When the final bout came, the last of the games, Cassander stood leaning against a post, spitting gobs of blood. His opponent was an Illyrian as tall as myself, a man of the phalanx.

"Come, nobleman!" the Illyrian taunted. "Come taste my commoner's shit and lick my ass!"

Cassander's face was expressionless as he walked out onto the sand and stood before the man.

When the referee signalled to start, the man drove his fist into Cassander's face, breaking his nose, and followed up with a knee to his ribs.

I heard the crack of breaking bone.

Cassander doubled over, but then he stood up, a smile on his face.

When the man came again, Cassander stepped lightly out of the way once, then a second time before bringing both his fists into the man's ears.

His opponent's balance off, Cassander's leg swept up into his chin, breaking several of the man's teeth as they crashed together. Cassander then walked about him, like a cheetah about a wounded ibex, waiting, breathing in the scent of blood.

The man still had strength however, and he drove like a runner from the starting line into Cassander's ribs with his shoulder, carrying him across the skama to crash through a rope fence.

Cassander instinctively reached for a shard of wood, but immediately threw it down as weapons were forbidden. Then he unleashed himself and seemed to strike all over at once so that his opponent felt simultaneous pain in his face, chest, kidneys and knees.

The Illyrian hobbled back to the middle of the skama, Cassander following slowly.

"Come…nobleman…" the man said through his savaged and bloody mouth. "Time to kiss my…ass!"

Quicker than I thought him capable, the wounded Illyrian struck out at Cassander's leg, tripping him. Then he lunged on top of him, his knee in Cassander's groin as they grappled. The latter, despite the pain that surely lanced through his body, reached up, took hold of the man's left ear, and ripped it off.

The sand about them clotted with blood, and before the referee could step in, Cassander hurled the man onto this back, jumped on top of him, and brought his fist down into his windpipe.

To everyone's horror, especially the Illyrian contingent, the man choked to death within a matter of seconds.

Cassander stood with the crowd staring at him in mingled horror and awe. Not even then did he yell or say a thing. He merely saluted Alexander as the king, and waded into the salt sea to soak his bleeding body.

The games had ended horribly and it took some time for the banquet that night to pick up.

You may ask why I have described these games in so much detail when they were such a fleeting moment on such a long journey. But I have done so to illustrate to you, the reader of this chronicle, my own private odyssey and the nature of the men in whose company I travelled, those warriors who helped Alexander to conquer the world.

The Hellenes of every nation could be both brutal and kind, highly intelligent and skilled, ignorant and base. They were the best and worst of humanity, and their vast army was a microcosm of the world in which we live. In a day, a man could beat the odds and win glory and honour, while another one tore apart and killed one of his fellows.

This was the world I moved through like a wraith who is himself haunted by demons. These were the men with whom the Fates had billeted me.

That day, Creon and Demophon had been far from my thoughts for once, until I hung the pouch with Eshe's finger back around my aching neck.

I knew I had fought, not only to keep going in my horrific mission, but also to punish myself for whatever Eshe and my daughters were going through.

When I left the banquet that night, quite drunk and in a

dark mood, I climbed the southern rampart of Tyre, near the temple of Herakles, and sat looking up at the black, star-pocked sky over my beloved Egypt in the distance. I prayed to Hathor, and then I wept until I passed out beneath my cloak.

When I awoke, the sun was high and burning. I found myself clutching Eshe's finger in the pouch. Though I could not recall them, I was aware of having had horrible dreams of pain laced with suffering and screams. I tried grasping out for some image of meaning or import, but all I could think of was the pouch at my neck.

I stood and leaned onto the battlements looking out to sea. My body was sore, vaguely so, but it dit not bother me. I wondered if I was still drunk, or if I was indeed becoming accustomed to pain, perhaps numb to it.

I relieved myself and then began to make my way along the wall walk, determined to go to Ra who was stabled with the Companion horses on the landward side, beyond the beach.

The sea was bright and the glinting sun pained my eyes. I could feel a tightness in my face where I had been hit the previous day. I walked farther until I heard a murmur of voices and spotted a small group on the west-facing rampart gazing out to sea and the mass of war ships at anchor.

The red cloaks, golden armour, and tall crimson-crested helmets of the royal guard caught my eye first, and then I saw Alexander standing with Aristander and Hephaestion. As soon as the guards noticed me, Hephaestion stepped in front of Alexander, his hand on his sword.

"Calm down," I heard the king say. "It is our friend of Egypt. Hanbal."

I bowed. "My lord, Pharaoh," I said without thinking.

"You see!" Alexander exclaimed to Hephaestion. "My

Egyptian subjects shall be among my most faithful. Hear how I am referred to as 'Pharaoh'?" He then approached me. "Hanbal, son of Akil."

I was sure that my appearance was unacceptable, but the king went on, friendly, warm, and welcoming. He led me to the others. "You fought very well yesterday in the games."

"Thank you, sire. Admittedly, I had no idea what I was doing."

"Ha!" he laughed. "I think Philotas would say otherwise, my friend." I could see that a part of Alexander was pleased with Philotas' loss to me. "And Craterus was still talking about it late into the night. You challenged him."

I still winced to think how the heavy infantry commander had flung me through the air.

Alexander laid his hand upon my shoulder. "Do not feel ashamed. I've seen Craterus wrestle a lion with his bare hands when we were out hunting. You did well." He smiled in that way that made men feel at ease. He went on, turning back to the men he had been with. "We were just looking at the sea, Hanbal. It has been our constant companion, our link to home. So beautiful…" He moved to the wall again, his gold and red cloak flapping softly behind him. "If I am truthful, I would say that I might never see them again, these wine-dark depths."

"Sire?" I stepped closer.

"We're heading inland now," Hephaestion put in, stepping close to me. He made me uneasy for he, above all others, truly had Alexander's well-being at heart. Whether Hephaestion was Alexander's lover or his best friend, I have concluded over time, is of no consequence. For he would have given his life in a second for Alexander. For me, he was perhaps the one true barrier to my mission. Hephaestion, I knew, was the king's selfless guardian. He was everywhere at all times. If he suspected me, my entire mission and my family were doomed.

"Just show me where the Persians are," I said casually, "and I shall take them down to the Underworld."

"There will be time enough for that," the king said, laying a hand on his friend's arm and drawing him away from me. "But Hephaestion is correct. We march north into Syria now."

"North?" I asked. "But Babylon is to the east."

"North," Alexander answered absolutely.

"Tell us, Hanbal…" Aristander spoke for the first time. "What dreams have the Gods sent you of late?"

I looked at him, taken aback. In the sunlight, up close, Aristander looked younger than he usually did. His grey eyes gleamed with the sun's light reflected off of the sea, and his hands appeared strong and youthful.

"None that I remember well," I said, not a little angry at the sudden intrusion. I struggled to bottle my anger and sadness like Pandora trying to reseal the box she had unwittingly opened in the Greeks' tale of her.

Aristander stared at me still, and I returned his gaze. Something had changed in the way he looked upon me since that day at blessed Siwa. He no longer frightened me, nor did he intend to. I was certainly not his peer as far as he was concerned, but there were traces of reluctant respect, even awe. He believed, as did many, including the king, that the Gods spoke through me.

How that could be, I do not know, for I remember little, and what I do recall is utterly terrifying. I heard Zeus-Ammon address his son, and though I tried to ignore it, that voice haunted my psyche like a far-distant roll of thunder. When I was near Alexander, I felt it, heard it…and then recalled the deed I must do.

I turned from the seer to the king who was watching me. "Sire, I have had no dreams of import, but, if I do, though I don't understand them, I will come to you and Aristander to relay what I have been shown."

Alexander gripped my shoulders tightly and smiled, his eyes fierce. "Good! I am glad of it, Hanbal." He let go. "The army marches in three days. I want you to ride close to us, with my Companions, in case I have need of you."

"I am honoured, sire."

"Today, go with Craterus to the armourers. We are going to war again, and you should be well-armed. Tell him that I have instructed you to be given a thorax and whatever else you require. A gift from your pharaoh for your honest service to this point."

"Thank you, sire." I bowed and departed down the stairs into the city streets. When I looked back I could see Alexander still gazing out to sea, Hephaestion beside him.

There was, I believe, real regret in the king's voice, at leaving the sea over which Homer's heroes had travelled, his idols, his family. Perhaps he felt the same now as I did when the Nile and sands of my beloved Egypt had receded behind me?

If even he felt he might not see those turquoise waters again, would I?

We were on the precipice now, each of us ready to step over the edge into the unknown.

A WAVE OF FIRE AND HOPE

Three days later, the army set out, an entire civilization on the move.

We left Tyre, that city brought-to-heel, behind. The fleet, unable to follow, had been augmented by one hundred ships from Cyprus and Phoenicia and were bound for Crete to carry out the punitive work against Sparta and the remnant Persian forces there.

For all the tales of courage and martial skill I had heard about the Spartans, it surprised me greatly that they had sided with the Persians against the rest of the Hellenes. One wonders if the campaign we were embarking on might have ended sooner had the men of Lacedaemon deigned to fight for Alexander.

At least they were honest. I could not say the same for the Athenians I was acquainted with to that point.

And so, like a singular leaf swept along a rushing river, I found myself marching north with the army, among Alexander's Companion cavalry with the King of Macedon, Warlord of the Greeks, Pharaoh of Egypt. From Damascus, we headed for Syria where we would cross at a polis named Thapsacus.

When I think of that time, it is difficult for me to pick out a specific moment, or any feelings other than the deep emptiness I felt without my family, the helplessness that frustrated me for my being forced to be there.

But it did feel good to be atop Ra again and, though he chided me at first by ignoring my commands, he quickly forgave me. I had left him too long unattended and realized that he might have feared I had abandoned him. When you have spent your life around horses, as I have, you learn that they think and feel as much as we. They can be happy or glum, jealous or aggressive. Ra was my dearest friend and I had left him alone, cared for but still alone, for days.

When I approached him in the stables, wearing my new thorax, he at first turned away from me, betrayed only by his ears which leaned toward me.

"Forgive me, Ra," I said softly as I approached. "I was wrong to leave you for so long. Father would have been furious," I muttered.

Ra turned then, sniffed the new armour of hardened linen and black bull's hide. The tanning and glue left a strong smell, but that would dissipate in time. Satisfied that it was me and that I felt remorse, Ra leaned over my shoulder and rested his muscular neck against mine. I put my arms around him, grateful for him and his calm, steady breathing.

Many Egyptians and Greeks have mocked me over the years because I believe horses are as people, and thus we have a natural affinity for one another.

Only Alexander really understood me when I talked of that affinity between a man and his horse, for he had the same connection with Bucephalus, the only other being whose courage and heart might have matched Alexander's when the screams were at their loudest, and the blood flowed at its deepest.

As we marched in the heat of high summer, I felt unused to the new armour and Ra, no doubt, was unused to the extra weight and stiffness of my riding style that resulted from it.

It was an expensive gift from the king which Craterus had insisted was of the best design. He had told me at the armourer's that the combined linen and bull's hide were far superior, lighter and more flexible, than the all bronze cuirass which many soldiers still used.

"This flexes and absorbs better," the big Macedonian said before hammering his fist into my chest, sending me back a few feet. He roared with laughter, but I could feel the difference. Such a blow would rattle me were I in bronze, and the flex of the new armour would better stop Persian arrows. At least I hoped so. "And you can move your arms more freely," he added.

"I must thank the king," I said.

"Our Alexander is beyond generous," he answered with his usual, big smile.

In addition to the black thorax, I acquired a dozen new throwing knives, and a kopis, a heavy, curved slashing sword that Craterus insisted I should have.

Thus armed, I marched with the rest of the Hellenes to war against Persia.

As I rode, touching the pouch about my neck, I imagined using my kopis on Demophon and Creon for what they had done. It was a pointless imagining, but then, it was a time to harden myself to everything around me. There was no room for sadness or regret, for both could sap the strength and get me killed. In those early days on the march, the intensity of the heat aided in keeping me distracted.

I used to think that there was heat unlike anything else in Egypt. I was wrong.

On the march, among thousands of men in armour, the dust churning up in great clouds all around us, beneath the summer sun of Syria, I experienced a heat unlike anything else. The terrain was rocky and dry, and our footfalls must have sent a dust cloud into the sky that Darius himself would have seen from his hanging gardens in Babylon.

Our pace was not hurried, but it was constant. We could tell that Alexander was eager to meet Darius, but on his own terms, and when the timing was right.

We made for the cooler, greener, high country, rather than cutting across the Syrian desert. Foraging would be easier and the heat far less punishing. And yet, I think Alexander had other motives.

He was keeping his enemy guessing.

There was a constant flow to and from the king's banner at the head of the column, scouts, engineers, philosophers, and friends.

Alexander was ever busy, his own mind moving the wheels of war by sheer will alone.

"The land is just as Xenophon described," Ptolemy said on the eleventh day out of Tyre as we approached Thapsacus at the crossing of the Euphrates.

"Xenophon…" I remembered the name. My father had had my tutor use Xenophon's work, *On Horsemanship*, as part of my lessons. "The Athenian writer," I confirmed.

"Yes," Ptolemy beamed. "A true Greek hero. Not just an Athenian though. He was a warrior and philosopher, an

Athenian by birth, but sympathetic to Sparta. He came through here with the army of Cyrus the Younger, and when that Persian prince was killed at Cunaxa, Xenophon had to lead his ten thousand fellow Greeks out of Persia and back home."

"The Anabasis?" I remembered.

"That's it! Xenophon chronicled the march and described much of the terrain. Alexander has been using his text as a field guide."

"But Xenophon marched south along the Euphrates," added Coenus who rode on Ptolemy's other side.

"Which is why we rode north," Ptolemy continued. "Darius will expect Alexander to follow Xenophon exactly and so-"

"Better to do the opposite," I finished.

"Precisely."

"But for how long will we march north?" I asked.

"Who knows?" Coenus said easily. "Persian spies will be reporting back to Darius. They'll tell him the opposite of what he expects."

"Persian spies in this army?" I was shocked Alexander would ever allow it to happen, despite my knowledge of the Athenians who had a hold over me.

"There are several, to be sure," Ptolemy added casually.

I did not understand. What if they killed Alexander instead? What if they betrayed him and the battle was lost before it began?

"Don't tell me the Egyptian is now a Companion!" The haughty voice that came suddenly from in front was Cassander's. He sat his horse as though born to it. He was still battered from the games, but he seemed no less dangerous.

"The king asked that I ride up front," I returned,

looking down at Cassander from my higher vantage point on Ra. "I do as Pharaoh commands." The words felt odd to utter, my tongue unused to such ways of talking.

Cassander smiled, looked me up and down with his cold, unyielding eyes. "Then you must do as commanded, Asp," he answered before riding ahead.

I noticed Philotas beyond him then. He had been staring at me all the while, and I knew I had an enemy in him.

"Careful, Hanbal," Ptolemy muttered under his breath without looking at me. "You don't want either of them as enemies."

I looked at him, but he stared straight ahead.

"We should train together to get you accustomed to that armour and kopis. You don't want to try them out for the first time on the day of battle."

"Good point," I said. "I would appreciate a lesson in Macedonian fighting and battle tactics."

"Done!" he said, finally looking over at me. "Once we reach Thapsacus, we'll train. Everyone will be drilling more now."

"When will we reach the city?" I asked. "Is it far?"

"Not far at all" he said, nodding to the northeast.

There, not so distant, stood a great polis baking in the midday sun beside the broad ribbon of the Euphrates river. The scene, the river with the city beside it, should have been a comforting sight to me, but somehow, this was not the case. The water did not speak or sparkle like the Nile, and my gods seemed far away. The Mother Nile always seemed peaceful, a part of things, even in flood. But the Euphrates was a sluggish stranger to me, the city of Thapsacus darker than Memphis, less welcoming.

A trumpet sounded and Alexander called a halt.

Hephaestion was to go ahead with three hundred horse

to ensure the city would welcome the king and that the river crossing was secure.

"Persians!" someone yelled, and as the army looked across the river, we could see a great cloud of horsemen racing south.

"Hya!" Hephaestion yelled from the front as he and his horsemen sped toward the city. They thundered off with their commander's red cloak and red-crested helmet at the top of a great arrowhead formation.

I wondered momentarily what the inhabitants of the town thought seeing our army appear. They had no doubt seen many armies over time, but I felt then that perhaps the whole world was holding its collective breath.

"To Thapsacus!" Alexander suddenly called back, his voice echoed down the line by heralds. "We cross where the Ten Thousand crossed!"

The Greeks and their heroes. The mere mention of that long-dead mercenary force would not have caused a twitch in Egypt, and so I was surprised when the army cheered heartily and banged their spears upon their shields.

We began again, ready to spend the night in that place.

"How long will we stay?" I asked Nearchus.

"Oh, a night…two at most, I should think."

WE STAYED FIVE DAYS IN THAPSACUS, JUST AS XENOPHON DID with Cyrus the Younger.

Many thought that Alexander should have pursued the Persians we had seen, but he refused. Instead, during that time, we took on new supplies and drilled beneath the wary eyes of our reluctant hosts.

Alexander was kind to the inhabitants, said to them that he knew Darius had held them under his boot but that he,

Alexander, was a beneficent, democratic king. "Our countryman, Xenophon, who passed through here," he said to the local council, "he called Thapsacus a 'large and prosperous city'. Well, under me, you shall be even more so for your past, present, and future kindnesses to the Hellenes and all my other subjects." He then approached the trembling elders and reassured them. "I thank you for not firing the two boat bridges across the river. If you keep them intact, you shall have my eternal favour."

Alexander was becoming more and more concerned with our supply lines the deeper into Asia we ventured, and sought reassurances that the way would remain open to him.

The council thanked the king and performed the proskynesis before him, laying themselves prostrate before Alexander so that their foreheads touched the ground.

The Hellenes scoffed to see these noblemen full-flat on the ground in obeisance to Alexander, but, for a moment, the king watched them with interest. Then, he said, "No, no my friends. You need not submit in this Persian fashion to me."

The men rose, confused.

"I require only your word, for *that* is a sacred thing."

The king had good reason to be grateful. The river was half a mile across and, though Cyrus' army had crossed on foot so many years before, the river having supposedly, divinely, held back for him, we all knew that the bridges would save several days of marching to find another crossing point.

The Persians had run so quickly that they had neglected to burn them, and so they had left the way open to Alexander and his army.

On the other hand, some believed it intentional, a ruse to draw Alexander further into the enemy hinterland where,

Alexander's scouts and spies reported, Darius was amassing an army from every quarter of the Persian Empire. It was an opportunity, an arrogance of the enemy's, that Alexander had to exploit.

I LEARNED LITTLE OF THE PLANNED STRATEGY IN THE evenings when I was invited to dine with the Companions and allied commanders.

The fact was that Alexander was adaptable.

We would not know the plan until the last moment.

I ate and drank among them and realized that, perhaps soon, I would have to carry out the mission forced upon me by the Athenians holding my family hostage.

I had certainly not forgotten Creon and Demophon, nor what they had done, and everyday that Eshe was captive was tortuous, a great failure on my part.

It seemed to take forever to bring the Persians to battle, but I knew that when it did come, it would be a fight the likes of which the world had never seen. The rumours of Darius' numbers were wild and never the same, ranging anywhere from two-hundred-thousand to over a million troops from across the Persian Empire. Wherever and whenever the battle took place, all I knew is that it was something I had to survive.

If I die, my family dies, I told myself constantly. *If I die, they die!*

That is why, on our first morning in Thapsacus, after a restless sleep billeted with a local elderly couple, I went to find Ptolemy and begin my training. If I was to survive, I had to be one of the best warriors in the army.

The Companions had set up a training area to the north of the city along the river. The clang of swords from hand-to-hand combat echoed above the thrum of marching feet and horns in the plains beyond where the phalanxes drilled harder than ever. No doubt the Persian spies took an interest, but Alexander was a master of surprise and not in the least worried.

We trained on horseback for a time, and I saw firsthand what excellent horsemen the Companions, Thessalians, and Paeonians were. It was exhaustive work with javelin, lance, and sword, our maneuvers precise as the dust swirled around our horses making it difficult to see, the grit coating our tongues. After some time at that, we rested the horses and began training on foot in separate groups.

"Come at me, Hanbal!" Ptolemy yelled, his eyes sharp and flinty beneath his bronze helmet.

The curved edge of the kopis was awkward at first, and I had several welts before I managed to get a feel for that brutal weapon. Beneath my own helmet, a shining bronze one with no crest and asps engraved upon the cheek guards, I found it difficult to breathe, to hear, and to wipe sweat from my eyes. Finally, however, I landed a couple smacks on Ptolemy's leg and back with the flat of my blade, the second sending him into the dirt.

"It's a good thing you're unused to that weapon," he said, laughing as he rose from the dusty ground.

I reached out to take his forearm but as I did so, a rasping voice broke in.

"Come on, Ptolemy! You let yourself be beaten by an Egyptian peasant!"

Philotas stood between us, his back to me. He was sweaty from his sparing with Perdiccas.

"Give it a rest, Philotas," Ptolemy dismissed him with a wave. "I've never known you to be such a poor loser. Hanbal beat you fairly in the games."

"Did he now?"

Before I knew it, Philotas' kopis had swung around, and it was only by Hathor's grace that I was quick enough to meet the sharp edge with the blunted one of my own blade.

It had been a killing blow, aimed at my neck.

"Philotas!" Ptolemy yelled, but it did not stop the young Macedonian's onslaught.

Philotas rushed me, cutting, slashing, looking for a bite of his blade. His rage made him sloppy, but he was dangerous and intent, and it took all my skill to deflect him. When the killing edge of his blade caught the top of my thigh, I was filled with such a hatred of him that I turned the sharp edge of my own kopis on him.

He was no better than a Persian then, and so I struck with a cut to his left arm, and followed with a sweep of one of my long legs to send him sprawling in the dust. I kicked his sword away and Perdiccas and Cleitus rushed in to pull Philotas away, screaming hate at me all the while.

It was then that Alexander, Coenus, and others came riding up.

Ptolemy went straight to the king who listened, an angry expression on his face.

I did not fail to notice the guards moving in around me, and so I sheathed my sword, crossed my arms, and waited.

Alexander ordered Philotas to contain himself, and brought him back.

We both stood before the king who stared down from high atop Bucephalus' back.

"My friends, the enemy lies on the other side of the river. Not here! Why then are you trying to kill each other?"

Neither of us spoke, and Philotas barely contained his rage.

"Philotas," Alexander continued. "Hanbal beat you in

the games fairly, and I know you've been nursing your anger over it. That is not noble, and indeed is far beneath you. I command you to let him be. He is our friend and has helped us greatly since he joined our ranks."

Then Alexander turned to me, no hint of friendship in his eyes. "Hanbal, I have honoured you and welcomed you among my elite, my friends. And this is how you repay me?"

I am sure shock registered on my face then, like a student unfairly chided by a teacher, as I looked to Ptolemy and back at the king. I knew that the men around me had grown up together, that they had been fighting side-by-side against the Persians for some time already, and that I was a newcomer, a xenos. But, it was difficult to contain my anger.

Beyond the king, I could see General Parmenion chaffing at the bit, outraged that his son had fallen to me again, and that I had been allowed to treat his son in that way.

Alexander looked at me and, swallowing my pride, I knelt to speak.

"Forgive me, sire. You have treated me most kindly with generous hospitality. Pharaoh, I was but defending myself. I have no quarrel with Commander Philotas."

There was an unbearable silence, broken only by the wind on the river and the rustle of dry grasses about us.

Hephaestion leaned over to the king to whisper something.

Alexander looked back at me and Philotas and spoke. "We cannot be fighting amongst ourselves. I need you both fit for the coming fight!" In that moment, Alexander's potential rage surfaced for the smallest of moments, but I could see that if he unleashed that rage, it would be more deadly than any storm at sea or upon the desert. He regained his composure quickly. "You are both at fault, and so the next one who provokes the other will be executed. That is my command, and if either of you ignores it, that will be the end of you."

"Your majesty, I protest!" Parmenion bellowed.

"You protest, General? I say the matter is closed!" Alexander wheeled Bucephalus to face the grizzled veteran. "When I say it is done, it *is* done."

Parmenion nodded curtly, grabbed his son by his wounded arm, and led him off.

All others dispersed for midday, leaving me standing alone with Ptolemy, the pages gathering the remainder of the gear about us.

"How can the king blame me?" I demanded.

"Be calm, my friend. Alexander did all he could do. You are a guest, yes, but you are also an Egyptian."

"So?" I found myself shaking with rage at my humiliation.

"So, Philotas is a noble Macedonian. If the king were to side with an Egyptian over one of our own, a Companion no less, he would meet with great resistance. And someone would try to kill you anyway."

"You paint a bleak picture. It is unjust, Ptolemy."

"It is politics, and Alexander needs Parmenion, his men, and his skill in the battle to come. I interceded for you, and told the truth to Alexander when he arrived, but it was Hephaestion who turned things in your favour. Alexander listened to him where Parmenion would surely have sought your death."

I took a cloth from a nearby page and tried to stanch my bleeding thigh.

"Let's get you to the infirmary and then get some food. Training with you, Hanbal, is hungry work!" He said it in such a jovial way that, in spite of myself, I laughed and followed him to find a physician.

Though exhausted by the training that day, I could not sleep.

Over and over again, my thoughts returned to my precarious position in Alexander's army and how my family's survival relied upon every interaction I had. I was angry with myself for letting Philotas bait me so easily. I had just escaped execution that day, ejection from the inner circle, or a flogging at the very least.

If not for Ptolemy and Hephaestion, I would have lost Alexander's favour. I had to stay in the king's good graces for as long as I needed to.

Why Hephaestion spoke to save me, was another question, and I could not help but conclude that it was not for kindness to me, but for love of his king that he might have whispered a way out. He also did not like Philotas, and many of the Companions were inclined to feel the same.

When I emerged from the home of my reluctant hosts the next morning, it was with shot eyes and a throbbing leg that I once again made my way to the training fields.

We were training on horseback that day and it was there that I excelled. No mount, save the king's own, adhered to every command like Ra. I was, however, greatly impressed by the Companions' skill, and that of the Paeonians who were lightly armed with two javelins each, bronze breast-plates, flared helmets and cloaks. The latter may not have been heavily armoured like the Companions, but they had no need of that, as I was to discover. They manoeuvred, turned, and wheeled with such swift precision that I was reminded of a flock of swallows wheeling and darting in the evening sky. Only, these birds had teeth. The Paeonians were so skilled with their javelins that not a one missed his target, even at a full gallop or after having passed a target.

I stood with Ra watching them while the Companions went through drills with the king.

When the Paeonians finished, one of their captains, a man named Ariston, dismounted near me. His white warhorse foamed at the mouth after the exertions.

"Nicely done," I said casually, admiring his mount.

Ariston took off his flared helmet and wiped his brow. "Thank you," he smiled and stared straight back at me. "You are Hanbal, yes?" His Greek was very thick and accented, and it took me a moment to register what he had said.

"Yes," I said suspiciously.

"Do not worry, friend. I'm not a spy. I've heard of you is all. I heard the story of how you led the king to Siwa."

"Oh."

"I also love horses and wanted to come and meet yours." He walked closer, his horse at his shoulder like a loyal hound, and looked up at Ra's face. "He's magnificent. What is his name?"

"Ra."

"Is that Persian?"

I was about to protest when he broke out in laughter. "I'm just kidding, Hanbal. I'm guessing Ra could trample many a Persian dog." He reached out gently to Ra who nosed his hand.

Ra could always tell if someone was friendly to horses.

Ariston stroked Ra's neck. "I've never seen his like, except maybe the king's horse. Your Ra is a wonder."

"Yes, he is," I answered proudly. "He is my best friend."

Ariston was silent a moment. Then he turned to his own

mount. "This is Apollo. He has saved my life many a time with his speed."

"He too, is magnificent."

Ariston smiled. "Two horses named for the sun! We will blind the Persians on the battlefield!"

I nodded, but did not smile. "Do the Paeonians ride with the king?" I asked instead, curious to find out more about the battles and how the Hellenes fought them on horseback.

"Yes. Usually," he said proudly. "We did at the Granicus and Issus, and I suspect that we will again soon." He gazed across the Euphrates as if staring at the enemy. "We are the wasps that buzz about the Persians' heads, stinging, before they are crushed by the Companion cavalry's relentless hammer.

"And which is the anvil?" I asked.

"Why, the phalanxes of course."

I was silent a moment and he spoke as though reading my thoughts.

"Where will you fight, Hanbal? Do you know? I hear the Egyptian contingent has been set to guard the baggage on route. But I don't see you with any of them."

"I do not know any of them. Nor do I know where I am to fight when we meet the Persians."

"No?" Ariston smiled, mischievously. "Let us see what you can do from horseback then." He whistled so loudly that it hurt my ears. Then, before I knew it, the training field near us was lined with Paeonian horsemen watching me.

"Now?" I asked.

"Why not? Show us what you and Ra can do." He put his helmet back on and indicated the avenue of targets they had been using. There were two rows, one facing the other, of six targets on each side.

"I only have two javelins," I told Ariston who had already mounted up again.

"What about those?" He pointed to the ten throwing knives that criss-crossed my thorax. "Just don't miss!" he laughed as he joined his fellows.

I had no choice but to accept the challenge, and began visualizing how I might hit every target either side of me as I rode. It was near impossible. I mounted up on Ra and he reared, his hooves making dust billow when they landed. I rode to one end of the targets, then back, ignoring the snickering to either side.

When I was a good distance off, I kicked Ra into a gallop and charged down the centre with a javelin in each hand, the reins loose on my saddle. I loosed and the javelins struck, right, then left and hit home before my hands flew to my knives and, with more grace than I have ever managed since, I threw the knives from sheath to target in one motion, right and left simultaneously.

A cheer erupted only as the final two hit home, and when I returned to my starting position, there was Alexander with the other Companions, cheering along with the whooping Paeonians. Ariston cheered the loudest of all.

When I stopped before the king, I had Ra bow as he had been taught long ago to entertain my children.

Alexander clapped and laughed.

I don't know why, but I felt immense relief at that.

"Well done, Hanbal, son of Akil!" the king said. "Perhaps we should call you a poisonous butterfly instead of an asp? Your outspread wings are deadly and beautiful in the execution."

"Thank you, sire," I said. "But if it is all the same to you, I think 'Asp' suits me better."

"Indeed it does. But where shall I put 'The Asp' in my ranks? Surely not on foot!"

"Place him with us, my king!" yelled Ariston with a smile.

"No, no… The Paeonians are too proud and awesome a power," Alexander teased. "Besides, you are your own breed of warriors."

"But, sire!" Ariston said, standing before the rows of his horsemen with outspread arms. "We're all bastards!"

The men behind him roared with laughter and raised their javelins high.

It was only later that I learned Ariston was of the Paeonian royal house, brother of King Patraus, but such was his humility and sense of humour.

"Very well," said the king. "Will you have an Egyptian asp among your ranks?"

"As snakes are sacred to our beloved Dionysus, so too is Hanbal's aim and evident skill," Ariston said. "Yes, we will have him!"

Another cheer went up and the king looked at me. "There you have it, Hanbal, son of Akil. Your place in Alexander's army."

"Sire,"I bowed from atop Ra and was immediately surrounded by my new comrades.

Of course a part of me felt guilty at deceiving Ariston and the others who had welcomed me at the time. How could they have known my true purpose? They loved Alexander, and he them. And so, a greater measure of trust was gained in my own campaign to get my family back.

As the Paeonians congratulated me and pat me on the back, I held the pouch about my neck tightly in my left hand in an attempt to ward off the lies I was selfishly sowing for the greater good of my family.

. . .

My new brothers-in-arms, I learned, were men of the mountain plains northeast of Macedon. They were gruff and sometimes surly, but highly skilled and loyal to Alexander. They and their neighbours, the light infantry Agrianes, always played a key role in Alexander's battle plans.

"The Thessalians are good horsemen too," Ariston conceded, "but they are not well armed. And those sun hats! I've never understood those!" He laughed and looked at me sidelong as we waited for our turn to cross the pontoon bridges over the Euphrates.

"Why have me in your ranks?" I asked bluntly, for I had been mulling over my new appointment in the elapsed time since Alexander declared it. I had come to worry that it meant I would not be close enough to Alexander, and so began to think that it was a mistake.

Ariston smiled, and shrugged his armoured shoulders. "Most men would have told me to fuck myself with that challenge on the training ground. But you, you just took up the challenge, chewed it to bits, and spat it back at me! I liked that!" he laughed his easy, joyous laugh, a sound which I came to enjoy.

"I wasn't sure I'd succeed," I said.

"Who could be sure? But you threw like your life depended on it. And anyway, surviving a battle is partly luck as well as the whim of the Gods." Here he looked me in the eyes, his own pale green ones unblinking. "From all I've heard, the Gods favour you, Hanbal, and where we're going, I'd like all the help we can get."

Just then, the trumpets sounded the advance, and our Paeonian cavalry set out across the first bridge.

Ra reared at the sound of the water beneath us, but kept

pace with the others who had grown accustomed to such crossings.

Our orders were to scatter and scout as soon as we were on the other side, until the army was formed up.

I looked ahead, feeling myself going farther and farther from Egypt with every step.

Ahead, the land appeared to be made up of vast plains as far as the eye could see, with mountains to the extreme northwest and northeast. When we looked south, we could see it… Vast carpets of smoke rising up into the sky.

"Scorched earth," said Ariston. "They're trying to shield Babylon."

"I guess we march north then," I muttered.

"That was indeed the plan all along!" Ptolemy reined in beside us.

I was glad to see him.

"Hipparch!" Ariston saluted and Ptolemy returned it.

"We weren't going to march south?" I asked. "From what I gather, your Xenophon did."

"Which is exactly why Alexander wants to go north. The foraging will be better there as well."

"Especially now," added Ariston.

"Exactly," agreed Ptolemy, looking at the blackening horizon to the south. "Each night on the march, you are both to dine with the allied commanders and captains." He said it suddenly, as if remembering the order he was to bring.

"We'll be there," I said, feeling a bit odd with the sudden formality from Ptolemy. I understood, however. Though loyal now, the Paeonians had been, in the early days of King Phillip's reign, one of Macedon's fiercest enemies.

The king had to walk a line between give and take, but such is the dynamic between conquerors and the conquered.

Each must be careful of the other without giving offence, especially if the one is expected to fight for the other.

I don't believe the Athenians cared for that way of thinking, especially after their humiliation at the battle of Chaeronea. My task was the ultimate evidence of that.

It takes a long time for the wounds of loss and humiliation to heal, and much longer for trust to be built.

Only Alexander could have nurtured such trust from the fierce hill-tribes after so short a time.

THE PAEONIANS, INCLUDING MYSELF, SCOUTED SOUTH FOR the better part of the day with nothing to report but blackened earth and an enemy that hid behind curtains of smoke.

We knew that the Persians were watching us as leagues of once-beautiful land lay burned and smouldering. The air was bitter.

The horses were champing at their bits, and Ra was uneasy beneath me. He pulled nervously at the reins when he spied stray tufts of grass that had not burned.

Ariston watched as the sun reached its zenith. "Time to get back," he said, looking up from the elaborate bronze folds of his cavalry helmet.

We set heels to our mounts and one thousand of us thundered north to rejoin the king, report, and continue the march.

The army was already on the move when we approached to trumpet calls signalling our return.

Ariston and Aerates, another Paeonian officer, approached the king where he rode with Cleitus and Hephaestion in the van. I rode with Ptolemy for a time, and was near enough to hear.

"What news, Ariston?" Alexander asked.

"They're burning all approaches to Babylon, sire. There's nothing left."

"Fools!" Alexander cursed them. "They burn their own lands."

"Don't you mean *your* lands, sire?" Coenus said from behind the king.

"Not yet, they aren't," Alexander replied. "Not until we defeat them and Darius is dust. Only then will this realm be mine."

"In the meantime, your majesty," Cleitus put in, "they're burning everything. Should we engage Mazaeus?" he asked of the Persian nobleman who had been Satrap of Cilicia. "He's the one doing this, certainly."

Despite the rumours of the size of the Persian forces that were amassing, I noticed that there was a distinct lack of fear among the men, or at least among the Companions and other cavalry. Like Cleitus, they all appeared eager to get on with it and engage the Persians. Whether they truly felt that confident, or whether they put on a brave face like one of their theatre masks for their king, I could not be certain at the time.

What I did know is that Alexander made them feel invincible.

But the fear would come later.

Alexander turned in the saddle to look at Cleitus. "Not yet. I will not rush this, Cleitus. The Gods will present us with the moment for battle, and then…" Here Alexander closed his eyes and looked to the sky. "Then we shall show them what the Hellenes are made of."

"What's on your mind, Hanbal?" Ptolemy asked suddenly as we rode. His red cloak whipped in the hot summer breeze, and the sun glinted off his polished helmet.

I looked at the Euphrates and the mountains of Syria to our left, the great plains ahead.

"I feel as though I am on the precipice of a great wave that is ready to break on the shore of an unknown land."

He smiled. "I think we all feel that way, my friend. Look at all of us." He turned and indicated the column of the march stretching back for miles. "This has never happened before. The world is about to change, and we can all feel it. We know it… We just don't know *how* it will change."

I could hear them all, the troops, singing their marching songs, the tramp of their feet, and the swish of their sarissas like impossibly high reeds in the summer wind.

"We all come from lands far away from these foreign fields," Ptolemy said. "Yes, we follow our king, but we also follow the shared dreams of our fathers and grandfathers of meting out justice to those who have bribed, murdered, and persecuted the Hellenes for generations."

I looked at this Macedonian who was the closest thing to a friend that I had.

Ptolemy spoke, unaware of those around him, alone with the ideals he had been raised to believe in.

I had thought I knew him well, but Ptolemy was indeed a mystery at that moment, as were all the Companions of Alexander who watched him speaking to me then.

"All of us in Alexander's army…all those in Darius's army…the people of countless nations…have lived under the boot, and dealt with the deceptions and betrayals of the Achaemenids for far too long. Darius and his ancestors burned parts of Greece as they now burn Mesopotamia. They defiled the great temple of Athena Parthenos, and sowed discontent among the Hellenes. They mocked our great heroes who checked their advance into Greece…Miltiades…Leonidas and others. They murdered our king,

Philip!" Ptolemy gripped his cavalry spear and pointed it eastward. "This war is not new. It has been dreamed of since before the first Persian set foot on the beach at Marathon, long before Thermopylae and Salamis. It has been waged in our hearts and minds, many times over, on behalf of all free people. Even by you, Hanbal, son of Akil with every Persian life you took in vengeance for the defilement of your ancient homeland."

I could see and feel the effect of Ptolemy's words on the men around us, their heads held high, their jaws set, their eyes like eagles' seeing their prey from a great distance.

"When the wave crashes, there will be a sound to crack the heavens and clog the shores of Tartarus with Persian dead."

"And when this wave crashes, Ptolemy," Alexander interrupted, turning in his saddle to face us, "I shall be at the front to cut off Persia's head."

"And us with you, sire!" yelled Cassander, the other Companions echoing the sentiment until it moved down the line of the army like a wave indeed.

As I rode away on the next reconnaissance with the Paeonians, I wondered if the Hellenes might be so inspired to greatness, if Alexander could do this impossible task, or whether Ptolemy's words were the brash ramblings of a young man who was trying desperately to beat back his fear, or Phobos, as the Greeks call that dark god.

I hoped all of our gods were listening then, for if we did not keep our footing, our resolve, and our courage when the wave crashed, we would all be swept away in a river of blood.

CHAPTER SEVENTEEN

FIRST BLOOD

We marched for days without another sighting of enemy forces. Many men were beginning to fear a trap. However, despite this rearing of Phobos' head, they still trusted the king and his instincts.

I learned that Alexander had never been outmanoeuvred by any opponent, that he had never lost a battle. The Gods were, it seemed, his constant allies.

In the dark of night, as we camped, I recalled the voice I had heard at Siwa, and I wondered how powerful Zeus-Ammon was, whether it was enough to protect Alexander's army against the might of Ahura Mazda and the forces of Persia.

Even with so much confidence, it felt like we were harried by ghosts.

The black smoke had gone, however, and we now found ourselves marching east through northern Mesopotamia. The world seemed so vast out there.

As I stood on a grassy rise, I stared at a world of long, level plains with low-rising hills teaming with life. It was not Egypt, but it seemed just as ancient, even paradisical.

I borrowed a scroll from Ptolemy of Xenophon's *Anabasis*, and it was exactly as he described it. The land was treeless, but full of low-lying vegetation, and the air smelled sweetly of spices and herbs at times, at least when the fires abated.

Ariston, myself, and several others hunted the wild animals that abounded - wild asses, ostriches, and antelope - that were caught between us and whatever Persian forces pressed them from the other side.

One of the antelope I had taken down with a javelin at a full gallop, and we ate well on that. Others dined on wild ass roasted over the camp fires. However, the only person to take down an ostrich was one of the Agrianes who managed to break the bird's legs with a sling. The man offered it to the king who, in turn, invited the man to eat it with him.

Everything was happening more quickly, despite the dread of waiting, and I was becoming more thoughtful.

Kneeling beside a small stream where Ra and Ariston's horse, Apollo, drank, I splashed my face with cool water. When the water stilled, I caught a glimpse of myself in the mirrored surface. In truth, the man staring back at me was a stranger to my eyes, the black and bronze armour foreign to me. Circles rimmed my eyes and my hair had grown, no longer the silky black my wife loved, but coarse and veined with grey. I washed my face of dirt and stood, rubbing my eyes before biting into a hunk of black bread I had taken from my satchel. I scanned the horizon in the orange light of evening as I chewed, comforted by the sound of Ra grazing nearby on sweet grasses.

Insects buzzed languidly in the grass where blood-red

poppies tilted their delicate heads. Their red reminded me of my mother's priestess robes so long ago, and for a moment I thought I could see her dancing for Hathor as she had, graceful as a swan or ibis.

"What's that?" Ariston's voice broke my reverie and I moved to look to where he was pointing east.

"Dust cloud," I answered.

"It's got to be Persians."

"Cavalry, sir!" said one of the young Paeonians, pointing with the tip of his spear.

Just then, Philotas came thundering up beside us. "The king orders you to pursue those riders immediately!"

"Yes, sir!" Ariston answered.

I said nothing.

"Take their leader if you can, and any prisoners." Philotas stared at me, but I ignored him and began to mount up.

We jumped into our saddles and then all one thousand of us thundered across the grassy plain to hunt a new quarry.

The grassy ground sped beneath us, quicker than dust in a sandstorm, all a blur as we pursued the enemy force south-eastward.

They moved fast, but our mounts were well rested and better than those of the Persians.

When Ariston gave the signal, we broke into two massive arrowhead formations.

Ra's stride never broke, and was as smooth as could be.

My memory of that first charge is still vivid in my mind - the battle cries of Ariston and his men behind us, the rushing scent of plains grass and herbs mixed with our sweat, the frothing of our horses' mouths, the snorting of their flaring nostrils loud - all of it has a place in my mind.

I also thought of Eshe, Femi, and Jamela.

Don't die! You die, they die! I told myself as a Persian arrow whistled by, ripping through my black cloak to skin the rider behind me. The Paeonian went down on his horse's neck, clinging on desperately.

The Persians were light-armed cavalry and wore only linen clothes and caps. They had no armour, and so refused to engage us.

Rather, they fired arrows at our approaching formations, one catching my arm, the other grazing my leg, but I did not even notice at the time.

"Ride them down!" Ariston yelled. "Persian cowards!" He rode straight for a giant of a man in green and yellow robes with a long black beard who appeared to be commanding the force.

As we closed with only a quarter of a stade left, I let my first javelin fly, taking one rider in the back and causing him to career into a neighbour sending both horses and riders crashing into the dust. I let out a yell as Ra leaped over them and I launched my second javelin into the chest of another who was turned in his saddle, bow drawn.

Now we were among them, like cobras in a rat's nest, and the world became chaotic.

I do not remember the number of Persians who fell to my deadly kopis. All I remember then is noticing and enjoying how that sword sliced through my enemies. At first it was about punishing the Persians for the past wrongs they had done to Egypt, to my family, but then my anger and rage at my plight, the very reason I was there, fuelled the violence in me. It became the fault of every Persian I struck.

The world spun and I tried to get my bearings.

The Paeonians were slaughtering those who went on fighting, while others herded those who had surrendered, cowering before their spears and the stomping hooves of their warhorses.

The smell of blood, urine and excrement was strong on the scene now, and I felt my gorge rise at the stench of my first true battle.

Suddenly Ra reared, an arrow in his hind leg. I fell backward and rolled, bringing my kopis up in time to block a Persian dagger. I punched my attacker's throat and rammed my blade down his mouth. Then, one of my throwing daggers found the chest of the man who had loosed the arrow.

I ran to Ra to check his wound and, though it was not serious, I knew it was my fault, for I had let my guard down.

A trumpet signalled the Persian retreat and a couple hundred of the enemy fled the field, screaming in their barbaric tongue.

I thanked Hathor for watching over me and dedicated the spilled blood to Zeus-Ammon who watched over us all. The latter, I know not why. It was a strong urge I had in the moment.

Then, cheering and taunting reached my ears and I turned to see a large group of Paeonians surrounding Ariston and the big Persian. They both faced each other on foot, but Ariston was a full head shorter than his opponent. The Persian flung insults at him, but the Paeonian crouched, focussed.

When the Persian's thrust came, Ariston was ready and stepped in, sideways of the blade, and grabbed him by his long, oiled beard to slam his forehead into the Persian's nose. This was followed by a dagger into the thigh which sent the Persian to his knees.

Ariston had the speed of a wrestler and easily avoided the desperately swinging blade of the kneeling Persian. He retrieved his kopis from the dirt and approached, his wild, green eyes cold and full of hate.

"To Hades with you, Persian. No mercy for you!" Ariston shouted.

The Persian mumbled something to the sky and made one last quick slash at Ariston.

Ariston parried him at the wrist, and followed it up with a back-handed slash that sent the Persian's head into the clotted dirt of the plain.

The men cheered, and so did I.

Ariston strode directly to the prisoners then and demanded the name of his vanquished enemy in broken Persian.

"Satropates…Satropates…" mumbled one man who had pissed himself.

"What was he?" Ariston demanded.

"Commander of…of horses…" came the terrified answer.

By nightfall, we met up with the army, the Companion outriders having found us. The camp had been heavily fortified and put on high alert. We were marched directly to the king's tent where Alexander, Ptolemy, Cleitus, Parmenion and others stood surrounded by guards and torchlight.

The king's eyes were wild with excitement as he stepped forward, motioning to one of the pages to give us watered wine. "I'm told you engaged the enemy!" he said. "What happened?"

"Sire," Ariston began, dropping the leather bag he had brought on the ground. "We charged them at full gallop, about one thousand Persian light horse. They wouldn't engage us, the cowards, but fired arrows backward as they rode away. We caught up with them though, and tore them to ribbons. Hanbal here was like a butcher at his work." He laughed and elbowed me. "I stopped counting how many he'd cut down."

Everyone stared at me.

Ariston continued. "Most of those who survived fled, but we did take thirty-odd prisoners as you commanded. They're under guard by the Agrianes."

"Excellent." Alexander came forward and put his hands on our shoulders. "You've done well, Ariston…Hanbal."

"Thank you, sire," I said.

Then, Ariston reached down to pick up the leather bag he had brought.

"What's this?" the king asked.

Hephaestion stepped up and took the bag. He reached in and pulled out the head for the king to see.

To his credit, Hephaestion did not bat an eyelid.

The blank eyes and cringing mouth looked even more horrific in the firelight.

"And who is this?" Alexander asked, waving it away so that the others could see it.

"This was Satropates, one of the Persian cavalry commanders."

"And where is the rest of him?"

"Outside of camp, sire," Ariston answered, aware now of a slight displeasure in the king's voice.

"Well, Ariston… You fought bravely and have my thanks. However…" Here the king stepped in close so only we could hear him. "Next time you have a Persian officer captured, keep him alive so we can gather what intelligence he can offer. Understood?"

"Yes, sire. Forgive me, sire," Ariston dropped down on one knee.

"Rise, my friend." Alexander smiled again. "If all were as fierce as you, we would end this war very quickly indeed!"

Ariston looked relieved.

"Tell me, what reward would you have of me for this gift?"

I thought Ariston would say that he wanted nothing, but that was not the case.

"Sire, might I have a new cup from which to drink? I lost mine in the battle."

Alexander smiled and nodded. He then turned to the page that was his own cup-bearer and took his own golden cup embossed with a lion-hunting scene from the boy. It was full of wine. Alexander drank, and then handed the half-full cup to Ariston. "I give you my own cup, Ariston, as a reward for drawing first blood."

"Thank you, sire!" Ariston said, accepting the cup with bowed head and then drinking the rest of the wine.

Everyone clapped at that.

"Go now, Ariston," Alexander said. "I offer wine and meat and rest to you and your Paeonians."

"Yes, sire. Thank you, sire."

Ariston turned to leave with Aretes and the others, and I made to follow.

"Hanbal, stay," the king commanded, before turning to Ptolemy. "See that Satropates' head and body are properly buried."

"Yes, my king," Ptolemy said before taking the sack with the head and going to the Paeonian camp.

"Cassander," Alexander turned to his companion and held his eyes fast and intensely. "Get to questioning the Persian prisoners. I want to know everything."

"With pleasure, sire," Cassander replied with a dark smile.

The men about us began to disperse and break into conversation.

Alexander turned to me. "Hanbal… Go wash the blood from yourself and then come back here. There are some people I think you should meet."

CHAPTER EIGHTEEN

THE OTHER EGYPTIAN

Once I found my tent among the Paeonians, and saw Ra safely stabled, I began to clean myself up at the bronze basin cradled upon a tripod beside my cot. I stood there, staring at my distorted reflection in the water for a moment before dipping my hands in and scrubbing my face. The water clouded immediately with blood and caked dust.

I then removed my leather thorax. It felt good to be free of it, as though I could breathe again. I was grateful for it, however, for I knew that it had saved me from several wounds. But I did not want to wear it more than was necessary.

My only thought as I changed into a clean black tunic was that the pouch around my neck was still there, that part of Eshe. I went to the entrance of my tent and looked up at the stars that now appeared brighter in the indigo sky. I held the pouch to my chest and prayed to Hathor that she continue to protect my family.

As I silently mouthed my prayers, I struggled against my tears, for they would take my strength which was my only defence, my only assurance of my family's safety.

I remembered that Alexander was waiting on me, and so I walked back to the king's tent at the centre of camp.

As I made my way, I found Ariston brooding aside from all others. His fists were bunched in frustration and the tensity of his clenched muscles was more than the force of a Syrian bow. "Ariston?" I called, approaching cautiously. "What ails you?"

He turned, surprised by my sudden appearance. "What ails me?" he repeated after a few seconds. "I have let the king down, Hanbal. I have lost face before him."

Truly, I had rarely seen a man so distraught, especially one usually so confident and companionable.

"I am sure the king has already forgotten," I told him. "He'll get the information he wants from the prisoners, and he will be happy. You should not worry so."

He scoffed. "Easy for you, Hanbal. You are not of a people whom the king once viewed as barbarians, nothing better than sheep-buggering mountain men."

"Aren't all non-Greeks barbarians to the Hellenes?" I asked.

He shook his head, annoyed. "The Paeonians are a great people, and we have fought hard to win renown with the kings of Macedon and other Hellenes. Years of humiliation, training, fighting, head-bowing and more…all for what? To have it all slip away, forgotten, because I lopped off a Persian's head?"

What could I say to him then? I could see he was angry with himself, and he seemed to need to do that. The Gods know, I am quite familiar with that sentiment. "I have been asked to return to the king's tent this evening. I will speak for you."

"Hmph! There it is, then… The day that an Egyptian needs to speak to Alexander on behalf of a commander of Paeonian cavalry.

I tried to ignore that. "The Gods work in mysterious ways, Ariston. Sometimes a stranger's word is clearer than that of a lifelong friend."

I laid a hand on his shoulder and turned to go to the king.

As I made my way among the tent rows lined with campfires around which the Greek allies ate and drank and boasted, I wondered if indeed Alexander would hold Ariston's actions against him.

I cannot say I would not have done the same, or that I would not have enjoyed putting the head of that bloody Persian on the end of my spear. In fact, I was, I realized then, quite jealous of Ariston's victory.

Had I really become so uncivilized? I wondered if indeed we were all barbarians.

I could see Hathor weeping at the person I was becoming. Then, I realized that perhaps that is how Alexander felt, as a god looking sadly at the actions of his mortal followers, all hopes for them dashed with one action, one disobedience, no matter how well-intended.

Before I could finish mulling it over in my head, I was before the king's tent.

"They're expecting you, Hanbal," Coenus said as I approached. This man guarded the king, but was more affable than Hephaestion. "Your sword and daggers, please."

"Of course." I removed my weapons and gave them to him.

"You can go in," he said.

As I parted the linen hangings to enter, Coenus spoke. "Hanbal?"

"Yes?" I turned back to him.

"Good work today."

I nodded my thanks and went inside.

THE KING'S TENT WAS FLOORED WITH REED MATS FROM Egypt and brightly lit by what must have been close to fifty lamps. A lyre could be heard in its depths, and a strong smell of frankincense moved about in waves of soft, white smoke.

I had expected to find a boisterous gathering of the Companions and allied commanders, but the only sound I heard was a single voice. The rest were silent.

I stood back, waiting and listening…

"Hektor with his dying breath then said, 'I know you, what you are, and was sure that I should not move you, for your heart is hard as iron; look to it that I bring not heaven's anger upon you on the day when Paris and Phoebus Apollo, valiant though you be, shall slay you at the Scaean gates.'"

One of Alexander's poets stood in the midst of the gathering, before the king, pausing upon those dread words, that tale I came to know so well of Alexander's ancestor, Achilles, and the world of sorrows shaped by his wrath.

The poet continued. "When he had thus said, the shrouds of death's final outcome enfolded him, whereon his life-breath went out of him and flew down to the house of Hades, lamenting its sad fate that it should enjoy youth and strength no longer. But Achilles said, speaking to the dead body, 'Die; for my part I will accept my fate whensoever Zeus and the other gods see fit to send it.' As he spoke he drew his spear from the body and set it on one side; then he stripped the blood-stained armour from Hektor's shoulders while the other Achaeans came running up to view his wondrous strength and beauty; and no one came near him without giving him a fresh wound. Then would one turn to his neighbour and say, 'It is easier to handle Hektor now than when he was flinging fire on to our ships' and as he spoke he would thrust his spear into him anew. When Achilles had done spoiling Hektor of his armour, he stood among the Argives and said, 'My friends, princes and counselors of the Argives, now that heaven has granted us to overcome this man, who has done us more hurt than all the others together, consider whether we should not attack the city in force…'"

Alexander raised his hand then, his eyes meeting mine, and the poet's voice trailed off.

A chill went down my spine then, a great cold, for the words of the poet, of Achilles, might have described the imminent meeting of Alexander and Darius, except Darius was no Hektor, and Alexander may well have been greater than Achilles.

What my part in the echo of that tale was, remained to be seen.

There was muted applause for the poet who bowed to the king.

Alexander then stood and kissed the man on the cheek. "Thank you, Agis," he said. "Ever you reveal to me the beauty of Homer's words."

The poet, Agis of Argos, bowed low and waited for a moment, as if in expectation of a reward for his verse.

Instead, Alexander turned to me where I stood at the

back of the gathering, near the entrance to the tent, and waved me in.

I saw Ptolemy and others smile at the poet's expression. None of them liked the man, for he was, I would come to learn, the worst of sycophants.

"Hanbal, come," the king said.

I approached and bowed respectfully though uncomfortably with all those eyes upon me.

"Thank you for waiting until the verse was finished."

"I did not wish to disturb, sire," I replied.

The king smiled and motioned me to a couch beside Ptolemy and his woman, Thais, where a man who was a stranger to me sat. He looked to be a countryman of mine, a hem-netjer, a priest of Horus by the look of him, for his tunic was adorned with red, blue, and gold falcon's wings, and a leopard skin cloak was draped from his shoulders.

The man turned his kohl-shaded eyes on me, and I found it odd that, among all the Hellenes, this Egyptian suddenly seemed so foreign to me.

He looked me over without speaking at first, observing my plain black tunic and the asps upon my forearms.

On either side of Alexander were Hephaestion and Barsine, the only other woman present. She eyed me coolly where Thais, the hetaira, looked me over with the same curiosity she had done previously. I believe the tattooed asps upon my arms fascinated her.

I was glad to have washed myself, for every person there was dressed in spotless linens or embroidered chitones, the women in clinging peploi. I would have thought it imprudent to expose those two women to so many men of war, that they would not be safe outside of that tent, but I realized that, if someone was close to Alexander, if they were in his favour, they were protected.

A page brought me a silver plate filled with roasted fowl, fresh bread and cheese. I was then handed a matching cup in which the boy poured watered wine.

I did not dare ask for beer.

It was odd, but I felt distinctly uncomfortable beside my countryman. Perhaps it was because he was a priest or, more likely, that he reminded me of home. His presence seemed to disturb the state of mind I had wrapped around myself like my Greek armour.

The priest was younger than me, and obviously had never been in a fight.

The king must have seen me eyeing my neighbour warily, for he spoke then. "Hanbal, I wanted you to meet Minkah. He is a priest of Horus whom the hem-netjer-tepi, the high priest of Horus, sent to accompany us on this expedition. He is one of our loyal subjects of Egypt."

I turned to the priest and nodded. "Iiti, sen Minkah," I greeted him.

"Iiti, sen Hanbal," the priest replied. He smiled slightly, but struck me as arrogant straight away, and inexperienced. He was a poor envoy from the priesthood of the almighty Horus, but many people had flocked to Alexander's army, and continued to do so. Especially young men seeking to make their names and fortunes in looting the Persian world at Alexander's side.

Minkah, however, was no warrior.

"Do you not miss your temple, Minkah?"I asked him when Alexander began whispering in Barsine's ear, melting her cool exterior.

"The Gods have seen fit to grant our pharaoh great victories to displace the Persians. The priesthood believed that our gods should be represented by those who could interpret the signs and omens if the king requires it."

The answer was smooth, and it was not the first time he had uttered it. I was still trying to decipher the personalities of all the Greeks I now knew, but this other Egyptian I could read as easily as a papyrus scroll. "Then you have met with Aristander," I nodded to the seer on the other side of the tent where he sat watching us in a swirl of smoke from a nearby tripod. "His knowledge of the Gods is vast and unequaled."

Aristander's eyes bore into mine then, and I could tell he resented having the Egyptian priest there, though he nodded politely to Minkah.

I ate some of my food and sipped my wine. It was good.

Minkah said nothing, but looked back at Aristander as his thumb and forefinger rubbed the large, golden Ankh that hung about his neck.

"Hanbal, my friend," Ptolemy leaned over, Thais stroking the tight curls of his hair. "How do you like our Paeonian brethren?"

I drank more wine before answering, giving myself time to think of how to answer, for the king and others were looking at me.

"They are magnificent horsemen and very strong fighters."

"Aye, that they are," Ptolemy said.

"I hear that you massacred a troupe of Persian cavalry today, Hanbal, son of Akil," Minkah said from my other side.

I eyed him and looked at the king. "We pursued them and fought them. And yes, we killed them once we got in under their bow range. If all Persians fight as they did, you shall have victory, sire."

"You are quite confident, Egyptian," Barsine's grey-green eyes were as fire in the light cast from the braziers.

She was formidable, I could see, and a likely consort for Alexander.

"I only know from that engagement, lady."

"There were no Immortals though," Ptolemy added.

"No. Though I admit to no knowledge of them," I answered.

"They are Darius' personal guard," Alexander said darkly.

"And his slaves," Barsine whispered.

"True, love," Alexander stroked her arm, and I could see the muscles in Hephaestion's jaw flex.

I brought it back to the Paeonians.

"I believe that, after what I saw today, with their skill as armoured horsemen, the Paeonians would be a match for any troops, including these Immortals."

"If they followed orders," Hephaestion said curtly.

I nodded, but added, "True, the blood madness was up, but we did take prisoners."

"And Satropates' head." The priest thought he ought to speak.

"It was single combat between two great warriors," I said. "Ariston was by far the smaller of the two, and won a hard battle. He faced his own Hektor."

Alexander smiled at that. "And who could blame him. I'm told the man was enormous." The king held out his cup for more wine. "I'm afraid my Paeonians can be more like loyal dogs than free-thinking men. Ariston brought me a head like a hound bringing its master a dead rat."

Ptolemy looked down at his food while Barsine chuckled.

"And yet, sire, I believe a dog to be most loyal and incapable of being bought." I could not help myself.

There was an intake of breath from the others, but the king laughed.

"Quite right, Hanbal! And who am I to rob a man of his victory in single combat?" He turned to Hephaestion. "Ensure a bag of silver is given to each of the Paeonians who fought today. Double for Ariston."

"It shall be done," Hephaestion answered.

"And for Hanbal?" Alexander asked.

"Sire?"

"Please, Hanbal. You survived your first battle with the most kills of anyone, from what I hear. It is a king's prerogative to be generous."

"Thank you, sire," I smiled, but could not help feeling that I had been robbed of my argument by being forced to accept payment.

"Sire!" Cassander entered the tent suddenly, wiping his hands with a bloody rag.

The frown on the king's face struck a chord of fear to puncture even Cassander's armoured arrogance.

Even I was surprised at the remnants of torture that had splashed Persian blood and guts over his person.

"Forgive me, sire. Lady," he bowed to Barsine, but not Thais. "I will wait outside. I've obtained news from the Persian prisoners."

Alexander nodded and Cassander went out.

"Perhaps Tyche will visit us once again?" Ptolemy said as he stroked Thais' thigh.

I noticed Barsine watching Alexander intently. He rubbed his temples and downed his wine.

"Perhaps, Ptolemy," Alexander said. "But let us go and see if this intelligence is the domain of Tyche, or of Fate." He took Barsine's hand then, and kissed it gently. "My dear, will you go to the Persian Queen, Stateira, for me?"

"What would you have me say?" Barsine asked, almost annoyed. "She has no love of me, or my father."

"Tell her I am sorry I have not seen her in months. That the business of war has all my attention, but that I want to ensure her comfort and all due respect. See to it yourself, Barsine, that she has everything she needs. Take food from my own stocks if need be."

"I shall, my lord."

"Good." Alexander smiled at her, a tired, but caring smile.

I knew then that she was one of the few who had an actual hold on Alexander's heart. How much of a hold, however, I could not say.

When Alexander motioned for Ptolemy and myself to follow him outside, I made sure to bow slightly to both ladies. They were highly influential with the two men.

The king went straight to Cassander who had been waiting with Coenus.

His impatience was plain, but Alexander ignored it, focussed as he was on the news.

Cassander, it seemed, knew his work.

Men standing about the king's tent watched and listened, but Alexander knew when to be cautious.

"What have you discovered?" he asked quietly, his grip on Cassander's arm anticipatory and intense.

"My lord… I questioned each of the prisoners. They were part of a scouting party and it seems that Satropates - the one that Ariston slew - was relatively close to Darius." Cassander smiled. "He was not as discreet as he should have been among his men."

"Where is Darius, Cassander? Where is his army?" The king fixed his gaze on Cassander.

"Several of the prisoners confirmed that the Persian army is on the other side of the River Tigris. Darius is waiting for you."

Alexander was excited, and that excitement radiated from him like a sunrise over the desert. "I knew it! What else?"

"Satropates was tracking our movements so that he could inform Darius of our crossing point where they would try to stop us coming over the river. But, Satropates and most of his men are massacred and can no longer report. The rest have fled."

"What about Mazaeus?" Ptolemy asked, coming closer to the king.

Cassander shook his head. "He's still far to the south of us, burning and watching the approach to Babylon."

Alexander laughed. "They think they've got us cornered. Fools!" He wrapped his powerful arms about Cassander and Ptolemy. "Soon then… Soon, we'll keep the boatman busy for a millennium."

"What do you think, Hanbal?"

It was only then that I noticed Hephaestion behind me, with Aristander and Minkah. I looked at each of them briefly and turned back to the king.

"I think the battle I fought today will soon seem insignificant."

Alexander nodded, then looked directly at Hephaestion. "Ready the army. We march fast for the Tigris before sunrise."

As Alexander and the others scattered to see to various things, only Minkah remained there before me. He stared at me and I thought that his look was one of disapproval.

"What is it, sen Minkah?" I asked him, my arms crossed.

"Only that you seem most at home among these Hellenes, sen Hanbal. I have heard of you, you know? The 'Asp of Saqqara'…that you live alone in isolation out in the desert where you come out to slay Persians in the night."

"I also kill them in the full glory of Ra's light," I replied, taking a step toward him. "Your point?"

He shrugged and the action seemed to make the falcon's wings on his robes flap. "Only that for one so adept at staying hidden, so skilled at killing from the shadows, you seem to have adapted well to being out in the open." He turned to watch where the king went back into his tent, then looked at me one more time. "Ankh. Udja. Seneb, sen Hanbal. May Horus guide you in the battle when it comes."

He left before I could answer and could only watch him disappear in the dark.

"Who was that?" Ariston said as he found me then.

"Another Egyptian," I answered.

"He looks like a priest."

"He is," I said.

"I suppose that's good," Ariston said. "The more gods we have on our side, the better."

"Horus is on our side," I replied, turning to him. "But I want nothing to do with that man."

PHOBOS AND THANATOS

It was dark when we set out with half the Companion cavalry, ahead of the main army led by General Parmenion. All units had been commanded to march at the double to the River Tigris, a day-and-a-half ride away without rest. There was an urgency in the air that I had not yet experienced, an excitement even.

I could not have imagined men going so keenly to a fight.

We sped across the plains of Mesopotamia as the darkness bled slowly away. The air smelled of crushed flowers and herbs beneath the thundering hooves of over two thousand horses across that dewy land. I had never ridden so far, so hard, but I found it invigorating, and Ra made me proud.

My mind was focussed by the rush of our journey, held back from thoughts of all I had to lose, and for that I was grateful.

When the sun finally cracked the horizon to the east, the yellow glow on the bronze and iron of our wave of war was a dread sight. Thousands of horses and battle-hardened men, silent, driven by will and their king's command to reach the Tigris and ford before the Persians could stop us.

At the head of our force was Alexander himself.

I suppose I had expected him to remain with the bulk of the army. But that was not his way. I could not imagine any other pharaoh, king, or general being the first in a fight. Would Agamemnon have been the first to throw himself against the high walls of Troy? Certainly not.

But King Alexander revelled in combat and needed to whet his anticipation. He had seemed slightly envious of our small engagement with Satropates, but I believe it was more than that. Alexander wanted to see everything fresh, to be the first to see the east, the sun on the rushing waters of the Tigris where the enemy might be waiting for him. Alexander was a man who wanted to be the first to see the dawn of each new day upon which he would scrawl his name, the same way he named so many cities after himself. I have never known another man to be so intensely curious.

If 'Curiosity' were a goddess, then she would occupy a very prominent position in the pantheon of deities worshiped by Alexander.

Alexander would be the first across the Tigris just as, I had heard it said, he had been the first to set foot from Greece into Asia at the beginning of the war.

BY EVENING OF THE NEXT DAY, WE ARRIVED AT THE TIGRIS to find the opposite bank deserted but for the flight of water fowl at our approach, and the wind in the bending reeds.

The river was a final barrier to Alexander who reined in Bucephalus beside Hephaestion, Ptolemy, Cleitus and the other Companions to gaze across the water at the plains beyond, with the mountains of Media and Armenia farther still.

"What are you orders, your Majesty?" Cleitus asked. "Should we wait for the army?"

"No!" Alexander said aloud, his head tilted like a lion sniffing at the air while on the hunt.

Bucephalus was eager also, attuned to his rider's will and energy as any good mount would be.

The king scanned the shore. "The terrain drops away to the north. We must find a ford and hold it for the rest of the army."

"But, sire!" Philotas spoke up. "The army. If we cross and the Persians attack, we'll be outnumbered and separated from the bulk of our force."

"Your father will get them here, Philotas!" Alexander responded without looking at him. "Besides, I'm not waiting around for Mazaeus to arrive. He's too busy burning his king's lands." Alexander pointed far to the south where the world sat smouldering, great plumes of black smoke writhing into the sky like serpents off a gorgon's head. "We need to capture and save any villages and supplies or livestock they're burning, before they go up in flames. Let's ride!"

With that, Alexander charged north along the river to find a crossing point over the rushing waters of the Tigris. It was a swift, dangerous current and a part of me dreaded falling in. I could swim, but with all my armour and weapons, staying afloat would not be guaranteed.

At last we arrived at a ford where the water would only rise to our chests, though the current was quite strong. We watched the other side for a time, wary of being surprised by a hail of Persian arrows from behind the low hills. But none came. We saw only the glint of new moonlight that revealed egrets and night herons like sleeping sentries among the dark reeds on the far bank.

Alexander urged Bucephalus forward and the stallion obeyed, the rushing water wrapping about him as though he were a giant boulder in the river bed. "Forward!" the king called over his shoulder.

Hephaestion, Cleitus, Ptolemy, and Coenus headed in. Philotas had been ordered to hold the western bank with five hundred men, to patrol the shore and keep watch for the army.

Riders were everywhere, like dragonflies buzzing among the rushes and over the water. They fought the current, which was stronger than expected. A few of the riders were swept away or pulled under, the sounds of their screaming mounts cracking the dark hours.

When I went in, the cold water was sharp as an arrowhead to my leg. Ra pressed forward, eager to be on more stable footing. He managed well, his breathing determined as his neck reached, straining to achieve the far side.

I was glad that there were no crocodiles in those waters as there would have been in the Nile. I never had Ra ford the river at home, so this was a first. Then again, I did not know how many 'firsts' lay ahead for the two of us.

On the other side, gasping from the effort, we formed up into groups of fifty horsemen. I dismounted to wash my face of dust from the ride and to relieve myself among the reeds. The cold water rejuvenated me and awakened my senses. I tried not to linger too long at the haggard face staring back at me, told myself not to think, but to keep going.

"Hanbal?" Ariston came to stand beside me. "We're to rest ourselves and the horses."

"How long?" I asked as I chewed a piece of bread.

"Till dawn. Rest and water Ra," Ariston instructed. "Then, we're on the first patrol." He left to spread the news among the Paeonians.

We set a watch and waited in the dark for what seemed days rather than a few hours. The king had patrols going in all directions at all times, but nobody reported seeing anything. Alexander had forbid fires, for fear of alerting the enemy to our crossing point.

I slept uneasily, my back against Ra's body, my own armour stiff and wet against me. The stars were bright above and I gazed upon them with the sound of plains wolves in the distant dark. I strained my ears for the sounds of an enemy army but could only hear the still-ragged breathing of man and beast all about me. Starlight shone off the helmets of men standing guard on every side of us.

As I watched and listened, exhaustion took me and I fell asleep beside the Tigris.

As I write this, I remember the dream that the Gods sent me.

I was in the desert, the moon full and yellow in a smoke-blackened sky. The moon kept coming closer, however, as if menacing me. I tried to dig deep into the rock and sand, to entrench myself, holding the great shield of Achilles which the king carried everywhere with him.

My fingernails ripped away as I dug in vain, and so I held the hero's shield aloft - it was of an unimaginable weight - as the great jaundiced moon bore down on me to crush me and all my hopes of seeing my family again. The veins in my naked arms and thighs began to run with fire from the strain, and I called out to Zeus-Ammon for aid.

Even then, I did not think to call on Hathor, and expected to be crushed for it. As I prepared for death, the metal of the shield burning me, a sound of exploding fire and screams rushed in. White light blinded me, searing my eyelids as I looked to see a great chariot-drawn sun collide with the rushing moon.

I awoke sweating and shaking, for fear not fever.

Ra lifted his great black head, turned to look at me, and nudged my shoulder.

"Sorry to have woken you, my friend," I said as I reached out to stroke his head between the eyes. He lay back down to continue his rest, and I stumbled to my feet and made my way to the water.

It was still dark, mostly, but dawn was near. I knelt down in the river mud and splashed my face. On the far side, I could see motion and realized that the first units of the army were arriving. How they had done it, marched so quickly, I do not know.

I stood up, my hair wet, my face dripping, and looked to the sky. There was neither moon nor sun to be seen. However, an orange glow pulsed not far to the south.

Then, I heard voices, and ran back to Ra.

"Hanbal!" Ptolemy called when he saw me and rushed up. "You and Ariston get your men! The scouts report that Persians are burning villages nearby!"

"Bastards are burning everything!" Ariston spat.

"There might be food in those villages!" Ptolemy said.

The thought of food brought me to. I had not realized how hungry I was, how vulnerable we all were on that side of the Tigris with the supply train so far behind the main army.

Within five minutes we were mounted again and charging south toward the fire's glow on the sky, one thousand of us, Companions and Paeonians. The rest, under Cleitus, were ordered to hold the ford for the army.

As we rode, the village came into view, the screams of women and children cutting into our ears.

Darius had begun killing his own people in his attempt to starve us.

The king was out front, his spearhead flashing as he pointed to the silhouettes of enemy horsemen in the dark. "Attack!" Alexander yelled as he raced after the Persian force.

We caught up with them and the day began bloody.

Alexander was unleashed now, and called out to the Persians to come and face him. When this happened, when the burning crews discovered that the King of the Hellenes was there in person, the banners turned and fled southeast.

But we caught up with them. We hacked and slashed at them like crocodiles rolling in the offal of fresh kills.

I slew five men myself, though their faces were hidden to me by the dark. I was grateful for my instincts, for they saved me in the chaos of the early morning battle.

It was over quickly, and we took many prisoners, wounded or trapped beneath their dead horses. They were put under careful guard.

"Now!" the king called. "To the village! Put out the fires so we don't lose the villagers!" He was off like a shot, his men about him.

Admittedly, I found myself confused by the king's intensity, his urge to save the Persian families in the village. I understood him wanting to save the food and supplies, but the Persians? I realized then that Alexander did not see all Persians as his enemy. Only those who stood against him. I was always surprised at how he sought to secure the safety of women and children, no matter where we were, or how far we travelled.

Everyone set to stomping out the fires or throwing buckets of water on them until the orange glow was gone and grey smoke swirled from wet ash. The air stank and stung our eyes.

When Alexander dismounted, some of the villagers rushed forward to kiss his hands and feet, much to Coenus and Hephaestion's worry, for any one of them could have had a dagger.

I stood looking at all the terrified children huddled together, and felt the lack of my own. One little girl's tear-stained face was almost too much for me to bear, for she reminded me of Femi and Jamela. Her grandmother saw me looking and came over to hug the child.

I wanted to say that I would never hurt them, but it seemed she was not thinking that. Suddenly, she smiled and came toward me with the girl. She whispered something to the young one who then delved into a nearby basket and offered me a small, flat bread and a bit of goat's cheese.

I shook my head but the woman insisted, the girl nodding at her side. I thanked them and ate, grateful for the meal.

After that morning, it was Alexander's will that all fires inflicted on those he referred to as his 'future subjects' were to be extinguished with great speed. He was already at work, winning over the people of Persia.

As I thought about my own family, of my parents' fate, I did not know how I felt about Alexander's kindness.

WHEN WE ARRIVED BACK AT THE FORD, MUCH OF THE ARMY had begun to arrive and the shoreline seemed to be straddled by a small metropolis, tents and avenues raised for what would be a four-day rest.

Alexander immediately sent wagons under guard to the village where some of the Paeonians were keeping a watch on a large grain store that had escaped the flames Mazaeus had set to destroy it.

The villagers were permitted to keep a portion.

It was not long before Cassander set to questioning the newly acquired prisoners.

Ariston and I were on our way to our tents when a shrill scream pierced the air near the river. Even above the din of tens of thousands of men and beasts, it could be heard.

"What in Hades was that?" Ariston asked.

I stopped Craterus who was running by. "Craterus! What's happened?"

The big man stopped when he saw me, out of breath. "The Persian Queen…she's died." Without another word, he kept running to the king's tent. Moments later, a cry of anguish came from the direction Craterus had run to.

It was Alexander.

"Is that all?" Ariston muttered, and then kept walking.

I asked myself the same question, but quickly realized the difference in civility between Alexander and most other men.

So, the Persian queen, Stateira, Darius' wife, was dead? What of it? At the time, I had trouble understanding the grief which Alexander displayed for his enemy's wife, and I was not the only one.

Many of the men did not understand the king's grief, for Alexander and Queen Stateira had not been intimate, and had barely seen one another since the battle of Issus when she was taken prisoner after her husband fled the battlefield.

Alexander, Ptolemy told me later that evening, disdained

the thought of making war on women. Even the wife of an enemy was to be treated honourably. More so because of the respect due to her station.

"Why should the king mistreat a woman who is married to the King of Persia, a title that will soon be his own?" Ptolemy went on. "It goes beyond that though. The king would not have accusing fingers pointed at him or his ideals. A part of him loves her."

"Loves her? The Persian queen?"

"Yes. He, in a sense, loves all women, and Queen Stateira is…was…a woman of great intelligence and beauty. We all long for immortality, do we not?"

I shrugged my shoulders, uncertain what Alexander's treatment of the queen had to do with his immortality. I remember thinking at the time that the Athenians viewed women with far less regard than did Alexander. I knew that my Akh would live for all eternity. I just did not know where I would end up when my heart was placed in the scales of the Gods.

"I long for immortality," Ptolemy admitted. "Alexander does not fear death itself, but being forgotten."

Ariston made a sign against evil on the other side of the fire.

Ptolemy continued. He was in a philosophical mood that evening. "Alexander fears mortality in others, and is saddened when beauty is quashed or fades from the world too soon, at the peak of its blooming."

"Does he feel that he locked her up in her final year?" I asked. "The queen, that is."

"I don't know." Ptolemy gazed at the flames. I could not make out his thoughts. "If his grief is anything to go by, then I fear his feelings of guilt are gnawing away at him."

· · ·

I had never seen the Persian queen, but rumours of her beauty and gentility abounded after her death.

For the Persians, the ceremonies after death were a private affair, and so I did not witness the rites for Queen Stateira. Alexander saw to these rites personally, in consultation with the Zoroastrian priests and the queen mother, Sisygambis, with whom he had a deeply personal friendship.

I asked Ptolemy if the queen's body was going to be given over to the crows and vultures upon the Persian 'Tower of Silence' which the Greek, Herodotus, mentioned in his writings, but Ptolemy shook his head. Not even he was privy to the rites. He only knew that Alexander presided over her funeral, clad in black. All was according to Persian custom, the queen being given all due respect.

After the funeral rituals, one of the Persian eunuchs who had been attending the queen escaped. Three days later, a messenger from Darius himself arrived with his ambassadors.

The army stood on a collective knife edge, suspicious and yet hopeful of a surrender from the no-doubt grieving Persian king.

Instead, Darius tried to pay Alexander off with thirty-thousand talents of gold and lands to the west with his son, Ochus, as surety. However, he also asked Alexander for the return of his mother and unmarried daughters.

Alexander scoffed at the offer and said that his clemency had not been out of a wish to be Darius' friend, but was who he, Alexander, was.

Alexander wanted battle, even more so when Hephaestion uncovered bribes sent by Darius to various elements among the army.

Part of me wondered if Demophon and Creon were

among them, but I knew they were far too cunning to get caught.

On the day after our crossing of the Tigris, the army set out to find the enemy, spurred on by the news gleaned so expertly from the prisoners by Cassander.

It seemed that Darius and his army were not far away, and that Persian allied forces were still arriving from all over the empire under the various satraps who bowed before Darius. There were Mardians and Sogdians led by Ariobarzanes, as well as Susians, Phrygians, Armenians, Babylonians and men of Parthyei. Cappadocians who had fled before Alexander previously were joining Darius, and Medians, Cadusians and many other nations, the names of which even now escape me.

The Massagetae were there with their stinging spears, as well as two-hundred scythed chariots. The latter I had never seen, but when they were described to me I felt horror at the thought of the damage they would inflict on us.

But of all forces in Darius' army, the most feared was perhaps Darius' cousin, Bessus, Satrap of Bactria, who had arrived, we discovered, with thousands of his heavy cavalry and war elephants from the farthest reaches of the empire. Bessus' force included Scythians, Arachotians, Hyrcanians, and Areians.

Alexander had the fortifications of his entire camp near the Tigris reinforced in order to protect the camp followers, pack animals, the wounded, the sick, prisoners, and the high status women, including Barsine, Thais, and others.

When we marched out for the great hunt, it was only the fit men of war who followed the songs of drum and trumpet, and then the seers and priests who proclaimed that the Gods of the Hellenes and Egyptians had sanctioned the coming bloodshed.

. . .

"WHERE ARE THE BASTARDS?" ARISTON POINTED OUT AS WE rode on a ranging mission among the low hills surrounding the line of march.

From where we were, we had a view of the army making its rumbling way in search of its quarry. The land was drier on this side of the Tigris, dusty and rock-strewn. My heart was racing all of the time now as thoughts from every quarter of my self gathered and collided inside me.

The battle to end all battles could well be upon us at any moment, and I had not stopped to make my peace with my gods, the task forced upon me, the pouch around my neck, the loves I had left behind…so far behind.

If I die…they die…

My dream of the other night still haunted me, and I felt dizzy beneath the imagined weight of Achilles' shield.

Then, I saw it. Some movement on a far hill.

"What's that?" I asked Ariston. "See? There!" I pointed.

Ariston strained to see, as did the others about us.

On a far hill, one, two, three and more dots appeared.

"Horsemen," I said.

"Persians!" Ariston called back, and sent a man to notify the column.

We all mounted up and raced down to the flats to form up. It was a couple miles to the enemy horsemen. We waited not three minutes before Alexander, Hephaestion, Cleitus, Cassander, Ptolemy, Philotas and the rest of the Companion cavalry came charging by, signalling us to follow.

Alexander was at the peak of the formation, his red cloak flapping behind him as he and Bucephalus led the way.

We rode hard, spears and swords at the ready, closer, more eager than ever before. When we were a mile distant from them, the enemy turned and fled, the sight of Alexander himself giving them pause.

"Mazaeus!" I heard the king roar. "Come and fight!"

But the Persians would have none of it. By the time we reached the top of that hill, they were but a distant dust cloud heading to join the real storm.

The king and Companions reined in hard to watch and observe. And it was no wonder, for when we finally reached the hill and the dust settled, a vast plain appeared before us, born from the haze.

On the other side of the plain lay the entire Persian army.

"My gods!" I heard Philotas curse. "This is madness!"

"Not madness, Philotas," the king corrected. "Simply our enemy already standing in battle order, waiting to be slaughtered.

"If you can call it orderly," Ptolemy said to Alexander.

"Slaughtered?" Philotas said, his eyes wide and full of fear. "You must be joking, sire? It's obvious the prisoners lied to Cassander. There are *not* two-hundred thousand men down there."

"Aye," agreed Cleitus, serious as he looked upon the massed nations of the Persian Empire. "Looks more like close to a million infantry and cavalry to our forty-seven thousand."

There were gasps from all around.

Alexander dismounted and walked to the edge of the cliff overlooking it all, his head tilted up to the sky. Then, he turned. "So much more the glory when we defeat such numbers!"

He stared at all of us, defied us to disagree, to expose our cowardice.

Cleitus laughed at the folly, but went to the king's side. "Majesty, we'll make what mince we can of them. But, by Ares, this will be a bloody fight."

Alexander laughed again, and leapt atop Bucephalus. "Come, my companions in war! Let them stand in battle order all they want. We will fight when *I* say!" Alexander stormed away, full of energy, back in the direction of the army and ordered them to make camp.

The fortifications would be heavy.

Hephaestion remained behind to watch the Persians a little longer. He had been silent the whole time.

Ariston and I moved beside him, and I wondered if he was afraid more for himself, or for Alexander.

"Do you think they'll move on us, sir?" Ariston asked.

"No." Hephaestion's gaze never left the enemy. "They need that broad plain with those numbers. Their chariots will be useless elsewhere. They're not moving until we do. But I want you to assign twenty of your men to hold this hill, Ariston. Any movement, and they are to ride to camp. Understood?"

"Yes, sir."

"I'll send out the Agrianes to spy the land and battle-field. Who knows what surprises are waiting?" With that, Hephaestion wheeled his horse - a dapple-grey mare with a long flowing mane and tail - and went after Alexander and the others.

When Ariston had assigned men to hold the hill, we returned to camp to join the general buzz of battle preparations.

Emotions ranged from excitement and bravery to panic and terror. Many boasted of how many Persians they would kill, and others retreated to a quiet spot to seek courage from the Gods.

Those hours before dusk that night were long and fraught with emotion. When darkness came, the enemy's fires set a glow on the night sky.

But nothing prepared me for what would happen next. I was with Ptolemy, Nearchus and others outside the king's tent when it happened.

"A million troops," Nearchus muttered as we sat in a circle, gazing at the fire. It would have been easy to drown in the wine of the Hellenes that night. "To our forty-seven thousand?" Nearchus laughed.

"You forget, Nearchus," Ptolemy said, rubbing his knuckles. "Most of them have linen clothes and wicker shields. Nothing to stand against bronze and steel."

"It's fucking mad, Ptolemy." Nearchus shook his head and plunged a dagger into the sand again and again.

I stopped sharpening the last of my throwing daggers and sheathed it across my chest.

"What about you, Hanbal?" Ptolemy asked. "What does the 'Asp of Saqqara' have to say?"

"It's not for me to say, is it? Crazy or not, we're here. All I know is that I don't plan on dying tomorrow." *If I die…they die…* "I only hope the Gods are on our side in the thick of it."

"How could they not be?" asked Leonatus who had sat down. "We've won every battle, escaped traps, and beat the odds many times over. Why not now?"

"Not even the Gods could shield us from a million arrows." Nearchus despaired, and Ptolemy said something to him that made him clamp his mouth shut.

These men were tough as crocodile teeth, even more terrifying at times, but the conversation showed me that even then, their courage was no easy thing to keep up. They clung to the belief that luck and the Gods were on their side, on Alexander's.

Then, it happened.

"What in Hades is happening?"

I looked over to Nearchus whose hands had begun to shake as each man jumped to his feet to stare at the night sky.

All over the camp, there were cries of fear and of desperation. Many men dropped to their knees, the names of their Gods upon their lips.

I stood too, and as I did so, Alexander, Aristander, Hephaestion, and Minkah came rushing out of the king's tent.

"What is happening, Aristander?" Alexander asked, gazing around, more dismayed at the fearful voices of his men than of the disappearing moon in the night sky.

"A bad omen!" someone cried, and others took up the same fearful call as panic began to spread like poison among the army.

That is when the buzzing rang out in my ears, deafening me to all else, such that I cried out. Aristander was suddenly beside me, and Ptolemy. I fell down, a pain wracking my head. For some reason, my dream came tearing back into my thoughts, violent and crushing.

The moon, that round, full, sallow moon had arrived to crush me. I held up my arms to push it away, and I yelled. "A shield! The sun!" I screamed at myself.

Then, the king was beside me. "What did he say?" Alexander asked Aristander.

"Majesty…the Gods are speaking!" the seer said, and they listened.

I was strangely present then, my body the only thing I

was unable to control. I could hear Minkah speaking brokenly of the cycles of the celestial bodies and the universe in a completely incoherent way, as he babbled through his fear.

But I felt none of that.

I do not know where the strength came from then, but I remember seeing Hathor, Zeus-Ammon, and my family on a desert plain, smiling up at the sun. Then, the great Charioteer came to burn my eyes, the moon, and light, and all the world.

"We should retreat, Alexander," I heard Philotas say. "The omens are clear!"

"NO!" the sound came from deep within my parched throat where bile rose and burned. I flipped over and spat, and pushed myself up on my knees.

"What, Hanbal?" the king asked, the others crowding in around me.

I coughed and tried to speak. "It is good…the omen… sire." *If I die…they die…*

I felt in my heart that we could not call off the battle, despite all the dangers, the incredible odds. I could not delay the fall of the Persians, as that would have meant I would not be able to kill *him*.

I grabbed for the King of Macedon's arms, his muscles straining like pythons to get me to my feet. Those golden eyes met mine and in my mind, the head of Zeus-Ammon turned and nodded.

Was it to me? To his son who held me up?

"Speak, Hanbal!" Alexander's voice was low, intense. "By the Gods, my friend, say it!"

I caught my breath. The ringing faded, and all the faces about me looked, stared, gawped. Only Aristander and the king were open to my words. "A good omen, sire…sent by the Gods." I shook my head, my mind reaching for words that came unbidden to me. "The moon is Persia, and the Chariot of the Sun is the Hellenes…your army…your Macedonian sun…"

"You hear?" Alexander said to those about us, around the fire of my vision like an ouroboros of doubt. "Say it again, Hanbal!"

I breathed, my voice strangely not my own. "The Greek army is the sun, and it will blot out the Persian moon."

Aristander then rose to his full, imposing height, his gaze raking over the host of men. "The Gods have declared that they are on our side!"

"Do you hear that, my brothers?" Alexander said excitedly and with great fervour. "Soon, the sun shall overcome! We shall, with our skill, discipline, and the courage I know is in each of you, win the day and free the world!"

The Hellenes erupted, all traces of fear or doubt sapped by the words of their king and the Gods' omens.

Alexander turned to me and his seer. "Aristander, stay here with Hanbal." Then the king handed me a cup of watered wine, and I drank deeply. "Tonight, make sacrifice to Helios, Selene, and Gaia that they will all look favourably upon us and bear witness to what is to come." His voice ended in a whisper. "Companions!" he shouted to his friends and the Greek allied commanders. "Into my tent for an emergency war council. I feel the time is upon us!"

With that, Alexander wheeled and swept into his tent, followed by Hephaestion, Coenus, Ptolemy, Parmenion, Cleitus, and all the others.

When the crowd outside dispersed, I thought I glimpsed Creon and Demophon before they too disappeared into the dark.

That night, fear would be each man's bedfellow.

. . .

I WAS NOT IN THE KING'S PAVILION WHEN THE WAR COUNCIL met. I was with Aristander.

He asked me about my dream, of the moon, of the sun, and of the shield of Achilles, that magnificent talisman of battle and heroism that Alexander carried everywhere except on horseback.

"How is your head?" he asked.

"The pain is subsiding."

"You are ever a mystery to me, Hanbal, son of Akil." The statement was odd, sudden.

"Why? I could say you are the same to me."

"True enough. And yet, the Gods speak to us both that we may better aid Alexander. I know there are those who doubt my own honesty and motives, but I like to think you could trust me and know I speak true when I say that I only tell Alexander what the Gods tell me."

For a moment, I saw a familiar sense of loneliness in Aristander's eyes. I understood and believed. He did not want to be who he was, and yet he accepted it, the incredible weight of being the seer and advisor to a king whom the Gods appeared to favour above all others.

"I believe you," I said.

"And I you. So, we have an understanding?"

"Of what?" My head was still foggy and all I could think of was the battle to come, and the finger bone around my neck…not dying.

"That we have a shared duty to Alexander and the Gods. That you and I can trust each other finally."

If only he knew. The Gods did, it would seem, speak to us both, but for whatever reason, my ultimate task was veiled even to their divine eyes, and to Aristander's. That, or the Gods did not want anyone else to know my bloody purpose.

"We have an understanding."

"Good." Aristander actually seemed relieved, for a moment at least. "See here, Ptolemy comes to check on you." The seer rose and turned to Ptolemy. "The council has met?"

"Yes." Ptolemy was white. "We attack tomorrow."

"It is as it should be."

"Parmenion wanted a night attack, but the king would have none of it."

"That is not his way," Aristander said with a slight smile.

"He said that he did not come to Asia to steal victory." Ptolemy smiled proudly.

I stood then, and he slapped me on the shoulder.

"Tomorrow, Hanbal, you and the Paeonians will ride beside the king's cavalry to strike at the very heart of Persia. Are you well enough?" There was genuine concern in his voice.

"I am well, Ptolemy." I clenched my fists and looked at the asps upon my arms. "I will ride and bloody my sword with Persian blood until there are none left, or the life leaves my body." *If I die…they die…*

Aristander made a sign against evil.

"The Gods keep us then," Ptolemy replied. "Go now. Sleep. Rest and eat until the trumpets ring and the crows gather for the feast."

"I shall go now," Aristander said, "to make due offerings." With that, he disappeared and Ptolemy too, for there was much to do.

I returned down the avenue dotted with cloaked figures huddled about campfires. Voices muttered prayers to the star-pocked sky, and blades and nerves were sharpened.

I stopped when I sensed them, just behind the horse lines. "What do you want?"

"A word, Hanbal." Creon's voice was cold, hateful.

"That was quite a performance, Egyptian," Demophon said. "I'm surprised you didn't add some foam at your mouth."

I tried to ignore him. I had to, for if not, I would have killed him then and there. Eshe's finger felt heavy about my neck as I stood near to the ones who had maimed her.

"What news?" Creon asked.

"I gripped the handle of my kopis and straighten myself, the thorax creaking as I did so.

"Don't think that because you are dressed like a Greek, Hanbal, that you are one, or even equal to any of us. All you should be concerned with is completing your task." He whispered the last bit. "You've been playing at Greek with the Companions and those Paeonian peasants with games and drills. But let me tell you something…" Creon stepped up to me so that I could smell the garlic on his breath. "If you forget yourself, you'll get your beloved wife back in little bits and pieces while she stays alive."

"Then we'll start on your girls," Demophon said with an dark grin. "Pretty little things-"

I could not help the fury in my soul then, but before Demophon finished, I had a dagger to each of their throats. "Listen, both of you!" I hissed. "I should kill you for what you have already done, but I won't. I know what I stand to lose. And I know what I must do." It was so tempting to slit their throats then, and I very nearly gave into the urge.

Then, I heard a bowstring pulled taut and the shuffling of two sets of feet.

Creon smiled. "Just this once, we'll forgive your rudeness, Hanbal. Once."

I stepped back from the two of them, and sheathed my daggers. I was afraid of myself in that moment, of what I was tempted to do.

Creon continued as though I had not just held his life in my hand. "Now, what news from the war council? I saw Ptolemy and Aristander speaking with you just now."

"We attack tomorrow." I crossed my arms, challenging them to make light. For once, they were taken aback.

"Attack?" Demophon asked. "In daylight? He's mad!" he said to Creon. "We're outnumbered a million to less than a hundred thousand!"

"Where are you in the battle, Hanbal?" Creon asked.

"The Paeonians will follow the Companion cavalry and the king. That is all I know."

"He'll go for Darius," Creon muttered. "Alexander wants all the glory." Then he turned on me. "You stay close to the king. Make sure he gets to Darius. If he kills the Persian king…then you know what to do," he whispered.

"You want me to do it while surrounded by the Companions?" I shook my head.

"If you want to see your family, you will somehow survive."

My head spun and I felt sick. It was impossible.

"But remember," Creon added. "Darius *must* die. If he doesn't, you continue on with the campaign, and we will keep your family longer."

Some of the horses whinnied as a group of grooms came around to feed them.

"Tyche guide you in the battle tomorrow, Hanbal," Creon said as he departed with Demophon and the other men whom I could not see.

I went down the road until I reached Ra.

"Some oats for your stallion, sir?" one of the grooms asked.

I nodded abruptly and thanked him. I stroked Ra's powerful flanks and neck, and when the boy was gone, I rested my head upon his ribcage and wept silently.

I fought hard then, for courage, for calm, for the strength that I knew was my only chance of surviving the battle. I was caught in a storm that would not pass, and drowning in feelings of helplessness. I looked through watery eyes at the great canopy of stars, the white river of the heavens that mirrored Mother Nile.

"Gods of my ancestors…watch over my wife and my children. Please keep them safe wherever they are, for however long. Let them know in their hearts that I am fighting for them, that I will come back for them…" I raised my hands. "Hathor, beloved goddess… Surround Eshe, Femi, and Jamila with your love. Care for them so that they will not know more pain. I…I honour you, and I give you my love. Forgive me my lack of prayers these past weeks. You are ever in my heart, and you have my undying loyalty."

I had no more words to give. I laid my cheek on Ra's side and then…she appeared…like a mist among the horses.

Hathor, Beloved and Loving, came toward me with an outstretched hand which came to rest upon my other cheek. I could not move or speak at her smile, but felt pain rush away from me. My heart was light, determined.

I remember her smile always, whenever I despair. Some say the Gods are unforgiving, but some divinities pity the flaws in their children, and care for them in times of need. I had been remiss in my offerings, and yet Hathor gave me peace and strength.

That night, when I laid down for sleep, I dreamed of

bright blue skies above golden dunes where beautiful swaying palms sprouted skyward. Beneath them, Eshe, Femi, and Jamila slept soundly, smiling as if back in our home in the land I had left behind.

Despite the world of fear and death that encircled me, it was a good dream.

CHAPTER TWENTY

BATTLE PLANS

"Hanbal! Wake up!"

Ariston cringed as the tip of my dagger touched his neck, just short of breaking the skin. "Stop! It's me, Ariston." He spoke more softly, and I pulled back quickly, realizing just in time what I had done.

He laughed. "Guess you've had your share of battle dreams too."

"Forgive me," I said, sitting up.

He sat across from me in the sand.

"Ach!" He waived it off. "Old Crix once stabbed his squad leader in the belly when the man woke him from a nice dream. I should have known better."

"Do we still fight today?" The casualness of my question was absurd.

"Oh, we're fighting all right. As soon as the king's awake."

"He's still sleeping?" I looked out and it seemed that the sun was very high in the sky.

"Yes. Seems the king needed extra sleep for his mighty victory, the one you told him was shown to us by the omen." He raised an eyebrow. "You sure you're right about that, Hanbal?"

"I can't explain it. It just feels right," I confessed. "It just happened."

"Well, that's why I wanted you with us. The Gods seem to be speaking through you and I wouldn't mind them watching our backs in the thick of it. But no need to worry. The king won't be sleeping anymore, what with the news I just gave general Hephaestion to take to him."

"What news?" I stood and splashed water on my face, drank, and spat in the sand.

"Two of our lads and some of the Agrianes just came back from patrol, scouting the enemy front. Seems that the plain…'Gaugamela' they call it…has been levelled by the Persians so they can use their horses and damned scythe-chariots against us. They've scattered caltrops everywhere too, to lame our men and horses."

The thought of one of those spiked objects cutting into Ra's hooves made me angry.

"The battle plans will change now, to be sure," Ariston said. "Alexander always changes things. The Persians have been standing there all night, thinking we were going to attack in the dark!" he laughed. "Anyway, Hanbal. Eat and then arm yourself. Battle is near, and I think the drums will be calling us soon."

I just nodded as he went out. I recalled my dream and was comforted by the thought of my family, before the reality of the day laid hold of me. I ate some hard bread and cheese, an egg, and drank some water.

I began to arm myself, Eshe not there now to ensure all the straps were tight, to tell me she would see me soon. I tried not to think of the yellow moon plummeting toward me in that awful dream, of the brilliant sun searing my skin. Instead, I focussed on arming myself for the fight of my life, a fight in which one million Persians lay across a foreign field, each ready to run me through, riddle me with their barbed arrows, or trample me beneath the wheels of their war chariots.

I said a prayer for Sekhmet, Goddess of War and Destruction, that she might help me to tap all of my skills in battle. The words to her were upon my lips as I checked every dagger. I asked her for vengeance against Persia, against the Athenians who had put me there, in that place, against my will.

I also asked the Gods for forgiveness for the slaying of King Alexander of Macedon, which I knew I must carry out the moment Darius was slain.

My black, Hellenic thorax was snug about my torso, and the black, pleated skirt dangled to blend with my breeches and boots. I gazed at the asps upon my forearms, remembering all those Persians who had persecuted my people, killed my family... Beside Hathor's love, there was indeed a phial of strong hatred in my heart which I forced myself to drink in full.

I slid my forearm guards over the serpents and laced them up, slung the daggers across my chest, over my armour, and hung the deadly kopis at my side. In the sheen of the rounded bronze helm that the Hellenes had given me, I spied myself and was reminded of Death and, for a moment, I saw the dread faces of Anubis and Osiris staring back at me, bequeathing me the power to take lives. It was a power I accepted in that moment, a moment in which they also judged me.

I lifted the pouch from where it hung and kissed it, imagining it was Eshe's hand, whole and soft and lovely.

When I stepped out of the tent, I was blinded by a high white sun and its glint upon the armour of thousands of men. It seemed the entire world was going to battle.

I joined the flow of men to the king's tent where Aristander waited for me to come and join the pre-battle war council, much to the surprise of the Greek warriors surrounding me.

It was crowded inside, stuffy with the smell of incense, leather, and sweat. A soft blanket of dusty light covered everything as the sun tried creeping through the material. It was midday already.

I found a space beside Ariston and Aretes, ignoring the disdainful looks from Parmenion, Philotas, Polyperchon, and other Macedonian nobles. Craterus gave me a friendly nod, as did Ptolemy.

On a makeshift dais, a hastily-sketched map of the battlefield was hung. Alexander stood before it, wearing a thorax of white and bronze trimmed with red and gold. Upon his chest was the hideous Gorgon, to frighten his enemies. His kopis was strapped tightly to his side. He looked strong and vibrant and full of confidence as he turned to speak to all present.

"Today is the day, my friends," the king began. "The Persians have been standing all night, fearful of a night attack…" Here, he glanced at General Parmenion who met his golden gaze evenly. "Now, with Zeus watching, and in the full light of Apollo, we will claim what is ours." He turned to the map, his voice now a rumble. "The Paeonian scouts have confirmed that the enemy is seven miles away." He pointed to a position on the map. "Darius has prepared the battlefield to his advantage by levelling it out for his cavalry and chariots. He has also had caltrops thrown down where he expects our own cavalry to attack." Alexander smiled. "But we will not do what he expects." The king took a piece of charcoal and began sketching on the map as he spoke.

Some of the men began to mutter, trying to decipher what he was planning.

Alexander continued. "Infantry will hold the centre and the left. Nicanor, Coenus, Perdiccas, Craterus, Amyntas and Polyperchon…all of your phalanxes will be under overall command of General Parmenion."

The old general raised his white-bearded chin then, staring down at all of the men around him.

"You'll be supported by the Thessalian allied and mercenary cavalry along with Sitacles and the Thracians, and Agathon's Odrysians."

Each man mentioned nodded to the king as he picked them out among the crowd.

Alexander continued sketching upon the map like an artist at a mural of war. "At the rear will be the allied and reserve phalanxes, ready to pivot if the enemy should try and encircle us. You've drilled the pivot enough, so I have no doubt that you will carry it out flawlessly."

The Athenian and allied commanders nodded gravely, perhaps even reluctantly.

That made me smile.

"On the right wing will be the Companion cavalry led by Cleitus. Ptolemy, Hephaestion, and I will ride in the van. Ariston…" Alexander's gaze settled on us. "You, Aretes, Hanbal and the Paeonians will stay with the Companions at all times. We need a solid wall of cavalry if we're facing off against the Bactrians."

The three of us nodded.

"Philotas, Meleager, Hegelochus, Antiochus, Heraclides, and Glaucus… Your cavalry squads will support and hold the right flank when we go in deep. Attalus, I want the Agrianes to follow us on foot, but the archers, spearmen, and other hypaspists are to harry and sting at Darius' left where they face us."

"What about the scythed chariots?" Parmenion suddenly burst out. "They'll cut our men to shreds."

Alexander smiled. "Simple, General Parmenion. We'll mouse-trap them, make a gap for them in the ranks, then surround them and kill the drivers. That way, the chariots will be immobilized right away. I'm not worried about the chariots." The king paced once then looked at all of us.

"The biggest threat is the Immortal bodyguard in the centre around Darius. There are about ten thousand of them."

Several of the men gasped, but Alexander shook his head and put up his hands to stay their worries. "But you, in the centre phalanxes will hold them off and crush their golden apples underfoot!" There was laughter and the tension eased a little. "If three hundred Spartans can hold off the Immortals, what can the thousands of men in our phalanxes achieve?"

There were murmurs of agreement.

I was struck then at how, with so little instruction, all men seemed to understand their roles. Of course I knew that they had been through many battles prior to that point in time, but still, it amazed me at how professionally they went about the fearful task of facing such odds. I wondered if such a battle had ever been fought before.

"Now," Alexander said when the voices died down. "Here, we come to it." He indicated that part of the plain before the right wing. "The field here is now littered with caltrops. They expect us to charge directly at Bessus who leads on Darius' left to meet us. But we will ride away from the battle, to the right, as if to envelop them."

The men began to mutter again, fearing that such an action would thin out and divide the army, but Alexander dismissed their fears.

"Darius will send Bessus and his Bactrians and Sogdians after us, I have no doubt. They won't risk envelopment. The gap will be covered by the other cavalry units while I go right with the Companions, Paeonians, and Cassander and Menidas with more mercenary cavalry."

"Then what happens, sire?" Cleitus stepped up onto the dais, looking at the map.

Alexander grinned and slapped the Companion commander on his armoured chest. "When we are far enough, and Darius' front line is sufficiently thinned, the Companion and Paeonian cavalry will turn sharply inward and make a direct line for Darius through the crack that will have opened up. Ariston, you and your men will deflect any who come at us so as to give us a chance to get to Darius."

"It will be our pleasure, sire!" Ariston said proudly.

Cleitus shook his head in amazement and was about to speak when Parmenion's gruff voice spoke up. "And what of the left?" the grizzled general asked.

"It all hangs, General, on whether you can hold out long enough against Darius' right - the Medes, Syrians, Cappadocians, the Greek mercenaries, the Hyrcanians, Parthians, the Sacae and whoever else is on Darius' right. Our countrymen, the Greek mercenaries, will be the toughest. They'll come at you in massive waves and you, Parmenion, will have to hold out long and hard to give us a chance at Darius' head."

Parmenion looked grave indeed, as though anger simmered violently within his aged body. His task was a brutal one, and everyone suspected he would lose a lot of men. But his pride kept him from protesting as Alexander stared him down for a few seconds before continuing.

"Cassander, Menidas…when we turn in and make the charge, you and the hypaspists must engage Bessus and delay him. Keep him from rallying back to Darius."

Cassander smiled, a violent glint in his unfeeling eyes.

"Are there any more questions?" Alexander scanned the tent, all the faces about him. Some seemed to hate him for his brilliance and arrogance, but most loved him for it.

I stared at the marks on the map and tried to picture myself in the fray. It was unimaginable.

"None?" the king asked again. "Then go, and tell your captains the plan. Gods willing, we will dine together again tonight."

When Alexander left, most following him out, I saw that Parmenion and Polyperchon, the oldest of the generals, remained. Their heads were bowed down now, as though they only now realized that they felt too old for war. I wondered if they missed King Philip in that moment, or whether they feared his son more.

It was a sad sight, but there was no time to think on it. The plan of battle was as clear as it could be, and Ra and I were to be at the forefront of the chaos and insanity to come.

Chapter Twenty-One

GAUGAMELA

Outside, the army had gathered beneath the white light of the sun. It was time for the sacrifices.

In a large circle that had been cleared by Aristander and the other priests and seers, a large black bull with gilded horns stood with garlands about its neck. On the other side of the circle stood a white heifer, similarly adorned. Both beasts seemed oddly sedate, ignorant of their imminent fates.

The king, now wearing his flowing red cloak, stood between the two beasts, a curved dagger in his hand as Aristander stepped forward to begin.

"To all you Gods of high Olympus… We pay tribute and ask for your protection in the battle that stands before us." Aristander outstretched his arms, his white robes flapping in the hot breeze. He raised his ivy-clad staff to the heifer and the king stepped toward it.

The beast eyed him, but could not see the blade, only

the handful of sacred grain which Alexander held above its head and let roll off.

"Accept our offering, Olympians!" Aristander said in the midst of thousands of silent men.

With a quick, deft movement, Alexander's hand shot out and cut deep into the beast's neck. Blood spattered his person, but he did not flinch. Rather, he watched it leak over the heifer's white coat as it stumbled to its knees and keeled over, eyes confused, then glossy and still. "Almighty Zeus…" Alexander prayed, "…Father…"

The king muttered silent prayers, as did all of the men watching.

I had already prayed to my gods, and so I observed the Hellenes with great interest. Their faith in their gods seemed unshakeable, absolute, as they stood upon the precipice of battle.

Then Alexander moved toward the bull where two men held it fast with ropes about its neck. The beast had become disturbed by the previous sacrifice, and so pulled hard.

"Great Father, Zeus!" Aristander began. "Mighty Goddess, Athena! Accept the offering of your devoted soldiers as they march to battle! Shield them from harm, and fill them with courage. Oh Ares, God of Battles, accept the coming offerings of enemy dead! Gods…guide our king, Alexander, to victory over the hordes of the Persian Empire, that he may rain glory upon your very names, now and forever!"

Aristander's staff pointed at the bull, and Alexander approached, mouthing, I could see, the names of Zeus, Athena, and of Ares. The bull thrashed against his bonds and pounded the dusty ground with his powerful hooves. But Alexander remained calm as he approached, meeting the beast's gaze

The animal stopped, and Alexander stroked its head with one hand, letting the grain fall, and then with the other hand he slit the bull's throat deeply. The bull howled but the legs buckled all at once and it crashed to the earth, a pool of crimson forming about it as if a gaping hole had opened in the earth, ready to swallow it up.

I thought of the voice of Zeus-Ammon at Siwa, speaking to his son, confounding the local priests. I thought of my role in all of this. *To kill a king…to kill the son of a god…*

I held the pouch about my neck and closed my eyes. I saw Hathor, her arms about my wife and daughters.

Bring me back to them, Beloved Hathor. Keep them safe until my return…may it be soon.

I had a couple of extra daggers in my belt for when the time of my dread task came, and that time would be soon.

THE SACRIFICES AT AN END, THE DRUMS OF ARES BEGAN sounding the call to battle. We all dispersed to our units to take our positions and march to the front.

I fell in to walk beside Ariston, Aretes, and other Paeonian horsemen. They wore flowing, knee-length cloaks of white, grey, or brown, and atop their heads now were the great cavalry helms of their people, open-faced with sharp and curling rims to deflect sun and arrow alike.

"Today is the day, Hanbal," Ariston said. May your aim be as quick and true as on the day we met you."

"And may your gods and ours guide us through," Aretes added, his face stern, focussed as we approached the horse lines.

"Mount up!" Ariston bellowed at his countrymen, the elite Paeonian horsemen. They mounted their war horses to a cacophony of man and beast.

Ra nudged me as I stroked his neck.

"Ride like the wind, my friend…for Eshe and the girls."

His great black lids closed and opened slowly. I held the saddle firmly and swung up, dropping my cloak out of the way and accepting the two spears and helmet which a groom had been holding for me.

"Gods keep you, sir," the boy said.

I nodded at him and then joined Ariston and Aretes in the van.

All around us the drums were beating, though I saw no drummers. It was as if the Gods themselves were the source of those sounds of war. It both inspired and unnerved me.

I HAVE SAID BEFORE THAT WHEN I THINK OF ALEXANDER, I think of the sounds…the songs…of glory, of the dead and dying, and the drums of war.

It was at Gaugamela, that vast plain of battle, where the drums of war sank deeply into every man's person, like a lion's teeth into flesh. No cry of horn or horse could drown out the driving force of battle.

I felt the drums as we marched to the front, as we crested the last, low hill to take in the sight of Darius' million-man force. My heart pounded within my ribcage, and my blood within my ears. My vision was blurred by it.

If I die…they die…

The words echoed within me as I watched the army of the Hellenes, Alexander's army, form up on the plain. Banners signalled the battalions into position, and orders were shouted as a vast forest of deadly sarissas sprouted up on the seemingly dead and dusty earth.

It took some time for all of the Companions to gather, and when they did, Alexander appeared before his entire army, red cloak flapping, his wild hair waving as he exhorted his men.

Of course, I could not hear him well from my position on the far right, but when he passed a section of the army, all noise died so the men could hear.

Everywhere Alexander went, he picked out individual men - Macedonians, Athenians, Corinthians and so many others - no matter who, and called them by name. He praised their deeds and wished them glory for themselves and for their families. He filled them with sunlight and courage by his mere presence, his respect, and when he moved on to the next group, he left those men ready to wrestle Hades himself on the very steps of Tartarus, all for their king.

Alexander reminded them that wicker and linen were no match for bronze and oak and hardened leather. He declared that he would be at the front with them as he always had been, fighting for their freedom and glory. And he meant it.

When he came to the Companions and others on the right wing, I could finally hear.

"My friends!" Alexander called, with Hephaestion and Cleitus beside him. "We have travelled far together, bled together. Not in my wildest daydreams could I have wished for a better band of brothers. Each one of you…" His golden eyes scanned the ranks of horsemen, Agrianes, and archers. "…each of you is dearer to me than life." Here, he circled Bucephalus. "It is, by Zeus, my honour to lead you, to fight for you and ALL of Greece!"

The men roared, and even I felt a chill, though I was a xenos among them.

Alexander swept his hand over Darius' milling army. "This will be the decisive battle that generations of our fathers have waited for! Granicus, Cilicia, Issus…they were but the prelude to this battle!" Alexander looked up at the white and blue sky, and at the sun where an eagle rose and fell on the thermals, high above the carrion birds who had already begun to circle. "The Gods are with us this day! Athena, guide us!" he called to the west.

Bucephalus reared and neighed violently, eager to run.

"Zeus! Grant us victory!" Alexander yelled, impassioned and wild.

"Hail Zeus!" all the men shouted. "Hail Alexander!"

It is a moment, a feeling, that is burned into my memory, for the fervent belief in Alexander and the Gods ran among us all, tied us together, as though we were in the centre of a great lightning storm hurled at us by Zeus himself.

If I die…they die… I thought again, kissing the pouch about my neck and tucking it beneath my thorax.

"Let us ride, Companions!" Alexander commanded. "Ride!"

The king dug his heels into Bucephalus' flanks and the stallion shot off like a swift black shadow, a match for Achilles' own immortal horses. Alexander's lion-mouthed helmet with red and white plumes streamed behind him as a few thousand horses galloped to the right in the hopes of luring the Bactrians away from the main army.

It had begun.

As Ariston, Aretes, myself and the rest of the Paeonians set off behind the Companion cavalry, and beside the mercenary horsemen, skirmishers ran after us. It was then that I caught a glimpse of the Persian lines, and two hundred scythe chariots taking to the field to slam into the Greek phalanxes.

Gods help them, I prayed for the men in the front ranks as the screams faded far behind us, choked by the dusty air.

Then, my vision focussed only on my immediate surroundings.

It was all confusion and chaos from then on, the dust from our movements so thick that I could barely see beyond the horse and rider in front of me. My Greek helmet restricted my vision, but I did not want to remove it in case the Persians rained down their arrows.

"He's following us!" I heard Ariston yell. "Bessus is following!"

Like a sandstorm on the far side of the plain, I could just make out the Bactrian cavalry who rode fast to prevent us enveloping them. The Persians had taken the bait, as Alexander had said they would.

Our pace quickened considerably and all became sweat, and speed, and dust.

My memories of that cavalry charge at Gaugamela are as broken as a fever dream, visceral and confused at the same time.

My legs gripped Ra, and my hands the two xystai - the cornel wood spears - as though they were my way to stay grounded in reality. Ever has the sound of horses' hooves echoed in my mind since that day.

Bessus' heavy Bactrian cavalry followed us, desperate to prevent what they believed to be an enveloping movement.

Occasionally, I caught a glimpse of Alexander's red cloak and plumes through the dust clouds, among the bronze glint of his companions' helms. I paced my breathing, knowing that the fight had not even begun for us, though I was somewhat aware that the infantry was knee-deep in the horrors of battle behind us.

Then, like a darting school of fish in the delta of Mother Nile, we changed direction.

"Left, Paeonians! Left!" Ariston and Aretes howled above the din, each of their fistful of cavalry spears indicating the direction to those behind and so on down the mass of horsemen.

To my amazement, I caught glimpses of the Agrianes, hypaspists, and slingers who had run along with us. They flanked Cassander and Menidas' cavalry who led Bessus a bit farther away before the Persians realized the Companions and us were already charging for the gap that had indeed opened up like a chink in the Persian armour.

It played out the way Alexander had envisioned it, the same way they say a Greek sculptor sees the finished statue within the rough block of marble before him.

The Companion cavalry cut across the plain like a deadly arrowhead, pulling away from us as though the Gods themselves drove them on, willing them forward after the son of Zeus.

Bessus was engaged with the skirmishers and mercenary cavalry, but then many Bactrians had realized the danger and rode hard to intercept Alexander who plunged head-long toward the masses of Persia where the dust of the main battle cloaked him, and the cries of the dying erupted in our ears to choke the air.

"Faster, Paeonians! To the king's flank! Ride! Ride!" Ariston lowered himself on his saddle and sped up.

I stayed close to Ariston, Ra's lungs heaving but steady in their breathing.

As we came abreast with the Companions, between them and the Persian lines, I was able to see more. A great whirlwind of dust rose to the heavens casting a yellow-brown light over everything.

Then, to our far right, I saw Bessus leading his cavalry. Their horses were armoured, unlike most of the Persian mounts, and they wielded great battle-axes. They were speeding directly toward Alexander.

Rage filled me, determination not to allow them to stop the Companion charge, for it all hung on Alexander reaching Darius in his golden chariot. I urged Ra more, desperate to break ahead, to see, to stop Bessus.

I heard Ariston curse as I pulled away from the group, but I did not care.

The distance closed faster now. I saw Cleitus come to flank Alexander in the van as Bessus closed.

With one spear held in my left hand, I raised the other in my right and came close, faster, louder with the pounding of thousands of horses as we prepared to crash like a titanic wave on that accursed Persian shore.

A Bactrian rode with a drawn bow meant for the king. Then, with all the force and momentum I could muster, I released my first spear shaft and took the bowman in the side. He collapsed and his horse tripped, taking down three more Bactrians.

I saw Aretes close with Bessus himself, his spear stabbing and stinging at the Satrap of Bactria, but other riders came between them.

"Paeonia! Hellada!" Ariston's voice cut through all else and his sword dispatched two Persians.

We pressed on, our weapons stabbing and slashing out to the right as more and more Persians came at us. It was all a blur of dusty colour, of screams, and of battle cries.

I spotted Bessus again, facing off with Aretes who had an arrow in his thigh. The satrap's battle axe whirled in a great arch, and then Aretes was no longer atop his horse.

I rode in and launched my second spear which grazed Bessus' shoulder.

It seemed then that ten Bactrians turned to me at once, and as they came on, I drew my kopis and charged them like one of the Greeks' Furies.

I killed quickly and easily, but felt myself suffocating inside my helmet.

"Hanbal, ride!" Ariston shouted and pointed to where the Companions were now engaged with the Persian infantry and Immortal bodyguard.

We charged into the fray again, hacking, screaming, chopping, leaving a stream of limbs in our wake. At one point, we just began riding down the Persian foot soldiers, even as arrows cut the air all around us.

Then, I saw it, the glint of Darius' great, golden chariot confronted with the rush of the Companions' dust cloud.

The Immortals and Persian cavalry swarmed about Alexander, Ptolemy, Cleitus and all the others like locusts, and slowed their progress.

But they did not halt it.

I could see it now, Alexander's lion-mouthed helmet and plumes, a raised spear, cutting through the mass of flesh and bone like a shark through muddy waters. The shaft soared high over the mass of fighters toward the Persian king, and for a moment, it seemed all in the vicinity held their breath.

The shaft came down into the wrapped head of Darius' charioteer.

Alexander now cut his way through, seemingly unstoppable.

Then, without warning, the great chariot was turning abruptly, crushing the Persians who were near it, and making to flee the field.

An arrow glanced off my chest, and then a Persian spear ripped a gash in my upper arm.

In battle, however, there is little noticing such things, and I pressed Ra in with the other Paeonians to engage the Susian infantry. Our horses' hooves trampled them and they had little time to use their bows.

I saw a great iron mace make for Ariston's head then, and reached for one of my throwing daggers which I planted in the man's neck.

Ariston turned back and howled, and then rode on. "To the king!" he yelled. "To the king!"

Then fear struck me, for I could no longer see Alexander.

A great scuffle ensued in the place where Darius' chariot had been and there, at the centre, was Alexander, on foot, fighting beside his Companions.

The Immortals, at the sight of Darius' fleeing form, lost heart and disengaged from Alexander. I could see Darius getting farther and farther away, and panic began to take hold of me.

The Persian centre was collapsed, but the battle, from the sound and the giant dust cloud, still raged on the Greek left. I saw Philotas screaming to Alexander above the cries of battle, and the king looking from the fleeing Darius to his own army's left flank.

"Coward! Darius, you coward!"

All could hear Alexander's ravening words.

The Persians seemed to lose heart, at least those who bore witness to Darius' actions. Without notifying the rest of his army, the Persian emperor was in full retreat.

In my own rage, I cut my way to where the king was, the stricken Persian heads rolling along beneath Ra's bloody hooves. "Sire!" I said, shall we pursue the Persian king?"

Ariston and the other Paeonians were now with me.

"The left is collapsing, Alexander! My father is overwhelmed!" Philotas cried out. "They're into the baggage train as well!"

Cleitus sat atop his horse beside Alexander, bloody and calm, with gore dripping from his black hair. "We can't risk losing now, sire!" the veteran said. "Send help to Parmenion, and we can pursue Darius later."

"AAAH!" Alexander screamed at the sky. Then, he regained his composure. "Mercenary and allied phalanxes to the baggage train for support!" He looked around at the rest of us. "Companions and Paeonians! To the left flank! Now!"

With that, Alexander turned his back on Darius and went to help Parmenion.

My hopes of returning home vanished.

The king and all the cavalry jumped into the dusty blood-soaked world of the left flank, passing by the forests of his advancing sarissas in the centre who were finishing off the remaining Persians.

From then on, I fought without feeling, out of a wish only to kill every Persian I could. It was massed confusion, but we took the Armenians, Cadusians, Syrians and Medians by surprise, and smashed them against the anvil of the phalanxes and the Thessalian cavalry.

Another wave of Persian cavalry slammed into us as they were retreating, and it became so congested that men were crushed between horses' bodies. The air stank of dust, iron, blood, sweat, urine and faeces, and in my mouth I tasted the grit of the plain mingled with blood that could have been my own, or other men's. I did not know. If one paused to contemplate the scene too much, one would have been dead.

If I die…they die…

And so I fought on, through bloodlust and exhaustion.

We hacked our way through to General Parmenion's phalanxes which were under attack on two fronts. The Thessalians were fighting hard, and rallied when the king's Companions appeared.

The Persian cavalry, which wreaked such havoc, was commanded by Mazaeus himself, who had burned Mesopotamia. The Thessalians then turned on Mazaeus' forces and pushed him back.

What Mazaeus' thoughts must have been when he found out that the Persian left and centre had collapsed, and that Darius had fled, I can only guess at now.

At one time, Alexander rallied all units to press forward and pursue the fleeing enemy.

Gaugamela was not to be a field of mercy.

While the Thessalians pursued Mazaeus, we followed the Companions and the king in pursuit of Darius once more.

We rode at speed without stopping, and only when midnight came and Alexander called a rest at the river Locus, did I realize that I was fully alive.

I dismounted Ra, and fell to my knees in the mud, my legs too weak to hold me up at first.

Inside, I was torn by emotion, the joy at having survived, the dread that Darius was yet at large. I still had a few of my daggers, but they would remain sheathed.

Darius had to die first. Then…then I would do it.

We rode for many more hours until we reached a village, but Darius was nowhere in sight. He had escaped, though his great golden chariot lay there, abandoned. Spears stuck out of its gilded hulk, making it look like a great, wounded beast. Blood spattered the paint, and great coffers of treasure lay scattered about.

The men hooted and laughed when they mounted the trophy, but I could not.

Nor could Alexander.

Darius had slipped through his fingers like sand in the wind, and Alexander had been robbed of the homeric face-off he had dreamed of.

Ptolemy and the others advised that Darius was well-crushed and that the army needed its king to deal with the aftermath of battle.

It was only Hephaestion who was able to turn Alexander's mind back to the army. The king's friend stood before him, bleeding from several wounds, his helmet under his arm, and told him that he, Alexander, had won the day and was now Lord of Asia.

"We'll go back to our friends and comrades, Hephaestion… But as long as Darius lives, I am not truly 'Lord of Asia'."

The great chariot was yoked to some horses and the treasure loaded into it for the journey back to the bloody plain at Gaugamela.

I HAVE ALWAYS FOUND IT ODD THAT THE RIDE BACK TO THE battlefield was no more than a blur in my memory, but that the battle itself lives on as clear and real in my mind as anything else. The charge, the blood, the rush of the wind are all branded onto my consciousness, but that silent, empty-handed return was a numbing experience of which all I can really remember is a feeling of helplessness.

I spoke to no one, not Ariston or Ptolemy who both approached me.

Each man deals with battle in his own way, I've found.

When we arrived at Gaugamela the following day, Persian prisoners had been rounded up, and Parmenion had occupied Darius' elaborate camp.

Though it was morning, the sky pink with dawn, a black cloud hovered over the plain of Gaugamela. Carrion birds had massed like bees around an apiary, picking at the dead without prejudice, leaving a field of corpses with empty sockets and savaged guts.

The Hellenes did their best to save the wounded, and to remove their dead before their remains were claimed by beak and talon.

For myself, I saw Ra well-taken care of, calmed after the horrors we had witnessed, and then I walked into the middle of the field, replaying it all in my mind, wondering where it had gone wrong.

I looked at the corpses of dead men and horses - Persians, Greeks, and those whose countries I did not know existed before then - and I found no answers. I had survived, but so had Darius. How much longer would my nightmare go on? How much time would the Gods put between me and my family?

The uncertainty was crippling and, in the midst of that bloody field where the gods of the Underworld feasted, I fell to my knees and wept into the night.

The weight of my failure pushed me down into the bloody earth until I wept and vomited my own blood and the hate that had consumed me. Body and soul, I felt wracked with pain and anger, despair and disappointment.

Hathor… Hathor…why? I asked, clutching the blood-soaked pouch that still hung about my neck…

. . .

IN REMEMBERING AND RELIVING ALL OF THESE MEMORIES, the pain that was ever present in my life back then has bubbled to the surface like a terrible sea monster from the deep. A 'Charybdis', as the Hellenes call her.

I must rest now, for as I have begun the telling of my tale, I realize that this chronicle will be much longer than I imagined.

There is still a part of me, of my Ka, kneeling on the blood-soaked plain of Gaugamela, filled with anger and weeping and the deepest of despairs.

I have pity for that man now, for he did not know how very long the road ahead would be. He had no inkling of the terror and beauty of his journey to the ends of the Earth, at the side of the son of Zeus-Ammon…Alexander.

Rest for now, Hanbal, son of Akil, for there is more to write.

The gates of Babylon are waiting…

Thank you for reading!

Did you enjoy *The Asp of Saqqara*? Here is what you can do next.

If you enjoyed this journey through the world of Alexander the Great, and if you have a minute to spare, please post a review on the web page where you purchased the book.

Reviews are the best way for new readers to find this book, and your help in spreading the word is greatly appreciated.

More novels in the *Killing a God* series, as well as other books set in the ancient world, are coming soon, so be sure to sign-up for e-mail updates at:

https://eaglesanddragonspublishing.com/newsletter-join-the-legions/

Newsletter subscribers get a FREE BOOK, and first access to new releases, special offers, and much more!

The Asp of Saqqara is vastly different from any other book that I've written and, for a long time, I didn't know if it would ever be published. I began this journey of remembrance with Hanbal, son of Akil, over ten years ago. I wrote the entire book long-hand, in several journals, during my one-hour lunch breaks working in the chaotic, dirty mess of downtown Toronto. Feeling quite alone during those dreary office days, I would make my way to the oasis of Toronto City Hall's rooftop garden to sit in the sun and escape to a world that was far more beautiful and terrible than most people can imagine: the world of Alexander the Great.

Those journals in which I had written down Hanbal's memories lay still and dusty in a box for years, like an Egyptian mummy in a dark tomb, while I was off writing other adventures. But the time has now come to dust them off, to let this story see the sun's light…

I had always considered writing a book about Alexander. Like so many Greek men and boys, he is my namesake, and the whole of my life he has been both an inspiration and an enigma. This was a young man who made a habit of achieving the impossible, of inspiring his people in a way no other leader in history has. He was curious, brilliant, violent, and touched by some power beyond our reckoning. The great generals of history were inspired by Alexander, including Hannibal, Julius Caesar, and Napoleon, and his tactics are a staple to this day in military colleges around the world.

The life and campaigns of Alexander the Great is one of the most exciting periods in world history. If there is one historic personage whose impact can be felt across cultures, for better or worse, it is Alexander.

I think that is why I held off writing this book for so long. How does one tackle such a titanic figure of history on the page? How does one do justice to the story of Alexander the Great? How does one properly relay the details of the life of a man who actually outdid some of the heroes of mythology?

I wrestled with this thought for some years, more often than not finding myself spitting sand as I was thrown out of the *skamma* of my mind.

And then it dawned on me, the idea to write this from the point of view of a single, fictional person who bore witness to the world of Alexander's army, his court, and his campaigns. This man would be forced to be apart from his family, the same way I felt I was during those tortuous workaday outings. As a result, the Muses filled me with inspiration, and breathed life into Hanbal, son of Akil who, in the later years of his harsh life, began to set down all that he had seen as he marched east with Alexander. As an Egyptian, the character of Hanbal is outside the sphere of Greek or Persian influence, and so he offers a unique perspective of the world and people around him.

When I say that *The Asp of Saqqara* is different from anything I have written before, that is mainly because it's the only first-person novel, or fictional-memoir, that I've ever written. Not only did this feel like a more intimate way to look at Alexander the Great and the events surrounding him, but it also seemed like the logical way for me to distill all that happened in that most exciting period of history.

When it came to the research, I was very lucky indeed, for much has been written about Alexander and his military campaigns. We are also blessed to have a few primary sources that have come down to us and, of these, I have made extensive use. The main primary source which I used as my guide through Alexander's military campaigns is the *Anabasis* of Alexander by Arrian of Nicomedia, a Greek general, historian and philosopher during the reign of Emperor Hadrian in the second century C.E. Arrian wrote his history quite deliberately on the model of Xenophon, aiming to provide a true historical account of that momentous age. He wrote his account of the campaigns of Alexander based on three lost, contemporary sources or accounts written by Ptolemy, Aristobulus, and Nearchus, all of whom were close to Alexander in life.

The next primary source upon which I leaned quite heavily was the *Historiae Alexandri Magni* by the first century C.E. Roman philologist, Quintus Curtius Rufus. Though the first two books of this particular chronicle are lost, the rest provide a more intimate look at some of the events of Alexander's life and, perhaps more importantly, a much more detailed and somewhat salacious look at the events and relationships in Alexander's court. Little is known of Curtius himself, and no other ancient works refer to his history. From references in Curtius' work, however, historians have supposed that he also made use of contemporary sources, mainly Cleitarchus, a chronicler in Alexander's entourage, and Ptolemy.

When it comes to secondary sources there are too many to name here. There are a few, however, that I would be remiss not to name. One work in particular does stand out, and that is the classic biography, *Alexander the Great*, by eminent British historian, Robin Lane Fox. This work is clear, detailed, and accessible and if you decide to read one biography of Alexander, it should be this one. Robin Lane Fox was also the historical advisor on Oliver Stone's brilliant, epic film, *Alexander*, and even appeared in a cameo as one of the cavalrymen during the battle of Gaugamela in the film.

Other secondary sources which were helpful in my research into the campaigns of Alexander were books in Osprey Military's 'Campaign Series', particularly *Alexander 334-323 B.C. - The Conquest of the Persian Empire*. This is an excellent series of books written and edited by former soldiers and professors at the top military colleges in the west. When it came to studying the siege of Tyre, and the battle of Gaugamela, every action during the fighting is expertly laid out for the reader. If you are interested in this aspect of military history, this is a wonderful series of books.

There is one more secondary source I would like to mention, this time in the form of a four-part documentary series, and that is the 1998 documentary *In the Footsteps of Alexander the Great*, by historian and broadcaster, Michael Wood. Admittedly, getting to the places and battlefields where Alexander marched and fought alongside his troops is no easy task. Doing so would be expensive and, in some places, very dangerous. Many of these places, such as modern Iraq and Afghanistan, remain war zones to this day. In this wonderful documentary series, Michael Wood follows the route of Alexander's life from Pella in Macedonia, northern Greece, to Egypt, Babylon and Persepolis, all the way to Bactria and India. He follows this route, sometimes risking his own life and that of his BBC crew's, to take us where Alexander marched with his army. Seeing these faraway lands, even if upon a screen, was more helpful than I can say, and only served to solidify my awe of Alexander himself.

As always, I have endeavoured to remain true to the history and primary sources in writing this fictional memoir, only veering from history when there are gaps, or when it serves the story. After all, why change history when the true events, people, and places are so very exciting and incredible on their own? Though Hanbal, the Asp of Saqqara, and the Athenians, Creon and Demophon, are fictional characters, the people and events around them come from the pages of history. Likewise, the feelings of the Egyptian people toward Alexander are true, so far as we know, as is the journey to Siwa, omens and all. The Paeonian cavalry commander, Ariston, with whom Hanbal becomes friends, likewise was a real person mentioned in the primary sources.

To learn more about the history, people, and places I researched for this book readers can check out *The World of The Asp of Saqqara* blog series.

The age of Alexander the Great was a new age of heroes that helped to shape the world, and Alexander himself was a man without equal. He was the most courageous, and always the first to face danger. He never asked of his men that which he would not do himself. He was also a visionary, though that meant he was often misunderstood by his peers, many of whom would later become jealous of the favour the gods showed him. He was a commander who did not condone the rape of women by his troops, but who was also capable of the mass slaughter and enslavement of people, such as at Tyre. Some believed he was a devil with horns, while many others truly believed him to be the son of Zeus.

What is certain is that Alexander the Great is one of the most interesting and controversial people in history. Mankind has loved and hated him for ages, but such is the fate of visionaries and Titans. And so the stage is set for the assassin, Hanbal, son of Akil, the Asp of Saqqara, to carry out his dread task. Will he kill a god to save his family? Only the Gods and this author know…

Thank you for reading.

Adam Alexander Haviaras
Stratford, Ontario
January 2025

Acknowledgments

Normally, I have a long list of people to thank for the genesis of a new book, but *The Asp of Saqqara* was a much more solitary endeavour. Nevertheless, there are a few people to whom I would like to express my gratitude.

First off, I would like to thank historians Robin Lane Fox and Michael Wood for their research which has made the life and times of Alexander the Great more accessible to us all. It is no small thing to tackle a Titan of history such as Alexander, and their work has been immensely helpful and inspiring over the years.

Likewise, I would also like to thank filmmaker Oliver Stone for his epic film, *Alexander*. Mr. Stone, of course, has a history of taking on controversial figures in his films, and with Alexander he did so with intent. No other film has come close to portraying Alexander in so accurate a way, and I would be lying if I did not say that this film was an inspiration.

I would also like to thank my wonderful patrons on Patreon for their continued and extremely generous support of Eagles and Dragons Publishing and my work. It truly is a privilege to have such dedicated fans who believe in what we are trying to achieve. My deepest gratitude to the following patrons at the time of publication: Edwin K. Gwaltney, Greg Hancock, John Meyers, and Bonnie Miller.

It goes without saying that I would like to thank my parents for encouraging my studies in history, but also for giving me a middle name to inspire me throughout life. Shakespeare may have said that 'a rose by any other name would smell as sweet', but I can honestly say that, for an idealistic historian, the name of 'Alexander' truly did bolster and inspire me.

To my dear father-in-law, Costis Diassitis, I offer my sincere thanks not only for our long ouzo-fueled discussions about Alexander's youth and origins, and my first visit to the battlefield of Chaeronea, but also for the veritable library of books he has continued to gift me over the years. He hunted down Greek books in English translation for me, and also helped me to discover the Osprey Military series of books which have informed all of my novels of ancient warriors and warfare.

To my daughters, Alexandra and Athena, I am ever grateful for their love and the purpose they have given me in this life. There are few things in this world that are so powerful and awe-inspiring. Thank you, my girls.

To my wife, Angelina, I owe everything that is good and loving in my world. With her at my side, I find that I am able to achieve heights of courage and strength such as only Alexander's men might have achieved. Not only is she my partner in all things, but she is also the very best (and toughest!) of editors (at Beautiful Ink Editing). I am forever grateful for her in all her many facets. Thank you, my love.

Lastly, this book is dedicated to my very good friend and fellow historian, Andrew Fenwick of Dundee, Scotland. From the time of our shared adventures in graduate school at the University of St. Andrews up until today, I have lost track of all the long conversations into the night that we have had about ancient history and warfare, not least about Alexander the Great and his campaigns. Andy has a truly encyclopedic memory for ancient history, but more so a passion for it that is truly exciting. He is my brother-in-academic-arms, and the greatest of friends, and I could not be more grateful for his presence in my life, even if we live on opposite sides of the wine-dark sea.

Andy, this one's for you.

Thank you for reading.

Adam Alexander Haviaras
Stratford, Ontario
January 2025

acroterion – decorative element at the peak of a temple's pediment

agoge – the Spartan education system and regimen to turn Spartan boys into men from the age of seven

agon – a contest or competition

agora – a central market place and administrative centre of a city

Akh – in ancient Egyptian religion, the spirit of a deceased person conceived as gloriously transfigured so as to reflect the deeds of the person in life

amphora – large clay container for storing and transporting goods such as olive oil and wine

anabasis – a march or expedition from the coast into the interior of a country

andreia – manliness; also courage, or fearlessness

aner agathos – a 'good man'

Ankh - symbol representative of eternal life in Egyptian religion

Ankh! Udja! Sencb! – a greeting or wish in ancient Egyptian meaning *Life! Strength! and Health!*

apodyterium – the change room of a palaestra or gymnasium

apotheosis – the process or experience of becoming divine or godlike

arete – the ancient Greek idea of 'human excellence'

aulos – an ancient wind instrument made up of two flutes

bouleuterion – an administrative centre or building where leaders meet

braca – short trousers or leggings

caltrop – iron, star-shaped spikes used to lame horses in war
cella – the inner sanctum of a temple
centaur – a mythological creature that was half man, half horse
chiton – a standard piece of clothing resembling a long shirt with short sleeves, reaching to the mid-thigh or knees; usually worn with a belt of sorts
chlamys – a cloak worn by most Greek men
chryselephantine – a style of sculpture that used ivory and gold (eg. the statue of Olympian Zeus at Olympia)

daemon – a benevolent or benign spirit
deme – a district or neighbourhood of a city
diaulos – the 400 meter race; roughly two *stades*
discobolo – (plur. *discoboloi*) discus thrower
discoi – throwing discs (a discus) used in athletic competition
dolichos – the long distance race; usually 5000 meters (24 *stades*), or 2400 meters (12 stades)
doru – (plur. *dorata*) the cornel or ash-wood spear that was the primary weapon of a hoplite soldier; about three meters (ten feet) long
drachm – an ancient silver coin; based on Attic *drachma*

embolon – the central spine or divider in a horse racing track, or *hippodrome*
Em heset net [name of god] – a wish to *Be in favour with* (insert name of god); eg. *Em heset net Horus*
Em hotep nefer – means *in great peace*
ephebes – adolescent young men
epinikion – a genre of poetry and sculpture dedicated to victories
erastai – the older man in a mentorship, or other, relationship between two men

eris agathos – 'Good Strife'; the useful, creative side of strife, that which fuels creative industry and is productive; applies to any trade or pursuit
eumorphia – to be 'in good shape'

gigantomachy – refers to the war between the Gods and the Giants
gymnasiarchos – the head administrator and overseer of a *gymnasium* or *palaestra*

hecatomb – a sacrifice to the Gods of 100 cattle
Heraia – women's athletic competition in honour of the goddess Hera; begun by Hippodameia
heraion – a temple or sanctuary dedicated to the goddess Hera
herm – a protective statue made up of a male head on a pedestal, sometimes with carved genitals
heroon – a shrine dedicated to an ancient hero, or heroes
hetaira – (also *haetaera*) a female courtesan or prostitute in Ancient Greece, often artistic, educated, and skilled in conversation
himantes – leather straps with rawhide or lead pieces used to cover ancient boxers' hands for fights
himation – a long cloak worn as a sole garment by men, or over a *peplos* by women
hipparch – an ancient Greek cavalry officer, commanding a *hipparchia* of about 500 horsemen
hippodrome – a chariot racing track; literally means 'horse road'
hoplite – an ancient Greek heavy infantry soldier; named after the *hoplon*, the large round shield used by these soldiers
hoplitodromos – the hoplite race in athletic competitions in which twenty men ran in full armour for two *stades*

hoplon – the large, round wood and bronze shields used by heavy infantry hoplites
hubris – excessive pride and self-confidence believed to be frowned upon by the Gods
hysplex – (plur. *hyspleges*); the starting gate in a *hippodrome*

iatros – an ancient doctor
Iiti – meaning *Hello* in ancient Egyptian

kakochartos – 'Bad Strife'; that which exults in bad things like war, dissent, and a lust for battle and bloodshed
kalos – beautiful
kinaidoi – boy whores; literally 'little buggers'
kopis – a heavy, forward-curving, single-edged sword often used by Greek cavalrymen
korikoi – punching bags filled with seed or sand
krater – a large clay bowl used for mixing water and wine prior to serving
kylix – a wide, shallow cup with a short pedestal, usually of clay, used for drinking wine
kythera – an ancient Greek lyre

larnax – a coffin used for inhumation/burials
linothorax – an ancient Greek breastplate made of glued layers of linen with leather; used from Mycenaean to Hellenistic times
lochos – the basic unit of an ancient phalanx; contained up to 600 men
lyra – an ancient Greek string instrument or harp

maeander – also 'meander'; the 'Greek Key' pattern in ancient art
maenad – female followers or consorts of the god Dionysus

naiskoi – little temples
Nike – Goddess of Victory

obol – a silver coin; 6 *obols* = 1 *drachma*
ostracon – shard of pottery on which names or symbols
were scratched

paiderast – a man who desires boys
paiderastia – a strong desire for boys
palaestra – a wrestling school; also where other fighting
sports were practiced
pentathlon – ancient competition involving running, jump-
ing, discus, javelin, and wrestling
pentekonter – the commander of a *pentekostys*, a unit of
about fifty *hoplites*
pentekostys – a unit of about fifty hoplite warriors
peplos – a long tunic without sleeves worn by women
phalanx – a rectangular, heavy infantry formation
composted of hoplites with shields and spears; originally
used by Sparta, followed by Argos, and then others; sizes
varied
philobolia – flowers, fruit, and greens showered on Olympic
victors during parade; literally 'love shower'
philoneikia – the love of competing
philonikia – the love of winning
phobos – fear, personified by the god Phobos
plethera – a unit of measurement equivalent to about one
hundred feet
polis – a city
ponos – toil or struggle
promachoi – first in the battle line of a military confronta-
tion or fight
propylon – a monumental entrance or gate

sarissa – a long spear or pike that was about five to seven
meters in length. This weapon was introduced by Alexander's father, Philip, and was used in the Macedonian
phalanxes which were several rows deep
satyr – a mythological creature that was part goat, part man,
sometimes with horse features; also a follower of Dionysus
Sen – ancient Egyptian for 'brother' often used as a prefix to
a name
Senet – ancient Egyptian for 'sister' often used as a prefix to
a name
skamma – the sand where fighting took place in athletic
competition, or in the *gymnasium* or *palaestra*
skiamachein – shadow-skirmishing; shadow-boxing
stade – a measurement of about two-hundred meters; the
sprint was the *stade* race
stadium – where athletic competitions took place, usually
dirt, with embankments for spectators on either side
stater – ancient Greek silver or gold coin; 1 *stater* = 2-3
drachmas
stele – an upright grave marker or monument
stoa – a covered walkway or portico for public use; usually
contained shops and other establishments, as well as space
to congregate
strigil – a curved, bronze hook for cleaning oil and dirt from
one's body when visiting the baths
strophion – a cloth or short undergarment women wore to
support the breasts; could also be a very short tunic that left
one breast visible
stylus – a wood or bronze pen for writing on papyrus or wax
tablets
synoris – the two-horse chariot race

taraxippos – literally means 'horse frightener';

tethrippon – the four-horse chariot race

thorax – a breastplate; body armour covering the torso

Tyche – the goddess of luck and good fortune

xenia – ancient Greek concept of hospitality; can also refer to foreigners (*xenos*, or *xenoi*)

xenos - a foreigner or 'non-Greek' person (plur. *xenoi*)

xyphos – the leaf-shaped sword of a Greek hoplite

xystis – the long, ankle-length chiton worn by charioteers; also known as an Ionic chiton

xyston – (plur. *xystai*) the cornel wood lance used by Greek cavalry

Yeh – meaning *hi* in ancient Egyptian, a greeting

Become a Patron of Eagles and Dragons Publishing!

If you enjoy the books that Eagles and Dragons Publishing puts out, our blogs about history, mythology, and archaeology, our video tours of historic sites and more, then you should consider becoming an official patron.

We love our regular visitors to the website, and of course our wonderful newsletter subscribers, but we want to offer more to our 'super fans', those readers and history-lovers who enjoy everything we do and create.

You can become a patron for as little as $1 per month. For your support, you can also get fantastic rewards as tokens of our appreciation.

If you are interested, visit the website below to go to the Eagles and Dragons Publishing Patreon page to watch the introductory video and check out the patronage levels and exciting rewards.

https://www.patreon.com/EaglesandDragonsPublishing

Join us for an exciting future as we bring the past to life!

Adam Alexander Haviaras is a best-selling and award-winning author and historian who has studied ancient and medieval history and archaeology in Canada and the United Kingdom. He currently resides in Stratford, Ontario with his wife and children where he is continuing his research and writing other works of historical fantasy.

Historical Fiction/Fantasy Titles

The Eagles and Dragons Series
The Dragon: Genesis (Prequel)
A Dragon among the Eagles (Prequel)
Children of Apollo (Book I)
Killing the Hydra (Book II)
Warriors of Epona (Book III)
Isle of the Blessed (Book IV)
The Stolen Throne (Book V)
The Blood Road (Book VI)
The Eagles and Dragons Legionary Box Set (Books 0-I-II)
The Eagles and Dragons Tribune Box Set (Books III-IV-V)

The Carpathian Interlude Series
The Carpathian Interlude - Complete Trilogy Box Set
Immortui (Part I)
Lykoi (Part II)
Thanatos (Part III)

The Mythologia Series

Chariot of the Son: The Story of Phaethon
Wheels of Fate: The Story of Pelops and Hippodameia
A Song for the Underworld: The Story of Orpheus and Eurydice
The Reluctant Hero: The Story of Bellerophon and the Chimera
Mythologia: First Omnibus Edition

Heart of Fire: A Novel of the Ancient Olympics

Saturnalia: A Tale of Wickedness and Redemption in Ancient Rome

The Etrurian Players

Sincerity is a Goddess (Book I)
An Altar of Indignities (Book II)

Killing a God - Novels of Alexander the Great

The Asp of Saqqara (Book One)

Titles in the Historia Non-fiction Series

Historia I: Celtic Literary Archetypes in *The Mabinogion*: A Study of the Ancient Tale of *Pwyll, Lord of Dyved*
Historia II: Arthurian Romance and the Knightly Ideal: A study of Medieval Romantic Literature and its Effect upon Warrior Culture in Europe
Historia III: *Y Gododdin*: The Last Stand of Three Hundred Britons - Understanding People and Events during Britain's Heroic Age
Historia IV: Camelot: The Historical, Archaeological and Toponymic Considerations for South Cadbury Castle as King Arthur's Capital

Eagles and Dragons Publishing Guides

Writing the Past: The Eagles and Dragons Publishing Guide to Researching, Writing, Publishing and Marketing Historical Fiction and Historical Fantasy

Stay Connected

To connect with Adam and learn more about the ancient world visit www.eaglesanddragonspublishing.com

Sign up for the Eagles and Dragons Publishing Newsletter at www.eaglesanddragonspublishing.com/newsletter-join-the-legions/ to receive a FREE BOOK, first access to new releases and posts on ancient history, special offers, and much more!

Readers can also connect with Adam on Twitter @Adam-Haviaras and Instagram @ adam_haviaras

On Facebook you can 'Like' the Eagles and Dragons page to get regular updates on new historical fiction and non-fiction from Eagles and Dragons Publishing.

To watch Eagles and Dragons Publishing's mini documentaries and other fun videos, be sure to follow us on TikTok and subscribe to our channels on YouTube or Rumble.

More from

EAGLES AND DRAGONS PUBLISHING

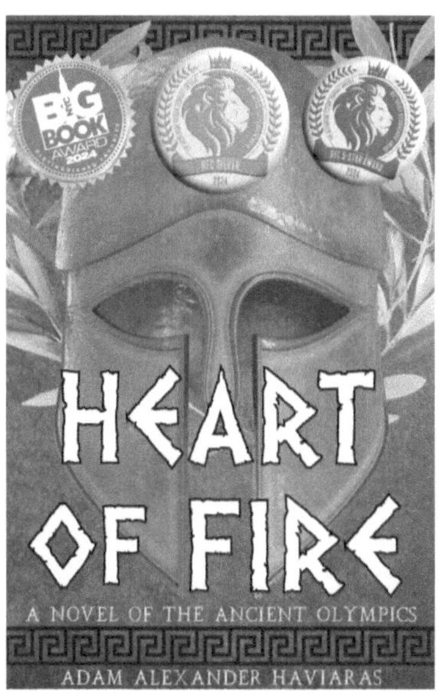

Step into the world of the ancient Olympic Games!

A Mercenary… A Spartan Princess… And Olympic Glory…

Heart of Fire is a book for all those who struggle to make their dreams come true.

Start your adventure today and set off on a gritty, mysterious, and emotional journey into the heart of Ancient Greece.

Available from all major retailers and public libraries in e-book, paperback, and hardcover editions, or direct from Eagles and Dragons Publishing at:

www.eaglesanddragonspublishing.com

Step into the world of Ancient Rome with the Etrurian Players!

Sincerity is a Goddess is a heartwarming story of friendship and love that takes you on a bawdy and hilarious journey through the world of ancient Rome.

If you like dramatic and romantic stories about second chances, misunderstandings, and a bit with a dog, then you will love *Sincerity is a Goddess*!

Read this book today for a theatrical adventure that will have you cringing, laughing, crying, and realizing that there is indeed hope for everyone. Well, almost everyone…

The Etrurian Players are coming! Brace yourselves!

DISCOVER THE *MYTHOLOGIA* SERIES TODAY!

Long ago, when gods and heroes walked the earth in triumph and tragedy, true love and epic deeds were set among the stars...

Do you love Greek and Roman Mythology?

If so, then you will love Eagles and Dragons Publishing's newest series!

In this unique, ground-breaking fantasy series suitable for all ages, you will discover a world of Titans, Gods and Heroes.

Start the series the First Omnibus Edition of the *Mythologia* series and escape into unique retellings of the poignant and epic myths of Phaethon, Pelops and Hippodameia, and of Orpheus and Eurydice.

New books are being added all the time, so you will never run out of adventures!

Begin the *Mythologia* series today and embark on an epic adventure with the Gods and Heroes of ancient Greece!

Available from all major retailers and public libraries in e-book, paperback, and hardcover editions, or direct from Eagles and Dragons Publishing at:

www.eaglesanddragonspublishing.com

START A NEW ADVENTURE TODAY!

Do you enjoy stories set in Ancient Rome?

If so, then you will love our marquee *Eagles and Dragons* historical fantasy series!

Start your journey today with the #1 best-selling prequel novel, *A Dragon among the Eagles* and experience the world of the Roman Empire like never before.

A Dragon among the Eagles is the first novel in Adam Alexander Haviaras' ground-breaking Eagles and Dragons series. If you like books set in the ancient world, then you will love this historical series that combines adventure, romance, and the supernatural.

Step into the world of the Roman Empire today!

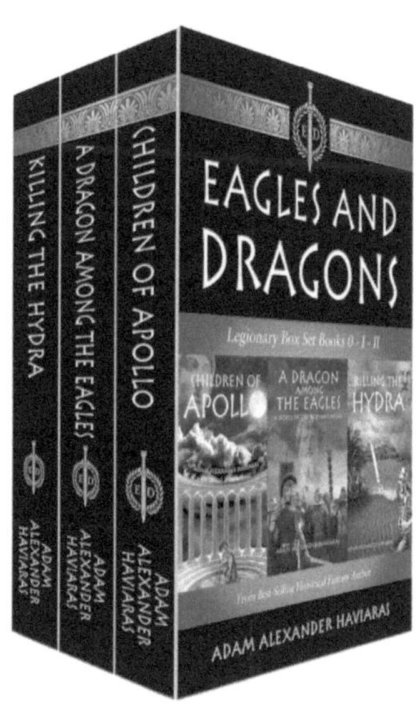

EAGLES AND DRAGONS LEGIONARY BOX SET

BOOKS O - I - II

Begin your adventure in the Roman Empire with a great deal!

Get the Eagles and Dragons series Legionary Box Set today.

This digital box set includes the #1 best-selling prequel novel, *A Dragon among the Eagles*, as well as Book I, *Children of Apollo*, and Book II, *Killing the Hydra*.

The Eagles and Dragons Legionary Box Set is available from all major on-line e-book retailers, public libraries, or direct from Eagles and Dragons Publishing.

EAGLES AND DRAGONS TRIBUNE BOX SET

BOOKS III - IV - V

Continue your adventure in the Roman Empire with another great deal!

Get the Eagles and Dragons series Tribune Box Set today.

This digital box set includes the reader-acclaimed novels *Warriors of Epona*, *Isle of the Blessed*, and *The Stolen Throne*.

The Eagles and Dragons Tribune Box Set is available from all major on-line e-book retailers, public libraries, or direct from Eagles and Dragons Publishing at:

www.eaglesanddragonspublishing.com

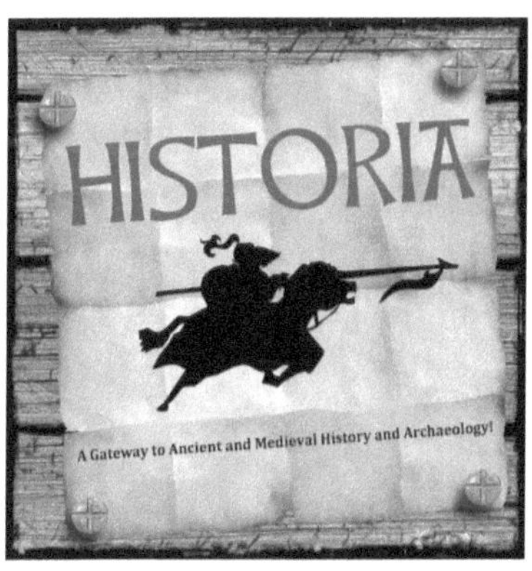

HISTORIA

A Gateway to Ancient and Medieval History and Archaeology!

Do you find ancient and medieval history and archaeology fascinating?

If so, then you will love Eagles and Dragons Publishing's *Historia* non-fiction series of books!

In this series, author and historian, Adam Haviaras will take you through such topics as Celtic mythology, medieval knighthood, and the search for the historical King Arthur and Camelot.

If you are interested in ancient and medieval history, and Arthurian studies, then you will want to check out the *Historia* non-fiction series.

Available from all major on-line e-book retailers or direct from Eagles and Dragons Publishing.

Do you love ancient and medieval history and mythology?

Visit 'EDPublishingAgora' on Etsy and on Amazon today to check out our array merchandise for history and mythology-lovers, including books, clothing, housewares, prints, collectibles and more. And all of it is designed in-house by Eagles and Dragons Publishing!

Check out Eagles and Dragons Publishing's AGORA on Etsy at the following link:

https://www.etsy.com/ca/shop/EDPublishingAgora

Visit our store on Amazon here:

https://www.amazon.com/s?me=A37SS2KKSCLCTB& marketplaceID=ATVPDKIKX0DER

See you in the AGORA, the marketplace for history-themed gifts and books!

Planning a vacation in Europe or the British Isles?

Visit Ancient World Travel for a wide range or helpful articles, travel tips, travel resources, and amazing deals on everything from airfare and accommodation, to car rentals, museum passes, and behind-the-scenes tours of the world's greatest historical sites.

Check out Ancient World Travel today at:

https://www.ancientworldtravel.net/

*Ancient World Travel© is a subsidiary of Eagles and Dragons Publishing©.

www.ingramcontent.com/pod-product-compliance
Lightning Source LLC
Chambersburg PA
CBHW061338310726
48974CB00001B/95